Double Honor

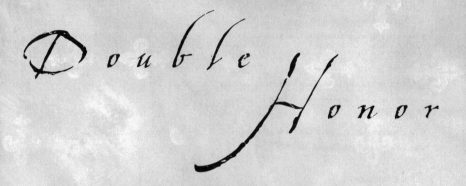

Double Honor

A NOVEL

Missy Horsfall *and* Susan Stevens

WATERBROOK
PRESS

DOUBLE HONOR
PUBLISHED BY WATERBROOK PRESS
2375 Telstar Drive, Suite 160
Colorado Springs, Colorado 80920
A division of Random House, Inc.

All Scripture quotations are taken from the *New King James Version.* © 1982 by Thomas Nelson, Inc. Used by permission. All rights reserved.

The characters and events in this book are fictional, and any resemblance to actual persons or events is coincidental.

ISBN 1-57856-547-2

WATERBROOK and its deer design logo are registered trademarks of WaterBrook Press, a division of Random House, Inc.

Library of Congress Cataloging-in-Publication Data
Horsfall, Melissa.
    Double honor / Melissa Horsfall and Susan Stevens.— 1st ed.
        p. cm.
    ISBN 1-57856-547-2
        1. Adult child abuse victims—Fiction. 2. Married women—Fiction. I. Stevens, Susan, 1961- II. Title.

PS3608.O495 D68 2002
813'.6—dc21

                                                    2001055940

Printed in the United States of America
2002—First Edition

10 9 8 7 6 5 4 3 2

This will be written for the generation to come,
that a people yet to be created may praise the LORD.

PSALM 102:18

To Victoria Kepler Didato, whose words of truth
ring through this book.
You have taught us, inspired us, and believed in us.
Thank you for showing us the very heart of God.

A Note to Our Readers

The topic of sexual abuse is an intense and complicated one. If we had given any deeper thought to how difficult it would be to address all aspects of it, this book in all likelihood would never have been written!

We are indebted to Victoria Kepler Didato, not only for her expertise, but also for her heart and her sensitivity to victims and offenders alike. Vicky, you shine as an example of God's unconditional love. Any mistakes or inconsistencies in our representation of the therapeutic process are ours alone.

We are also grateful to the many women (and men) who have shared their journeys of healing with us and whose lives have been transformed by God's restorative love. Lest we do a great disservice to these remarkable individuals, or to other survivors who have suffered, we would like to make it clear that healing is a lifelong process.

Double Honor is fictional. It is in no way intended to be a statement of how recovery should or will happen. The devastating effects of sexual abuse impact every area of its victims' lives—physical, emotional, mental, and spiritual. Mallory's story is not meant to suggest that a quick fix is realistic, nor to diminish the difficult and painful task most survivors face in dealing with their pasts. We do not wish to imply that forgiveness is instantaneous, nor do we intend to say that all who have been abused need therapy. Forgiveness is a process, and faith an individual journey.

If you are a survivor of sexual abuse, it is our prayer and hearts' desire to extend hope to you and to all who read this book. May each of you meet Jehovah Rapha, "the Lord who heals."

Acknowledgments

My heart is overflowing with a good theme;
I recite my composition concerning the King;
my tongue is the pen of a ready writer.

PSALM 45:1

To the real and unseen author of this book
who allowed us to be His pen.
Thank you Abba, Daddy.

The "real story" behind any book can be found in the acknowledgments. Without the input of some very special people, this project would never have been completed.

To the women connected with the Child Sexual Abuse Institute of Ohio (CSAIO) and the hundreds whose lives they have touched by their courage to face the truth: "Instead of your shame you shall have double honor, and instead of confusion they shall rejoice in their portion. Therefore in their land they shall possess double; everlasting joy shall be theirs" (Isaiah 61:7). May this book tell of the double honor you will receive at the Lord's hand.

Thank you to:

- Erin Healy—for seeing our heart. *Double Honor* is as much yours as it is ours.

- Karen Ball—you caught the vision and had the passion to bring out our very best.
- Everyone at WaterBrook Press—what a great ride!
- Angie—your insight as well as the first editing launched us on our way.
- Jackie—your input was invaluable.
- John—for your generosity. Your photos are wonderful.

To the many who have lifted us in prayer and especially those at God's House, we are in your debt.

From Susan's heart:

Mom, for all those nights you ate alone and always left a plate on the table. I love you. My friend Ned, thank you for letting me borrow Missy on those very long, late nights. I love you, man! And to all of my friends who insisted that it could be done and should be done, thank you.

From Missy's heart:

Ned—for always. My precious sons, J. T. and Ryan, and Emy, my beautiful daughter—you are my joy. Thanks for your encouragement, for your many sacrifices, for cleaning the house and cooking your own dinner!

One

The darkness was overpowering.

Oppressive…closing in.

She swept her hands through the emptiness until her frantic fingers touched a cold, moist wall. Was she in a tunnel? Was she blind? Though she could see nothing, she sensed the room was small—and getting smaller. Walls don't move. She shivered and wrapped her arms tightly around her body. Was this a prison cell? It smelled dank and musty, like the dungeons in the storybooks her daddy used to read to her.

But Daddy wasn't here now.

Where was she? She opened her mouth to scream, but the sounds only vibrated inside her head. She felt along the wall until she came to a door. She began to bang and pound, but no one could hear her. No one could see her—

Wait! There was a window, and she could see people walking past. They were laughing and calling to each other. Relief coursed through her, and she beat on the glass of the small window, but no one paid any attention. They were out there! Why wouldn't they answer her?

She turned her head and searched the darkness but still saw nothing. She pounded on the door, harder now, with growing panic. They had to hear her—they had to! Prickles of fear tingled along the back of her neck. There was a different odor now…sweet, pungent—stinging her nose. She shivered again. It was…repulsive. Something—or someone—was behind her. In this room. In this darkness. She could hear him breathing.

Her heart was pounding so hard—could he hear it? She couldn't breathe, she couldn't move…

But she must! She had to run and hide—quick—before he found her, before he—

Mallory kicked her legs, fighting the bonds that held them. She screamed, jerking herself awake. Her ragged breathing and thumping heart rate broke the nighttime silence. Cool air touched her damp skin, and she pulled the sheet closer, her eyes searching the darkness.

It was just a dream. She sat up and forced her fingers to relax their grip on the covers, willing the numbness away. The red numbers of her alarm clock glared with the hours that remained until morning light.

She lifted her eyes to the ceiling and tried to pray, but the heaviness of the dream persisted so that all she could manage was a whispered "the Lord is my shepherd" over and over. She lay back down in the king-size bed. It was too big and too lonely without her husband's strong presence to ward off the terrors of the night. She curled her arms around his pillow and buried her nose in the downy softness. His scent remained even though he was gone.

"Jake"—she whispered into the darkness, caressing the pillow— "I need you." The minutes ticked by, and Mallory's eyes grew heavy with sleep.

Her world was moving. Bouncing up and down…

"Mommy! Wake up!"

Mallory rolled over and came into contact with knees and elbows. She opened tired, heavy eyes and stared into the face of her enthusiastic six-year-old.

"Mommy, I want pancakes, 'kay?"

Renee's warm body draped over her shoulder did much to dispel the lingering fear that followed Mallory out of sleep. She smiled at her daughter. "What? Not even a good morning, first? Just, *Mommy, I want?*"

Renee grinned back. "Morning, Mommy. I want pancakes."

"Is Angel up?" Mallory scooped her daughter up into a hug.

Renee's dark hair bobbed in wild disarray. "She's watchin' cartoons. I told her she wasn't allowed, but she wouldn't listen."

Mallory reached for her robe and shuffled to the bathroom. Dark smudges pocketed her eyes. She rubbed them and looked again. Not even Jake would find these eyes sexy this morning. Usually he called them his beautiful emerald jewels…

She leaned against the edge of the sink. *It was just a dream; it didn't mean anything.* Stress, overtiredness, eating pizza at midnight—a lot of things could have caused it. She hadn't been plagued with nightmares since she was a little girl and had to sleep with a night-light. *It's nerves. That, and Jake being out of town.* Mallory splashed frigid water against her heated skin.

"Mommy, will Daddy be home today?"

"No, sweetie, not until Tuesday. Two more days." *It feels like forever.* Mallory headed for the comfort of a hot shower.

"Are we goin' to Grandma's today? Can I take my bike?" Renee's never-ending questions, shouted over the rush of water, kept her disturbing thoughts at bay. "I want breakfast! Mommy, are you ready yet?"

Tossing her wet towel toward the hamper, Mallory opened the bathroom door. "Yes, we are going to Grandma's today, but later, after church. It's Sunday, remember? And I'm almost ready for breakfast."

"Mommy, Angel tried to dress herself again. She put her shirt on backward! I tried to tell her she's too little to get dressed by herself." Renee planted her small hands on her hips.

Mallory laughed, glad to leave her tortured thoughts and self-doubts and face the familiar tasks of another day, even if it did mean playing referee to her two energetic daughters. "Then I guess there's nothing to do but go help the squirt, is there?"

Renee raced out of the room. "Yeah, and hurry up 'cause I'm *hungry.*"

Mallory followed Renee down the mauve-carpeted hall. Probably a bad color choice for a house with active children, but she had loved the plush texture and color. She straightened a photograph on the wall. It was one Jake had taken of the girls chasing her along the lakeshore. Jake had captured Mallory with her head thrown back, Renee tugging on the edge of her T-shirt, and Angel right on her heels. All three of them were laughing. They had gone to Lake Erie for a week last summer.

Was that only seven months ago? It seemed much longer than that now. She touched the frame once more, then hurried to the girls' room.

The long, spotted neck of a giraffe peeked out at her from the window of an enormous wooden boat angled on the side of a mountain. When she had painted the mural of Noah's ark, complete with life-sized animals parading around the walls, her mother had shaken her head, Jake had laughed, and the girls had loved it.

So did she, and that was all that mattered.

"Mommy, I dressed myself!" Angel stood on the bed with both arms outstretched.

Mallory laughed. Her three-and-a-half-year-old's shorts were twisted, and her shirt was indeed on backward. "And you did a wonderful job, sweetheart, but let Mommy fix your shorts for you." Mallory lifted her off the bed and kissed the top of her head. She went downstairs to make the girls pancakes. By the time she'd cleaned the kitchen, dressed the girls for church, and then sat them at the table with crayons and large sheets of drawing paper, she had just ten minutes to spare before they needed to leave.

She studied the clothes in her closet and pulled out the green jumper. It would do for today. Her priority in clothes was comfort first and style second. She pulled her long, straight hair back and clasped it at the base of her neck; no time to fuss with it this morning. She reached for her Bible and glanced at the devotional book beside it. She was four days behind in her read-the-Bible-through-in-a-year commitment. She had planned on trying to catch up this morning, but she was late.

They arrived at church, and Angel balked at going into the nursery when she found out that Renee had been promoted to junior church. When Mallory finally slipped into a back pew and took a deep breath, the service was well under way. The pastor, James Gates, was preaching from Isaiah. "In the sixty-first chapter, we find encouraging words…"

A narrow, stained-glass window rose from floor to ceiling behind the pulpit. It depicted Jesus' baptism, with Christ rising out of the water. Mallory loved the way the startling white dove was arrested in midflight, seeming as if any second now it would come to rest on Pastor James's head. For Mallory the dove was more than a sign of the Holy Spirit. It was a sign of peace. *Peace.* That was what she needed this morning.

"He has sent Me to heal the brokenhearted, to proclaim liberty to the captives, and the opening of the prison to those who are bound."

Mallory shivered. A prison was easy to imagine after her nightmare. She glanced down to follow the Scripture reading: "To comfort all who mourn…to give them beauty for ashes, the oil of joy for mourning, the garment of praise for the spirit of heaviness." The spirit of heaviness—that's what she felt. A cloud of unease, unrest that was so nebulous she couldn't even describe it.

Why do I feel this way, Father God? I want to find Your joy, but all I sense is a dark cloud all around me. Don't let it consume me, please.

With a start she realized the music for the final hymn had started playing. Mallory glanced around and snatched up her bulletin to find out what page everyone was on.

After the service she collected the girls and their papers and hurried them to the car. She checked her watch, fighting the urge to honk her horn at the line of cars in front of them. All she needed today was a dose of her mother's wrath for being late.

"Mommy, Angel took my doll!"

Mallory looked in the rearview mirror and saw her daughters locked in a tug of war over the toy.

"Girls, that's enough. We're almost at Grandma's. Look out the window. There's Willow Hill, the park Grandpa takes you to." The afternoon's pale light glinted off a spinning merry-go-round. Two girls lay on their backs, hair flying straight out as another child ran, small legs pumping hard.

"I want to go to the park."

"Me, too."

"No. You always do what I want to do."

"Mommy, Renee's being mean!"

Mallory glanced in the mirror in time to see Angel reach over and slug her sister.

"Ow! That hurt!"

"I said that's enough. Both of you." Mallory pulled into her parents' driveway and parked beside her brother's red Jeep. She turned the key and listened to the cooling engine's *ping, ping, ping.* The three-bedroom bungalow her parents lived in was the home of her childhood.

She gripped the wheel of the car, then massaged the bridge of her nose and clenched her jaw. She could handle this. She would not cry. If only her mother hadn't insisted this birthday celebration be today. Not even Jake being out of town had gotten Mallory out of it.

"Let me ring the doorbell, you're not old enough."

"Am too!"

"I'll get the door, girls, move back." Mallory got out of the car and followed her daughters to the front porch. *Please, dear Lord, get me through this day.*

Before she could reach for the latch on the door, it swung inward, and Mallory sucked in a breath. Her eyes darted up the six-foot-plus frame of her older brother to land on his bearded face.

"Well, well, the princess has arrived."

Mallory frowned. Eric knew how much she hated that child-hood nickname. Which was probably why he used it.

"Hi, ya rug rats!" Eric chuckled as his eyes shifted past Mallory, down to his nieces. Like a big, burly bear he faked a growl and chased the squealing girls into the house.

Mallory slipped out of her coat and hung it on the hook behind the door as Eric swept Angel up in his arms, turned her upside down, and planted a loud raspberry on her exposed belly before swinging her around in a circle. Angel squealed in delight, and Mallory cringed. Eric flipped Angel upright and carried her into the living room.

"You don't have to carry her, Eric." *She knows how to walk.*

He set her on the floor. "What's with you?"

"Nothing. Jake and I are just trying to break Angel of believing she needs to be held all the time." *Ease up, Mallory. Don't let his teasing ruin your whole day.*

"Angel didn't seem to mind my carrying her."

Mallory rolled her eyes and followed her brother through the archway and into the living room. "Well, that's just the point…"

"What are you two squabbling about now?" Her father was stretched out in his favorite easy chair, suit jacket, tie, and shoes discarded beside him. Lazy curls of smoke rose above the section of newspaper he held. The rest of the *Cleveland Plain Dealer* lay scattered across his lap.

"Hi, Daddy. Smells like Mom's been busy this morning." Mallory leaned over the back of the chair and kissed his receding hairline. She smiled and greeted Eric's daughter, Lindsay, who was in the corner of the living room surrounded by a three-sided dollhouse and miniature furniture.

Her dad rattled his paper and spoke around his pipe. "Yes, she has. Roast beef, mashed potatoes, noodles, green beans, and fresh rolls." He patted her hand and pointed to the paper. "That fool zoning board gave the Simon Company a permit to build down on Broadview. Mark my words, there'll be trouble over that one."

"Building is growth, growth is business, business is progress." Eric dropped his bulk onto the couch and propped his feet on his mother's glass coffee table.

"Humph." Her father's teeth clicked against his pipe stem.

"If you don't like how they handle things, maybe you need to run for city council. Then you could straighten things out. You're good at that…"

Mallory decided to leave before Eric's needling got the anticipated response. Her father and brother had been arguing ever since she was old enough to remember. The subject matter changed, and the volume sometimes rose, but the result was always the same.

"Smells good in here, Mom." She dropped a kiss on her mother's high cheekbone as she entered the kitchen.

"Are you all right, dear? You look pale." Her mother tucked a strand of blond hair back into the French twist she always wore, then patted her hands on her crisp apron.

Mallory tossed her purse onto the kitchen counter. "I'm fine. I've just been fighting a headache all day."

"You're late. What happened?" Her mother tapped the last of the mashed potatoes off the beaters and dropped them into the sink.

"I'm sorry." She tucked her head, refusing to look at her mother, and fought back another round of tears. "Church was late getting out, and I forgot about the detour."

"Well, you're here now. Help me get the food on the table so we can eat before it gets cold." Her mom's voice was clipped as she thrust the steaming serving bowl toward Mallory. "I hope the meat isn't too dry. It sat longer than I wanted it to."

The sharp click of her mother's high heels and her ramrod back spoke for themselves. Yet again, without even raising her voice, the indisputable queen of "how could you do this to me?" had made her disappointment in her daughter painfully clear.

"Everybody come to the table. Martin, see what you can do with this roast." Her mother slipped off her apron and straightened the belt on her print dress. "Girls, wash your hands. Marty? Eric, where is that boy?"

"In the basement. I'll get him." Eric opened the door to the basement, the floorboards creaking under his weight. "Christopher Martin! Get up here. And remove that thing growing out of your ears." Eric held the door wide for his son, snatching the earphones off his head. "Put your CD player up. Your grandmother has dinner ready."

Mallory smiled in sympathy at her nephew's scowling face. It was tough to be a teenager in this house. She tucked the napkin under Angel's chin and sat down, giving Renee a stern warning to sit still. "We're going to say grace."

"Lord, we thank You for what we are about to receive. Amen!" Angel's shout at the end of the prayer said in unison rose above the other voices but was ignored in the bustle of passing the serving dishes.

"Your centerpiece is gorgeous, Mom. Did you get it at Avery's Florist or at that new place downtown?" Mallory wiped a streak of gravy off Angel's chin.

"Your brother sent it; Geoff hated to miss today."

"And I'll bet the flowers got him off the hook too." Eric reached for the card tucked in the spray of roses and baby's breath. "Money and charm. The kid always knew how to get what he wanted. Where is the jet-set playboy anyway?"

"Eric. That's no way to talk about your brother." Her mother's reproof was mild.

"He's in Las Vegas," her father replied. "One of his clients needed him to go repair one of those new computerized slot machines. I don't know why he has to take on clients that run gambling casinos. I thought we raised him better than that."

At his words, an awkward silence fell across the table. Mallory bent her head to her food, letting the chatter of the children and the clink of silverware against china flow over her head. She passed the mashed potatoes when Marty asked for seconds, buttered a roll for Angel, and sipped her water. If only Jake were here. His stories had a way of keeping a conversation going.

Why is it so hard to connect with my family? Sometimes just talking to them is impossible.

"When do we get to eat the cake?" Lindsay asked.

"I'll get it." Mallory scooted her chair from the table, and the screech of wood across her mother's polished floor earned her a frown.

"Just sit still. I'll get it. Marty, why don't you get the ice cream out for me?" With less grumbling than usual, Marty went to help his grandmother.

"It's too bad Jake couldn't be with us today."

Mallory eased her chair back to the table and smiled at her father. "There was some kind of delay with the photo shoot, but he thinks they'll be back by Tuesday." She pulled her hand from the spoon she had been playing with and laid her hand in her lap. "Bad timing, I guess."

The plate holding the double-tiered chocolate cake tipped as her mom set it in the center of the table. "I know Eric and Marty's birthdays aren't for another week and a half, but this was the one free weekend we could have their party."

"Ma, this is fine. So what if everybody can't make it?"

"Eric's right, dear. We should just be thankful to have whatever family here we can." Her dad handed his wife a pack of matches from his shirt pocket, and she lit the candles.

Mallory was grateful for the distractions of singing "Happy Birthday" and coping with the melting ice cream. Any further down this conversational path and her mother would be harping on how much Jake was away from his family.

Not that she would be wrong.

It wasn't long before the girls clamored to be excused from the table. Mallory pulled Angel's chair out and watched her run from the room after Renee and Lindsay.

"Yes, well"—her mother gave a quick glance at the open doorway and Marty's departing back—"children need both their parents…"

"Don't even start, Ma."

"Eric! In this house you will speak to your mother with respect!" As usual, her father's sternness didn't faze Eric. Mallory began gathering her daughters' dirty dishes and stacking them.

Her mother sniffed. "I just meant your divorce is so hard on the children, and heaven knows what the Ladies Aid will think. It simply isn't proper…"

As her brother let it be known what the people at church could do with their opinions, Mallory slipped out of the room and escaped to the safety of the kitchen, which hadn't changed in fifteen years. She slumped against the country-print wallpaper. Proper. That's one thing the Benningtons always were: proper. God forbid anyone in the family should be improper.

Mallory leaned her head back against the wall where she and her brothers had been disciplined as children. She could still see her mother lining up her three naughty children against the small ducks printed on the kitchen wall and could still hear her mother's firm, disapproving tone…

"Your father's position is important, and you will be on your best behavior at all times. This family has a reputation to uphold. Is that clear? We will put our best foot forward for Daddy, to make him proud of us." Mother leaned down to within inches of Mallory's face. "Is that understood?"

"Yes, Mama."

The hand that touched Mallory's arm startled her, and she knocked over her purse as she tried to squelch the tremor running through her body. The contents of her handbag scattered over the counter, and a small container of pills rolled across the Formica.

"You okay, honey?"

Mallory nodded at her father. "I'm fine, Daddy."

As he went to pour himself a cup of coffee, she began picking up the contents of her purse. Her mother's dining room clock chimed the hour, and Mallory turned back to the sink, drew a glass of water, and reached for the bottle of aspirin. If she could just get through cleaning up, she could get out of here.

"Mom says you're not feeling well today." Her dad squeezed

her shoulder and started back toward the dining room. "Oops." He bent to retrieve an envelope from the floor. "Looks like a bill. You don't want to lose this one."

I'd like to lose them all. Mallory looked at the envelope in her hands. She knew what it was and how angry Jake would be. The thought drove her to rip apart the envelope and look at the contents.

Her whole being stilled. She thought for a moment her heart might even stop, but it kept right on beating. *What am I going to do?*

How could she have done it? She knew it was easier to spend money using a credit card, but forty-six hundred dollars? The tears Mallory had held in check all day silently ran down her cheeks.

Jake was going to kill her.

March 21

*I bought this journal today. I had to. Who else am I going to talk to?
Not Jake. I'm not sure God is really listening, and even Geoff wouldn't
understand And anyway what would I tell him? That I jump at the
slightest sound, that I'm afraid of my own shadow and I don't know
why? He would think I was going crazy.*

Am I?

*Yesterday I almost wrecked the car and had to pull off the road. It
felt as if a giant rock had fallen on my chest. I tried to breathe, but I
couldn't. I couldn't even move. It seemed like hours, but it was only
minutes. I'm frightened of something I can't even name.*

What's happening to me?

Two

Jake's home.

The thought drew Mallory from the cocoon of sleep. She rolled over next to his warm body and wrapped her arms around his broad back.

His response was a rumbled grunt.

Even tucking her cold feet next to his didn't rouse him. He didn't even flinch. He'd gotten home after midnight last night. The girls had long been asleep, and Mallory had fixed a candlelight dinner. She smiled at the memory. It had been a great welcome home party, just the two of them.

Another grunt came from the other side of the bed, and her husband shifted onto his back. The sound of his deep snores brought her wide awake. She needed to shower before the girls got up, but she was far too comfortable to move. The soft edge of the blanket snuggled against her cheek. Her Bible and devotional lay on the nightstand right in her line of vision. She was still more than a week behind. *I'm sorry, Lord. I promise to do better.*

The bed moved as Jake rolled toward her and dropped his arm over her stomach. His steady breathing was right in her ear, and Mallory pushed down a rush of annoyance when Jake pulled her against the solid wall of his bare chest. What was the matter with her? She wanted to be close to him, needed to be close to him, but…

With a sigh she slid from Jake's heavy embrace and headed for the master bathroom.

When steam rolled out of the shower stall, Mallory stepped beneath the spray and tilted her head back, letting the warm liquid roll down her face. Lately her emotions had been on a wild roller coaster. Even now tears threatened to spill. Her fingers scrubbed her scalp, and the foam from too much shampoo plopped to the floor of the stall.

Even worse than the emotional upheaval were the overwhelming bouts of terror that struck for no apparent reason and left her numb, unable to think straight. What was she so afraid of?

As she leaned back to finish rinsing her hair, a dark figure loomed through the blurred glass. Panic seized her common sense and held it hostage when a bulky figure crowded into the stall behind her. She screamed and bolted from the enclosed space.

"Mallory! Honey, it's just me."

Jake. Relief swept through her, then anger. "Jake!" She grabbed a towel from the rack and wrapped the thick terry cloth around her. "You scared me. I thought you were still asleep."

"I'm sorry, hon." Jake reached out to hold her, and she backed away.

He followed her into the bedroom, clutching a towel around his waist with one hand and running his fingers through his hair with the other. The short strands stood straight up, and his face was drained of color. "Mallory? I…I just thought we could share the shower. Honey, it never dawned on me that I would frighten you."

Trying to still the trembling of her body, Mallory curled up on the end of the bed. *This is silly! Get hold of yourself.*

Jake ran his hand through his hair again and took several tentative steps toward the bed. "What spooked you so bad? You act like you don't want me anywhere near you. Is that it? Is it…is it me?"

She shook her head. "You know I hate it when you sneak up on me! Why you insist on these childish antics is beyond me."

"First hot, then cold. Make up your mind, Mallory. You're the one who's acting childish." He turned on his heel. "I'm going to take a shower."

The bathroom door slammed, and Mallory inched off the bed. She tugged on her clothes and worked at cramming her anger and fear back into the space from which they erupted. It took several minutes of pulling the brush through her hair for the calming effect to take place.

She really shouldn't take her bad moods out on Jake. She didn't see him enough as it was, and being angry at him for something so trivial wasn't doing her or their marriage any good. She should apologize but…

She pressed her lips together, then left their room and went to get Renee up for school.

Mallory was just setting a steaming platter of omelets and a plate of toast on the table when Jake joined her in the big, airy kitchen. She started to tell him how foolish she felt for overreacting, but he turned his back on her, reached into the refrigerator, and pulled out the milk and orange juice.

"Daddy!" The girls flung themselves against his legs. The last of Mallory's irritation fled as she watched the reunion between father and daughters.

"Who are you and what did you do with my two little girls?"

"Oh, Daddy! It's *us*." Renee giggled and covered her mouth.

"Can't be. You're much too old. My daughter is this high"—he gestured with his hands—"had her front tooth missing, and was a total tomboy. Wouldn't be caught dead in a dress."

"But, Daddy, I had to look nice. I'm having my picture taken at school today!"

"In that case how 'bout a dance with the prettiest girl in the school?" Jake lifted Renee into his arms and smacked his lips against her cheek, then swayed around the kitchen, bobbing her arm up and down in an exaggerated tempo.

"Me too, Daddy."

Jake reached down to swoop Angel up in his arms with Renee. He danced them over to their seats at the table.

"Can I say grace, Mommy?" Renee bounced up and down on her seat. She clasped her hands in front of her forehead. "Thank You, God, our daddy's home and can take us to the park. Amen. Oh, and for the food, too. Amen."

Jake helped himself to the eggs and smiled at Mallory. "This is nice. It smells wonderful." He drank a third of his glass of orange juice. "What are your plans today?"

"Take Renee to school, Angel to preschool, take some illustrations to Paxton's, pick up a few groceries, then come back here and finish some drawings." *I hope Dorothy has another assignment for me.* The illustrations she'd just finished for the children's book were good. She just hoped the author approved as well. "Why?"

"I thought I'd run into work for a little while. I need to check in, and I thought I'd just develop my negatives there instead of at home. It shouldn't take me too long. Then I'll come back and take you all out to eat at Pasano's." Jake wiped Angel's mouth with her napkin.

Angel's pigtails bobbed as she bounced up and down. "Yeah! I want 'scetti."

Jake tugged gently on the blond strand. "You always want 'scetti." He stood and began to clear the table.

Mallory started to take a drink, then set her glass on the table. Jake stacked the dishes into the dishwasher, and Mallory frowned. What was this? He never cleared the table without being asked.

He saw her expression and shrugged. "Can't a husband be nice to his wife? How about if I take the girls to school this morning?"

"Thanks." Mallory carried the last of the dishes to the sink.

He tossed the dishrag across the room to Renee. "Wipe the table, love, then run upstairs and brush your teeth. We want to see your beautiful smile in those pictures. And hustle; we need to get going."

Above the noise of their daughters' feet clunking up the wooden stairs, Jake leaned toward Mallory. "Still mad at me?"

She shook her head, staring down at the sink as she wiped it out, then folded the dishrag and laid it over the faucet. "I'm sorry. I know I'm jumpy. And grouchy. I'm sure it must be driving you crazy, because it is me."

"It's okay, babe."

Mallory turned to wrap her arms around Jake's waist. He smelled fresh from his shower and the musk cologne he always wore. She shifted and pressed her nose against his neck.

Jake's finger sought out her chin and lifted her face to his.

"Eewww!"

Renee's disgust was echoed by her sister's "ucky."

Mallory pushed away from Jake's chest. "We've got an audience."

"So I noticed." He pulled her back for one more hug.

"You'd better go." Mallory stepped away.

"Come on girls, get a move on. We don't want to be late for school."

She watched Jake follow the two giggling girls through the mud room and out to his 4Runner. It was a special treat for Daddy to take them to school. He buckled them into their seats, then got behind the wheel. He waved and tooted the horn as he backed the car out of the garage. Mallory pushed the button to bring down the garage door and snapped the light switch off. She closed the door and returned to the empty kitchen.

The house was silent without the girls. Without Jake. Even knowing he would be home later didn't lift the melancholy that suddenly engulfed her. What was wrong with her? Mallory took the dishtowel and wiped at a spot on the table.

Maybe it was a good thing she had this time alone. She had things to do. She could draw for a while, then do her errands. She needed groceries…

Too bad she didn't feel like doing any of those things.

Mallory folded the towel and laid it on the counter. Her gaze drifted toward the paper…and the ads. There was a sale at the mall today. She reached for her purse to make sure she had her checkbook and wallet.

Her work and errands could wait. First, she'd go shopping.

March 22

Abandoned. Alone. Infinite nothingness. Jake used to be my anchor; now I am a derelict drifting in the world, going through the motions of life, but never connecting to anyone or anything—not even You, Jesus.

    I weep for no reason. I long for what Jake and I once had, but don't know how to tell him what's wrong. Is this what insanity is like?

Three

"Carlisle! In my office!"

The deep, raspy voice boomed through the intercom system and reverberated through Jake's small darkroom. He swore when a bottle of chemicals tilted and almost spilled its contents into the developing tray. He nudged the wall intercom button with his chin while his hands removed the roll of film from the canister. His mind's eye knew the layout of the darkroom so well that even in pitch-blackness he could find his way around.

Jake inhaled a calming breath, then spoke into the intercom. "Karl, I'll be in as soon as I'm finished."

"Now, Carlisle!"

"That would be a little hard to do. I got a roll of film halfway out. I'll be there when I'm finished."

Karl Stiles muttered something unintelligible and broke the connection. Jake fought down his growing annoyance at the man responsible for giving him a chance in the photography world.

When Jake started his job at Point of View Images, it was nothing more than a deserted warehouse in Cleveland's dock district manned by a couple of photographers with big dreams. Now it was one of the fastest growing studios in the country. Karl Stiles had seen Jake's news photos of the destructive force of Hurricane Iris and had commissioned him to come on board. What Jake hadn't known at the time was that Stiles was a driven man. Too driven. In fact, he was driving Jake crazy.

Maybe it was time to move on—but to what?

He set the timer, flipped on the lights, and began to develop the roll of film. The smell of developing chemicals was as intoxicating to him as rare perfume.

Modern technology had all but made the need for a darkroom obsolete, but Jake still preferred to develop his film the old-fashioned way. There was something satisfying in watching his creative instincts come to life.

Jake quickened his movements, determined to get the negatives developed and the proofs on Stiles's desk so that he could spend some time with his wife and daughters. He'd promised Mallory to take them out to celebrate his homecoming. The last thing he wanted to do was disappoint her.

She had been so moody lately. First the candlelight dinner…and then a cold shower. Women! He didn't even begin to understand them.

He veered his thoughts away from his wife and toward what Stiles had in store for him now. Another assignment? He'd just completed the last one. He could almost hear the old man rasping out his retort if Jake complained: *"Sacrifice, Carlisle. You want to be a winner. You want to succeed. Then you better be willing to sacrifice. That's the way it is in this business."*

Over the last few years, Mallory and the girls had taken a backseat while he tried to make a name for himself. He knew his compromises were wreaking havoc on his home life, but what else could he do? It was just the nature of the beast. A steady beat began to throb at Jake's temples.

The timer went off, bringing him back to his task. Twenty minutes later, he scrutinized the strips of film as he clipped them into the slots in the film dryer. *Not bad.* He cleaned up the darkroom, wiped his hands on the chemical-stained apron, and reached for the door.

The outer office was in systematic confusion. The other photographers scrambled to complete their various projects. Jake pitched his stained smock onto the desk in his cubicle and headed toward Stiles's office.

"Hey, boss man, how'd the negs turn out?" Jake's personal assistant, Joey Peterson, fell into step beside him.

Jake kissed the tips of his fingers. "Great."

"Now, if Snarly Karly will just agree, you may be able to get home to your woman and show her just how much you've been missin' her."

Jake cast a glance over his shoulder. "Watch it, Joey. Stiles catches you calling him that, and we're both history."

"Dude, I didn't know you cared!" Joey's blue eyes widened, and he flung a skinny arm around Jake's shoulders. Jake backed out of the one-armed embrace.

"I care about having to train a new person on the delicate handling of my equipment and having to spend days teaching them how to open a camera back. It took me long enough to teach you."

Jake tapped on Karl's office door and peeked around its edge. Karl stared down his nose past his half-moon glasses and waved Jake inside, before turning his attention back to the person on the other end of the phone. "Yes, we can do that for you. Yes, he's available."

Jake shook his head and motioned with a cut of his hands. "No, Karl, I'm not."

"Hang on a minute. Jake just came in." Stiles clamped his hand around the mouthpiece. "Do you know who I've got on this phone? *World Graphics,* that's who. They want you, Jake. Don't blow it."

"*World Graphics*! They want me? Why?"

Karl shook his head. "Because of your shots of the Haitian refugees. Here, talk to them." He pressed the phone into Jake's hand and sat back with a grin on his round face.

Jake listened to the photo editor explain his desire for an exclusive shoot. The monsoon season had begun in Malaysia, and one had just ripped through the country.

Jake tried to process what the photo editor was saying. Their regular staff photographers were tied up on assignments, and the editors wanted shots of the devastation before cleanup began. *World Graphics* wanted him, Jake Carlisle! For a moment he was tongue-tied at the ramifications. This was it! The career breakthrough he had been waiting for. How could he turn it down?

"Yes sir, I'd be interested. I'll let you give the details to Karl while I go round up my assistant and make some plane reservations. Thank you for the opportunity, sir." With deliberate calm he handed the phone back to Stiles. He didn't even mind the smugness on the other man's face.

Jake closed the door behind him before letting out an ear-piercing shout. His colleagues turned to stare, but he didn't care. He spotted Joey at the vending machine and caught him around the waist. His coworkers shook their heads as he waltzed Joey around the room.

"Care to tell me what has you flying so high that you'd risk your reputation to do the cha-cha with me?"

"Pack your gear! We are headed to Malaysia!"

"Where's Malaysia?"

"Who cares? Doesn't matter, 'cause when *World Graphics* calls, you go."

"No way! *WG*? Congratulations." Joey flopped down in a chair and tipped it back. "When do we leave?"

"Tonight. They want us to cover the effects of a monsoon."

The front legs on Joey's chair hit the tiled floor. "You promised Malo a night on the town tonight. We just got home. How's she going to take the news?"

"She'll take it just fine. We've been waiting for this for a long time. This is it, Joey! She has to understand. I'm going to call her right now."

The simultaneous sounds of a child's shrieking wail and the strident ringing of the telephone made Mallory's hand jerk. The abrupt movement spread a thick layer of India ink across the sketch she had been working on. She raced toward the sound of the piercing screams, and skidded to a halt inside the doorway of the kitchen where her youngest child stood frozen in a sea of slivered glass. Mallory sagged against the door with relief when she saw Angel was unhurt.

The slight change of pitch in Angel's cries assured her that the child was more afraid of punishment than of the broken glass. Mallory's tense nerves were strained even more by the continued ringing of the telephone.

She picked her way through the shards of glass and lifted her baby into her arms, then reached for the wall phone in the kitchen. She yanked it off the hook halfway through its ring.

"What?" Mallory took a deep breath and tried again. "Hello?"

She cuddled Angel's head against her shoulder to muffle the child's screams. She whispered against the little girl's cheek, "Angel, hush. You're fine. Shush, Mommy needs to talk."

"Hi, babe. Sounds like World War III there. What am I missing?"

A strange combination of tension and relief curled through her at the sound of her husband's baritone. "Jake, hang on a sec." She turned to the still-clinging little girl. "Sweetie, you're not hurt, and Mommy isn't mad at you. Why don't you go and play? Mommy needs to talk to Daddy."

She kissed the little cherub cheek and set Angel onto the safety of the carpet in the dining room. Big green eyes, identical in color to Mallory's, stared up at her. Mallory watched the child wipe her eyes with her shirtsleeve and shuffle further into the other room.

Mallory sighed and sank onto one of the padded barstools. She pulled a notepad in front of her and began to doodle as she talked with Jake. "I'm back. What's up? I thought you'd be home by now."

"Mal, something came up…"

"Jake—"

"I'm sorry, honey, but I just got word of another assignment." Jake's voice was a mixture of guilt and excitement. "*World Graphics* called!"

She knew he loved his work. And he was good at it, Mallory had to admit, very good. But she wanted him here, at home. She closed her eyes and could see his image. The thick, sandy blond hair cropped close to his head would be mussed by this time of the day. The suit jacket and tie would have been discarded a long time ago. The sleeves of his pale blue shirt would be rolled to the elbows.

She heard him give a muffled response to one of his colleagues. Maybe he was winking or breaking into his big, easy smile. Even now there would be a twinkle in his hazel eyes and excitement over the prospects of a new assignment.

"They aren't even giving me time to air out my bag. You know how much I hate dirty clothes keeping me company. Look, I need to know how much is left on the MasterCard."

Mallory gripped the phone. *What do I do? I can't tell him.*

She skirted the mess on the floor, stretching the cord across the kitchen to her small, cherry wood desk in the breakfast nook. She cradled the phone to her shoulder and reached into the pigeonhole for the checkbook, then flipped through the pages of her register. But she already knew the balance.

"Mal? Did you hear me?"

"Do you have to use the MasterCard? Don't you have any money in your checking account?"

"Yeah, but it's easier to use the card when I'm traveling."

Mallory curled the phone cord around her fingers. "The bill hasn't come yet." She winced at the lie. "Where are you going that you can't use one of your other cards? Why don't you just use your American Express? Or traveler's checks? Where are you off to now?" She had to distract him before he started asking questions.

Jake picked up the file folders that were at his elbow and slung them out of his way. They skidded across the slick surface of his desk. What was the problem with her? Why, whenever he mentioned money, did she get defensive? He worked. He brought in a paycheck. That's what this assignment would do. It would take care of his family. Didn't she understand that?

"So, where are you off to now?" Mallory's halfhearted attempt to show some interest couldn't stop the zing of adrenaline that rushed through Jake.

"Malaysia, then Indonesia. They want me to photograph the destruction from a monsoon that just hit. I'm sorry about dinner, but this is a great opportunity… I'm doing it for us, Mal."

A hand touched Jake's back, and he tipped his head to see one of his colleagues giving him a thumbs-up. "Way to go! Got the *Graphics* people looking your direction. Congratulations!"

He lifted his shoulder to hold on to the phone and did a two-handed champion wave. He cupped his hand over the receiver. "Thanks, mate." He turned his attention back to the phone. "Listen, babe…"

"Jake?"

"Uh, sorry. I was just talking to a colleague."

"I asked how long you would be gone."

"Um, couple weeks. Three tops." Jake found himself stumbling for words to fill the sudden void in his conversation with his wife. Why couldn't she be happy for him? The silence stretched between them.

"I guess you're too busy to talk."

"No, I—"

"I'll talk to you when you get back. Have a good trip."

"Mal…babe?" No one was there.

Jake glared at the receiver, then dropped it into its cradle. Its silence mocked him.

Mallory hung up the receiver.

Oh, Jake. I just want you home. With me. With your girls.

Her hand was still on the phone. Should she call him back? She swallowed the thick tears that lodged in her throat.

She retrieved a broom and dustpan from the pantry and began sweeping up the fragments of glass that were scattered over the kitchen floor. The dark blue bowl had been an antique given to her by her grandmother. She banged the dustpan into the trash can harder than was necessary.

"Mommy, are you mad at Daddy again?" Startled, Mallory looked up into Renee's brown eyes.

"No."

"Are you mad at Angel? She didn't mean to break Grandma's dish."

"I'm not mad at Angel either." Mallory gave one of Renee's brown curls a tug, then leaned around the doorway. Angel was standing in the corner, her nose pressed against the wall, her hands behind her back as she ran her toes back and forth through the deep plush carpet. Her tears had receded to residual hiccups and an occasional sniffle.

"Angel, come here, honey. Mommy's not mad at you."

The tiny back stiffened, and Angel's little head turned to look over her shoulder. Streaks of tears remained on her cheeks, and Mallory went to wrap her arms around her daughter. She reached out a hand to draw Renee into the embrace.

"Mommy, if you aren't mad at Daddy or Angel, who are you mad at?"

Who are you mad at, Mallory?

She didn't know. And that terrified her.

April 7

It must be hormones. Maybe I should see a doctor, or maybe Pastor Gates. But some of what I feel is so embarrassing. What could I tell him? That I weep at the oddest times? That I love my husband, but sometimes he repulses me? That my children kiss me and I fly into a rage?

I can't go to Heather, she'll only ask questions I can't answer. I get so angry when Jake's gone, but I'm annoyed at him when he's here, too. What's the matter with me?

Four

Mallory clamped a brush between her teeth and squatted down in front of the old toy chest. She had decided to try her hand at the French painting technique of trompe l'oeil after seeing it done in an art magazine. If it was successful on the trunk, she thought she might get brave enough to do the three-dimensional procedure on the hallway wall. Maybe a trellis leading down a garden path.

Mallory was leaning close to the trunk, painting in the fur of a teddy bear falling out of a drawer, when the side garage door banged shut. She jumped, then gritted her teeth. "How many times do I have to tell you not to slam the door?" She snatched a clean brush and dabbed at the smeared paint.

"Sorry." A quiet female voice spoke from the doorway. "The wind grabbed it from my hand. I couldn't catch it."

Mallory flung the brush into the container of water and twisted around to face her best friend. "I'm sorry, Heather. I thought you were the girls." Leaning back, she stretched her legs out in front of her and studied her friend.

Heather North was picture perfect. A pair of sunglasses rested on top of her blond, windblown hair, held away from her oval face by a wide headband. Her eyes were a perfect azure blue, and her petite frame sported a denim work shirt and khakis. She was dressed to play.

Heather stepped closer and scrutinized Mallory and her work. "The trunk is nice, but you don't look so good, mi amiga."

"Well, thanks! You, on the other hand, look great."

"What's on your agenda for today?"

"The girls, and work on this chest." She nudged it with her foot. "No work for you today?"

"One of the perks of being self-employed. How about you and the girls coming with me to the stables to ride, then I take you all out for lunch?"

"The girls are playing. How about you just stay here with us?"

"Even better."

Mallory rolled to her feet and moved to the galvanized sink near the mud room door to wash her hands. If only she could wash away all the turmoil and confusion as easily as she was ridding her hands of paint. "I'm thirsty. Come on in. We'll get something to drink."

"So how's it going?"

Mallory shrugged and reached for the refrigerator handle. "Iced tea or soda?"

"An answer would be better." Heather blocked her path. "You look pretty frazzled. What's wrong?"

Mallory pulled glasses from the cupboard, then peeked past the dark green gingham curtains to check on her girls. Angel and Renee were playing on the wooden swing set in the backyard. Mallory's focus shifted and she caught her reflection in the glass. It took her a moment to realize that those big green eyes were her own. The dark mass of hair that fell just past her shoulder obscured part of her profile, and she tucked it behind her ear. "I think I need a change."

"What kind of change do you have in mind?"

"Haircut, maybe."

"Why? Looks good right now."

"I don't know. Maybe get it back to chin length, like I used to wear it years ago. Jake always liked it that length. He said I had a kissable neck."

Heather groaned. "He would."

Mallory continued staring out the window, trying to ignore the saddened eyes that stared back at her.

"Does your current mood have anything to do with Jake?"

Tension curled deep in Mallory's gut, and she fought hard against the tidal wave of conflicting emotions. She didn't know whether to punch the wall or curl up and cry. Instead, she just swallowed hard. "What mood? I'm not in a mood. What makes you think that?"

Heather lifted a blond brow and stared her down. "I know you, Carlisle. I have since our freshman year of college."

Mallory squirmed against the compassion on Heather's face, torn between the urge to flee and the desire to fall weeping into someone's arms. Why was she reacting this way? It didn't make sense. She hugged her arms across her chest.

Heather lifted one shoulder in a shrug, but her words were arrows shooting straight to Mallory's vulnerable heart. "You're tense. Sad. Moody. What happened to the carefree, nonchalant Mallory I've known all these years?"

"That girl seems like forever ago." Mallory sank onto one of the barstools, pulled the notepad in front of her, and picked up a pen. Heather's hand on hers stopped the pen from moving.

"Talk to me."

"Jake's leaving."

"What?"

"No! Not like that. He's on an assignment, and on top of that he's going to miss our anniversary." He hadn't even mentioned it when they talked on the phone, and she'd been too angry to remind him. *He'll probably forget all about it.*

"He's missed it before."

"I know, but he promised me he would slow down, take some time off to be at home with us."

Mallory hated the whine in her voice. It shouldn't bother her that Jake was going to be gone for two or three weeks. It never used to. He had a job to do, and the travel was part of it. Besides, when he was gone, she was at her creative best. She and Heather could play without her worrying about someone else's timetable, and she had the freedom to indulge in shopping sprees.

She used to be strong, independent. She had always detested clingy, demanding, fearful women.

When had she turned into her greatest fear?

"Have you tried praying about it?"

I can't. Mallory traced the beaded drops of condensation on her glass of iced tea. She wanted to pray, to feel close to God again, but He seemed so far away, and how could she admit that to Heather? *She never seems to doubt God.* "Of course I have."

"It doesn't seem to have brought you much peace."

"I'll tell you what would bring me peace. Jake getting his act together!"

Heather's brow creased. "Mallory, what's going on? This isn't like you."

It *wasn't* like her. She and Jake adored each other. They had always loved being together and sharing their hopes, their dreams. She had always welcomed his affection, his touch. But now…

She shook off the dismal thoughts. She'd always known it would take more than a great passion to keep Jake at home. It would take chains.

Now there's a thought…

"I know Jake needs to travel. He needs to take pictures like I need to draw them. It's part of who he is."

It was true. Jake's photos spoke more powerfully than her artwork ever could. She'd always understood that, and they'd always supported each other in their careers. So what had changed?

A wave of dread hit her. What if their marriage was wearing on…and the passion was wearing out?

"So?" Heather's arched brows spoke volumes.

"It just…it feels like he's moving on without me." Mallory left the counter and rummaged through the cupboard to dig out chips and cookies. "You want the truth?"

"Don't I always?"

"I don't know what's happening to me anymore." She dug into the refrigerator and pulled out a package of lunchmeat. "Or to us. Jake and I fight. He growls if I go out and buy a few things."

"You have your own checking account. Why would he complain about your buying stuff?"

"He says we need one more thing like we need a hole in the head."

Heather looked around at the organized clutter. Open poplar shelves held an array of expensive baskets and tins, a collection of crystal stemware was displayed behind the glass cupboard doors, and deep purple glass grapes lay draped across a wicker basket.

"You've got, what? Maybe fifteen Longaberger baskets in the kitchen alone?"

"Don't you even *think* about agreeing with him!"

"Who? Moi?"

The ringing of the telephone saved Mallory from answering. "Hello?"

"Mally?"

"Geoff!" The stress of the day evaporated at the sound of her brother's voice. "I thought you were somebody selling light bulbs or insurance."

"Bad day, huh, Sis?"

"It could be better. Starting anytime now would be fine." Her brother's chuckle soothed her ragged nerves, and she envisioned the laugh lines around his wide mouth. "Are you home yet or still off playing man of the world?" She smiled.

"Well, Las Vegas was nice," he drawled, "but I got bored with the slot machines and came home early."

"What? Not enough women out there to keep you entertained?"

Heather stopped midway to the kitchen door and wiggled her eyebrows. "*I'll* keep him entertained."

Mallory just shook her head and shooed Heather outside.

"Oh, the women. You know what they say, 'They're all the same in the—'"

"Geo!"

"Yeah, yeah, you know I was just twisting your tail. Listen, what about stepping out with me tonight? You can bring the old man, too, if he insists."

"He's gone on another assignment."

Geoff's whistle pierced the air. "Doesn't let much grass grow under his feet, does he? Hey, tell him I saw his shots in *Scenic*. Not bad." His voice held a note of admiration.

"At least he's good at something."

"Sounds a bit nippy at the Carlisle home today. I take it this latest job has blown in the Arctic winds. An even better reason for me to take you out tonight. Get a sitter," he demanded, "and tell the cuties I bought presents. Be there about five. Ciao."

"Geo," she protested, but only the dial tone heard her.

Heather held the back door open with her hip and pointed Renee and Angel toward the bathroom to wash. She looked at Mallory. "What's up with Lover Boy?"

"He just got home from Las Vegas."

"Worn out by all the show girls, I'll bet."

"I guess not. He asked me out for dinner tonight."

"Ooh, that sounds like fun!"

"Knock it off, already. If you want to be helpful, you can tell me what I should wear."

"I'll do better than that. I'll take the girls down to the park so you can have a couple of hours to unwind."

"Feel like staying and baby-sitting?"

"Don't push your luck! I'm leaving when Geoff gets here. I've got big plans of my own for the evening. Hot bubble bath, bowl of popcorn, and the latest Mel Gibson movie."

Mallory appreciated the hours of solitude. By the time Geoff arrived and Heather left, it was 6:15. It took Mallory an extra twenty minutes to settle the girls down from their uncle's roughhousing so she could leave them in the care of the high school senior who watched them.

"You're incorrigible," she told Geoff as they climbed into his '64 white Mercedes. "It will take Sheila hours to get them to bed."

"I do what I can."

"Oh, grow up!" Geoff drove fast, but Mallory knew he was a competent driver, and she relaxed against the leather seat.

The exclusive French restaurant her brother had chosen on the east side of Cleveland had an excellent view of the lake. Mallory wasn't surprised. Geoff bought only the best—from the antique cars he loved to restore to his tailor-made suits.

His dark, wavy hair held just a hint of gray at his temples. A childhood fight with Eric had left a jagged scar running through his left eyebrow to his temple, but even that didn't detract from his charm. "It gives me an air of mystery. Women love it," Geoff told her once. With his looks, his wealth, the grace with which he moved…Mallory had seen firsthand how women were drawn to her brother.

She smiled now as she studied his impeccable suit, with matching silk tie and handkerchief. She was glad she had made the extra effort to dress up. She straightened the swirled print skirt of one of the few dresses she owned. It was worth its price tag.

They arrived early and decided to stroll out to the restaurant's pier. The sun had lowered but hadn't set. A sweet, fresh breeze was blowing, and Mallory breathed in the intoxicating lake air as Geoff led her to a wooden bench placed for scenic viewing.

Her brother paid little attention to the palette of color before them, turning instead to Mallory. "Okay, kid sister, spill it. What's going on with you and Jake?"

She refused to meet his eyes and picked at the hem of her full skirt as she reassured him. "Not much. I'm just tired of being a journalism widow, I guess."

"Mmm. Been gone a lot, has he?"

"Too much. He promised me he would never put his work before the girls and me. I should have known better." Her words were clipped as she stared out onto the lake.

"Maybe it's out of his control."

Her brother's masculine logic added to her irritation. "Maybe he just doesn't care."

Geoff held out his hands. "Hey, I'm on your side, remember? Shoot the enemy, not me."

"Oh, Geoff, I'm sorry." She patted the sleeve of his gray suit. "Anyway, don't worry about me. We'll get by."

"I'm not convinced, Mally." Geoff lifted her chin to look into her eyes. "You can't fool your big brother."

She turned toward the water, then finally gave voice to the truth she'd been trying so hard to hide. "Geo...I'm in trouble."

April 13

If it weren't for Geoff, I don't know what I would have done. I know Jake will use his MasterCard overseas. I can't let him find out. I can't. But how long can I continue to play these games? Why am I doing these things? I don't understand what is going on inside of me, but it terrifies me.

Five

"It's gone."

Jake lifted his finger from the shutter release. "That kind of light comes around once in a lifetime!" He lowered the camera, then tugged his sweat-soaked shirt away from his back. What an intense week! The devastation of the monsoon seemed to worsen the further he and Joey got from the airport in the capital of Kuala Lumpur. At first it had been broken windows, downed power lines, and some localized flooding. But as they progressed northeast, Jake had been stunned at the flattened buildings and the thick, muddy water that coursed down the streets as a rampaging river. It flowed through buildings and piled up debris against the stronger structures. And the people…

He hadn't seen such shocked hopelessness and despair since the Haitian refugees.

Jake had witnessed his fair share of ruin, but nothing had prepared him for what he found along the coastline of Malaysia. The town of Pantai Dasar Sabak looked as if a giant had thrown a temper tantrum. What hadn't been knocked flat lay under fifteen feet of water. Traditional bamboo boats, the method of travel throughout the islands, had been commissioned down the streets of the small village.

By early afternoon Jake and Joey had left the flooded lowlands and traveled here into the hill country, where the storm had blown itself out against forested mountain peaks.

Jake glared at the darkening sky and for long moments took in the destruction wrought upon the terraced rice paddies scattered down the side of the mountain. Uprooted nipa palm trees lay like broken toothpicks spilled on a table, their shriveled leaves waving lethargically in the warm, humid air. In the distance, workers removed the debris from the fields.

Chaos. It was utter chaos…like so much going on in the world around him. Jake shook his head. The God Mallory tried to get him to serve must be a distant and uncaring one to allow such wanton destruction.

Jake studied the scene below him. A tiny, dusky-skinned boy struggled to move a small tree off the mountain path. His tongue was clamped between his lips in solemn determination as he wrestled with the piece of wood. Jake leaned over the outcropping at his feet and focused his camera.

"That photo's gonna knock ol' Karly off his ancient caboose." Joey stepped back from the edge of the cliff and pulled his flaming red ponytail over his shoulder, then grabbed a bandanna from his back pocket to wipe the beads of perspiration off his face. He twirled the handkerchief into a long skinny rope and secured it around his forehead.

"I could give him a Pulitzer Prize–winning photo, and Karl still wouldn't be happy." The last of the sun's rays were shrinking behind the distant mountains, stitching saffron and crimson streaks through the pearl gray sky.

Jake turned when no retort was forthcoming. Joey stood on the edge of the cliff, his hand outstretched, his lips moving. Jake took a step to the side and tried to read Joey's expression. The reflection of the sun shimmered on a tear sliding down his assistant's face.

"They need bulldozers more than they need that prayer."

Joey shook his head. "They need both, boss. They need both."

Sure they do. "Come on. Let's get the gear packed up. We've got a long day ahead of us tomorrow."

They stored the lenses, camera bodies, light meters, and collapsible reflective screens into foam-insulated bags. Jake straightened and shoved his fist into the small of his back. He flipped his Indians baseball cap around and pulled the bill low over his eyes.

With a grunt he slung one of the bags onto his shoulder, then turned to retreat down the hillside. "You got the information on our next destination?" He received no answer and asked again. "Joey, where are we headed next?" Only the sound of chain saws and distant voices broke the silence of twilight. Jake turned around in time to see Joey climbing back over the cliff followed by the dusky-skinned boy Jake had photographed earlier. Joey dusted off his hands and rested his palm on the boy's thin shoulder.

"Boss, we need a guide and a place to stay for the night, don't we?"

Jake raised an eyebrow. "Been recruiting for God again, Joey?"

"Just helping a person in need, boss. Couldn't turn away without giving the kid a hand. Wouldn't be right to snap his pic and then just walk away and leave him to his struggle. Know what I mean?"

"I suppose."

The boy beckoned. "Come. You sleep." He pointed behind Jake.

Jake hesitated, then shrugged. "Seems he wants to earn his keep. Lead the way, kid. Joey, grab those bags and let's go."

Joey jogged to keep pace with Jake's long-legged stride as they followed the scampering child in front of them. "Thanks, man! God just smiled on you."

"Sure He did. So how come wherever we go, you end up befriending every waif that comes along?"

"Dude, it's in my blood. Can't be helped." Joey's smile was unrepentant.

Jake shook his head. "Peterson, what am I going to do with you? You have this annoying habit of throwing off my schedule and routine."

"Schedules are overrated."

"Not if we want to get paid. Speaking of schedules, what's ours for the rest of the week?"

Joey reached into his back pocket and removed a crumpled piece of paper from his worn Bible. "Bali. Then off to Surabaya."

Jake squinted in the gathering dusk as he made his way down the stony path. The air here was damp and fragrant with the whisper of the sea and exotic flowers he had yet to identify. One sweet-smelling bush reminded him of Mallory. His gut twisted at the thought of their phone conversation. She was so distant lately…and it had nothing to do with geography. He remembered how it used to be…when no matter how far away he was, her spirit was with him. Now, no matter how close he was, he couldn't seem to reach her.

Jake shook away the disturbing thoughts. *Get the assignment over with and get home to your wife.* It was this place that had him tied up in knots. The fear, the desolation, the hopelessness. *Mallory isn't slipping away from you.* Then why did he feel this distance in his heart?

"You okay, boss man?"

Startled from his thoughts, Jake stared at his assistant. How did Joey *do* that? His ability to read Jake's emotions was downright unnerving.

They paid their young guide his wages and carried their gear into the small room they'd rented. Joey slipped off his shoes, then moved across the rice straw mats to the terrace door, opening it wide, so the sticky breeze could dance inside. Jake stared beyond Joey, into the growing darkness. The unfamiliar night noises blended with the muted conversations in an unknown tongue from the street beyond the courtyard.

Joey hummed a melody of his own making. His hand lifted in front of him, and his body began swaying.

Jake shook his head. "You're weird, you know that?"

"Yeah, man, I've been told that on occasion." Joey stepped away from the door and flopped backward on the bed. "Rather be weird for Jesus than normal for the world."

Jake shook his head and reached for his camera case, pulling it close.

Joey tugged the rubber band from his ponytail and brushed out the tangles.

"I don't know why you don't get that mane cut."

"Are you nuts? The first recorded haircut in the Bible, the guy ended up blind. No thank you."

The hot air closed in on Jake, and he yanked his shirt over his head and flung himself down on the twin bed closest to the terrace.

His gaze slid to his watch and he calculated the time difference. It would be early in the morning at home…would he get Mallory out of bed if he called right now? "If you got your hair cut, you might end up with a girlfriend."

"Yeah, just like old Samson. If I recall, his girl was the one who cut his hair and the reason he ended up blind. No thanks. I don't need that kind of hassle." Joey rewrapped the rubber band around his hair and pulled his Bible out, flipping it open.

Hassle. That's what it feels like…a hassle even to connect with Mallory anymore. I just don't understand. "You may be the smart one after all. There's something to be said for freedom." Jake sat up on the bed and began to clean his camera lenses with a chamois.

Joey lifted his eyes from his Bible. "Boss man, you wanting some freedom now?"

"I didn't say that." He leaned over his equipment and sprayed compressed air into one of the camera bodies.

"What are you saying?"

"Look, it was just an observation."

"Dude, you don't make casual remarks like that. The way you talk about wedded bliss sometimes makes me want to either gag or go huntin' for a woman. Not sure which yet." Joey rummaged in his backpack and came up with a sorry looking candy bar.

Jake chuckled, but it was a short-lived sound. Wedded bliss. It used to be that. Now it was just…painful. Silence descended between the two men, and Jake looked up.

Joey reclined against the headboard, his eyes closed, his hands resting on his crossed knees, palms up. Good night, the man was praying again. Jake sighed. He didn't really mind his assistant's sometimes peculiar behavior. Joey had been a good friend for the last five years, but sometimes the younger man's forceful views got annoying. His T-shirt said it all: "Live a Radical Life—Pray."

Joey opened his eyes. "Is it this place that has you in a funk, or is it something else?"

"What're you talking about?"

"Boss man, you usually fly high when you're shootin' negs, even if the subject is depressing. You want to talk? I'll listen."

Jake laid the camera down and rubbed his eyes. Maybe he did need to talk. Maybe just saying the words would help show him how absurd this feeling was. "I don't know, Joey. I get the feeling that Mallory and I are…drifting apart."

"How so?"

"It's like we aren't together anymore."

"You're thousands of miles apart, dude."

Jake ran a hand down his neck. "That's not what I meant." He stood and paced the cell-like room. "There was a time when we were connected, in here." He pointed to his heart. "Now there's…nothing. I liked to travel because I knew when I got home things would be even better than before. I couldn't wait to get back and share my adventures with Mal. She was the best friend I had." He paused to stare out the window. "Now she's like a stranger. She doesn't talk. She doesn't listen. Nothing I say or do makes her happy."

He swore and threw a pillow off the bed, then reached again for his camera. "She's really changed. And I don't know why. I've tried to talk to her, but she keeps insisting that nothing's wrong. That she's fine, and that whatever is going on is my fault because I'm always on the road."

"So do you think she could be partly right?"

Jake glared at him. "You taking sides with my wife? Some friend you are."

"I'm just trying to get you to think." Joey held up his half-eaten candy bar. "Maybe it isn't your fault and it isn't her fault. Maybe it's both of you."

"You into marriage counseling now? Maybe you should try the blessed estate first, before you proclaim yourself the expert."

Joey lifted his hand. "Musta hit a raw nerve. Sorry, boss. I don't claim to be a counselor, wouldn't want the job of trying to straighten out someone else's head. Got all I can handle right here." Joey tapped his temple.

Jake reloaded his camera and shut the back. "I just want things to be the way they used to be. And I don't know what to do."

"We can never go back."

"Wonderful!" Jake pushed his palms against his eyes.

"We can move forward though."

"All I ever wanted was to make Mallory happy. Do you think she got the package I sent out?"

"There's the phone—you could find out."

"Might as well."

"That's my cue to hit the nearest grub joint and see what the action's like. Tell Malo I said 'hi.'" Joey grabbed a couple of granola bars and a handful of candy along with his wallet. "Boss man…"

Jake paused with his hand on the phone.

"Just something to think about. Is it your job to make Malo happy? Seems to me that whatever is going on, she's got to resolve it herself, just like you gotta deal with whatever is eating at your soul."

Jake stared at the door long after Joey walked out. Shaking his head, he dialed the long string of numbers that would connect him with his family half a world away. Because of the storm damage, the phone lines had been sporadic at best, but maybe it was time for his luck to change. Tension drew his muscles tight while he waited for someone to answer. He couldn't wait to hear Mallory's reaction to the gifts. She was as bad as the girls when it came to getting presents.

"Hello?"

He couldn't believe the connection. She sounded as if she were right beside him. His body responded to the sound of her sleepy voice. "Hi. It's me. I've missed you." He hesitated. "So how are things going?" He swallowed hard.

"Okay. Renee spent the night at a friend's house. Angel and I decided that we were going to have a slumber party and stay awake all night. We made it all the way to ten o'clock, but this morning we decided that we'd pretend we had stayed up all night."

"Hmm, sounds like fun. 'Course, you know if I had been there, we both would have managed to stay awake all night."

"You made your choice."

Her comment was worse than the ice-cold shower he'd had to take that morning. He wanted to swear. Couldn't she see he was trying? Why wouldn't she meet him halfway?

"What's that supposed to mean?" His back ached as muscles contracted all the way down his spine, and lead settled in the pit of his stomach. It was going to be one of those conversations. He tried again. "Look, I'm sorry I wasn't there for our anniversary."

"Anniversaries are meant to be spent together."

"Give me a break, Mal. You know I'd be there if I could. I did send a—"

"Don't you understand that I want more from you than a package?"

Jake frowned. Was she crying? He thought she wanted him to show that he cared about her.

"I need you, Jake. I don't need the gifts, beautiful as they are. I need more from you than phone calls from halfway around the world and presents that attempt to appease my anger or buy my affections."

"Buy your…? Is that what you think I'm doing? You used to love getting gifts from me. What in the world is going on with you?"

"The gifts cost more than we can afford."

"No, they didn't. I put it on the card and will pay it off when I get home. It's no big deal." Jake rubbed his eyes. "Yes, I bought something to show my affection for you, but it was more than that. It symbolized my love for you. I'm sorry it wasn't what you wanted."

"Oh, Jake!" Mallory's voice was full of contrition. "I'm the one that's sorry."

She was crying. Jake clenched the receiver. Blast the miles between them!

"It's so hard. I just miss you so much."

"Mallory, I don't understand what's going on. I've been gone on assignment over our anniversary before."

"I know. I just…I miss you." She sniffed. "Thank you for the vest. It's beautiful. Where did you find it?"

"I saw it in a shop in Singapore. The saleslady told me that the design symbolized the binding of two hearts as one. It just seemed the perfect gift for you."

"It really is beautiful." Her warm voice washed over him, easing the tension from his aching muscles. This was the woman he remembered. He could picture her in their huge, four-poster bed, wearing one of his T-shirts, warm from sleep, her dark brown hair tousled against his pillow.

Jake tightened his hand on the receiver and sighed. "I miss you too, sweetheart. I should be home in about five days. Five long days." Jake ached to be with her. He needed to see her face, to see how she was responding. Dare he tell her about his other gift?

"The girls loved their gifts too. The dolls are exquisite. I'm having trouble explaining to them they aren't the kind you drag around and play with." Her light laugh rippled across the miles between them.

"Did you get the carvings?"

"The water buffaloes? Sure. The mama is right here on our dresser. The girls put the babies in their room."

"Go get it."

"What?"

"Go get the water buffalo."

"Okay." He heard the soft thump of the phone. "I got it."

"Take off its head."

"Take off its head?"

"You heard me. You can unscrew the head. It's hollow inside."

Jake smiled to himself, anticipating his wife's reaction when she found the ring. It wasn't a typical solitaire. The center gem was an oval, crystal-clear, blue-sheen moonstone—Mallory's birthstone. Hugging either side were two small, rectangle-cut diamonds. It was gorgeous. Perfect for Mallory. It had taken a little wheeling and dealing, some bargaining and fast-talking to the owner of a small, dim jewelry shop in a crowded market in Singapore, but he'd managed to make the deal.

He listened to the muffled sounds on the other end of the wire. The ring's band was wide enough she might want to wear it on her other hand. Her sharp gasp pulled his attention back to the phone, and he sat forward and tried to suppress his grin.

"Jake!"

"Do you like it?" His grin widened.

"It's breathtaking. But, Jake, this thing cost a fortune!"

"Not really. And even if it did, who cares? You're worth every penny." No reply. The warning bells clanged… Mallory wasn't pleased…but why not?

"Jake, the amount you paid for this ring is nothing to joke about!"

He stiffened at the tone in her voice. "I'm not joking."

"We can't afford this."

"Sure we can. Don't you understand that with this job I'm breaking into the big league? I'll be able to do so much more for you and—"

"All I ever wanted was you, Jake."

He rubbed his forehead, then wrapped his hand around the base of his neck. Her tears were back, and he was again at a loss. A thousand negative emotions were in her voice. Why was she so upset? And angry?

"Babe, you have me. You know that." Anxiety coiled through him as he dropped his hand from his neck and smacked the skimpy mattress. He didn't know what to do. He wanted to make her happy. He had tried to make her happy. Yet every attempt failed.

He couldn't win.

"Mallory? Tell me what I can do—"

"Nothing, Jake. Just don't buy me anything else. I don't need it. I don't want it." Her voice was flat, void of emotion.

What was she thinking? Jake couldn't tell. A shiver ran down his spine, and he hung up the phone after a stilted good-bye.

Tears misted his eyes, and he fought them off. He fell backward on the bed and whipped the pillow from under his head to fling it at the closet door.

"I don't get it. I just don't get it at all!"

July 1

This will take some getting used to—Geoff's serious about someone. He's never dated anyone for longer than six months, and now he's bringing someone to the family reunion? I wonder what she's like— petite, feminine, batting her eyelashes and breathing, "Oh, Geoff!" every other sentence?

Meow! I'd better pull in my claws. So Geoff's found someone— that's good. I'm just feeling left out and alone, abandoned by my husband, who has better things to do with his time than spend it with me.

Am I being selfish? I've tried to support Jake's dreams. But the girls and I have already given up so much. Yet if I don't let go—will I lose him?

I ache with a longing I cannot define.

Six

"And now, some late breaking news. A seven-year-old girl was found murdered today in Willow Hill Park. The police—"

"Renee! I told you to quit playing with that remote and turn the TV off. We have to leave for the picnic." Mallory punched the Off button and pointed to the stairs. "Go up, and get your sister, and pick up these toys like I told you a half-hour ago."

She watched her daughter grumble her way upstairs before going to finish the fruit salad. Where was Jake? It couldn't take that long to get ice. He had promised to help with the girls this morning but had forgotten to get the bag of ice she had asked for last night. She checked the driveway once more. If he didn't hurry up, they were going to be late.

When Jake pulled up to the house fifteen minutes later, Mallory had food, children, and necessary essentials ready to go out the door. To her relief they made the drive to her grandparents' farm in less than thirty minutes. A wave of midsummer heat washed over her when she opened the door of the car. The air was laden with the smell of mowed hay mingled with the scent of her grandmother's cherished roses. The grass was cool and soft beneath her feet.

Home. She was home.

Mallory's nerves began to loosen their viselike grip. For the first time in days she could breathe without anxiety coiling through her.

"Girls, carry your own chairs; Daddy and I have our hands full." Mallory handed the girls their miniature lawn chairs, then reached into the backseat of the car for the picnic basket. Jake, carrying the cooler, had already followed the girls.

In preparation for the party, the lawn was mowed and set with colorful tables. Chairs of every type sat under the leafy arms of the elms and oaks that guarded the backyard of her grandparents' rambling farmhouse. The Fourth-of-July picnic was an annual event, a chance for cousins to get reacquainted and for the adults to reminisce and embellish their telling of all the old stories.

Mallory carried her burden to the overloaded table and had just put it down when she was engulfed in a firm hug.

"Gran!" Mallory pressed her face against the silver-white curls, and the scents of lilacs and yeasty, fresh-baked bread tickled her nose—fragrances she forever associated with her grandmother. Vibrant energy still flowed from Eleanor Bennington's eighty-two-year-old frame. Mallory guided Angel and Renee to their great-grandmother for their own enthusiastic welcome.

"How's my best girl?" Jake set the cooler down beside the table and reached out to give Gran a kiss.

"Who's the young whippersnapper flirtin' with my wife?" a gruff voice called across the clearing. Jake turned and grinned. Gramps rose from his chair, and even from a distance, Mallory could almost hear his joints groaning in protest as he plodded toward them. At eighty-four, her grandfather's body suffered from arthritis, and his hearing had failed enough to require a hearing aid, but his eyesight remained sharp.

Mallory met him halfway and kissed the white-haired man on his weathered cheek. Gramps lifted one bushy eyebrow at Mallory.

"This young punk takin' care of ya, is he?" His still-strong hand gripped Jake in an unbreakable hold.

"Yes, Gramps."

"Paul, you leave Jake alone now," Gran scolded, and Jake grinned at her.

"Just makin' sure," Gramps said, fixing Mallory with a twinkling gaze. "Now, let me have a look at you, to see for myself. And where are my two little lollipops?" Both Renee and Angel giggled as he looked over their heads and across the wide expanse of the yard. He scratched his stubbled chin. "Hmm. Don't see 'em anywhere."

"Gramps! We're right here!" Renee exclaimed.

"No. Can't be the ones I'm lookin' for." Gramps wrapped both hands on his cane and bent toward them. He looked toward the picnic table where Gran was setting out food, and placed a finger against his lips. "Don't tell Gran." He reached into his shirt pocket and handed them each a sucker.

"We won't." The girls wrapped supple arms around his neck before running to join their cousins by the rusty swing set.

"Don't go too far. We'll be eating soon," Mallory called after them, then scolded her grandfather. "Gramps! You spoil them."

"Humph! Thought that's what grandpas were for. I can see it didn't hurt you none." He gave her a wink, tucked a raspberry sucker in her hand, and ambled back to his chair.

She shook her head at the man who had indeed spoiled her all her life, then turned her attention to the table where Aunt Patty was in full dictator mode, telling everyone how to arrange things. Her plumpness attested to the fact that she loved food—cooking it and sharing it. Mallory laughed as her aunt chased Jake away from the table and then turned at the sound of her father's hearty laugh across the clearing. He and his twin brother had teamed up to play against their sons in a game of horseshoes. She lifted a hand in greeting to her father and called out, "Who's winning, Daddy?"

"We are! Who else?"

Martin and Michael Bennington were as identical as they had been in their youth—except for the well-trimmed beard Uncle Mike sported and the slight paunch her father had grown.

"Mallory, where are the girls?" Mallory turned to see her mother coming up behind her. Jake followed her and plopped down on a bench beneath the crab apple tree.

Mallory glanced around, then indicated the girls. "They're over there with the other kids. Geoff not here yet?"

"You know your brother." Mallory watched her mother straighten the neat lines of her linen skirt and ruffled yellow blouse. "He never shows up on time."

"Oh, Mom, you know Geoff isn't that bad."

"Yeah, right." Eric had wandered over from the horseshoe pit. "Geoff will probably be late for his own funeral."

"So speaks the man who was late for his own wedding."

Eric made a face at Mallory. "I had a flat tire. You know I hate to be late—"

"Whoa, dude! Check out those wheels!" Marty interrupted his dad. A low-slung, candy-apple-red sports car pulled up the long lane.

"I'll be—*uhn!*" Mallory cut off the swear word with a jab to Jake's ribs. He mumbled an apology as he rubbed his side, then spoke again. "Leave it to Geoff to surprise everyone by being on time."

"What is that?" Lindsay leaned against her father's leg.

"A car, stupid!"

"Marty! That's enough." Eric reached down and stroked his nine-year-old daughter's head. "Sweetie, that is a '55 Triumph convertible. Only your Uncle Geoff can afford one of those."

"Everybody knows that's a classic, dope!" Marty swished his sister's ponytail and took off in the direction of Geoff's vehicle. Geoff opened the door for the woman who had arrived with him. The copper highlights of her hair glinted in the afternoon light, and he wrapped his arm around her waist to escort her to the group congregated in the large yard.

"Everyone, this is Holly Marshall. Holly, meet the clan."

Holly's warm smile and quiet hello were echoed with a chorus of greetings. Marty's "What a babe!" earned him a light cuff on the back of his head from Geoff.

"Welcome to the zoo, Holly." Mallory shook Holly's hand, then kissed Geoff's firm jaw. "Forget trying to learn everyone's names. I've been in this family for thirty years and I still haven't done it."

"You must be Mallory. Geoff's talked a lot about you. I'm glad to meet you at last."

Her eyes were light brown, almost the same color as her hair— nothing like the syrupy blond bombshell Mallory had envisioned.

Eric dropped an arm around Geoff's shoulder. "You show up at the family picnic with a new car and a new woman. This must be serious, little brother. I don't recall you bringing someone to the reunion since your college days. She must be pretty special."

"I think so."

Eric turned to Holly. "You wouldn't happen to have a single sister that you'd like to introduce me to, would you?"

She laughed. "Sorry. I have one sister, and she's married."

Eric shrugged. "Figures."

"I'm starved, when do we eat?" Geoff asked the question just as the large bell on the back porch resonated its message across the yard down to the edge of the creek and out to the surrounding woods.

"Gather round for the blessing." Gramps waited for the group to quiet, then continued. "Precious Lord, we thank Thee for family and for this time that we can gather together around Thy table and fellowship with one another and with Thee. Bless this food, we pray in Thy Son's name." Chaos erupted as soon as the *amen* was heard. Mallory and Jake settled their daughters at one of the children's picnic tables, and then returned to get their own meals.

Jake took his heaping plate of food and sat opposite Geoff, who was digging into Aunt Patty's famed potato salad. Mallory sat across from Holly, whose plate held carrot sticks, celery, and a plastic cup filled with fresh fruit. She was drinking bottled water, as was Geoff. Mallory raised a brow at her brother.

Jake asked Mallory's unspoken question. "What, no wine cooler?"

"A new woman, a new lease on life. She's got me converted. You're looking at a new man."

"Please! I'm gonna throw up."

Mallory listened as her husband and brother fell into their easy banter. They were so similar—good-natured, slow to anger. Two of a kind. Jake and Geoff were on a roll as they each topped the other's stories of airplane flights. Holly seemed to be content listening, shaking with laughter at one point when Jake described trying to find the rest room in an airport in a Third World country.

When the meal was over, several cousins convinced Geoff to join them in a game on the basketball court in the old barn. Geoff and his cousins engaged in the male ritual of backslapping as they moved off in the direction of a large, stone structure set near the front of the house.

Jake slipped an arm around Mallory, kissed her on the cheek, and said in a low voice, "See you later." With that, he loped off after the others.

"Mommy, Mommy!" Breathless from her headlong flight, Renee dropped in her mother's lap. "Can we ride the horses? Can we? Gramps said we could if Lisa and Brad would take us. Pleeease?"

"No, honey."

"Pleeease?" Angel cajoled, echoing her sister's intonation perfectly.

"They'll be just fine. Lisa and Brad have been around horses forever," Aunt Patty assured Mallory. "Sunny and Prince are too old to do much more than walk, and the kids will just lead them around the corral." Aunt Patty smiled at the girls, who jumped up and down with excitement. "If it makes you feel any better, I'll go down and supervise."

"Okay, okay." Mallory laughed. She was outnumbered. "But be—"

"Careful!" Renee and Angel shouted in unison, drowning out their mother.

"My, they are getting big, aren't they?" Her father's younger sister sat down beside Mallory. Aunt Liz was a slight woman, too thin by even today's weight-conscious standards, and reminded Mallory of a small squirrel; her graying red hair was frizzed and her hands never rested. "My two young ones ran me ragged when they were that age. Why, it seems like yesterday. I was just saying to your Uncle Ken that we…"

Liz jabbered on, and Mallory only had to "Uh-huh" and "Um-hum" a few times to keep her going. Holly had to turn away to hide her grin, and Mallory hid her smile in her coffee cup.

It wasn't long before Mallory's mother joined them at the table. Mallory saw her eying Holly. *Here it comes.* Her mother might be tiny, but she packed a powerful punch. *I wonder how Holly will fare against Mom's verbal assault. This should be interesting.*

"Now, dear, tell us about yourself. How did you meet our Geoff?" Her mother's syrupy voice grated on Mallory's nerves, and had it not been for her own curiosity, she would have gotten up and left. Without pause, her mother continued. "Why, you haven't eaten a thing. Here, have some of this luscious chocolate cake. I took it, but I don't think I could eat another bite. You could do with a little more padding. Why, look at your thin arms and legs!" The remark held a scorpion's sting as Mallory's mother looked at Holly's jeans shorts and cropped T-shirt.

"Thank you for the offer, Mrs. Bennington, but I don't eat chocolate." Holly smiled. "Some people think I'm a health nut, but as a nurse I know how important nutrition is."

Mallory sat back, watching with increasing respect as Holly parried her mother's barbs with a firm kindness that drew the line at answering questions that were too personal. Before long, Gran rescued Holly from the verbal sparring match by insisting that she come and meet more of the grandchildren.

Mallory's mother flitted away as well, stopping to talk for a moment with her husband. Mallory's father frowned and said something. Her mother patted his arm. Her dad still bore the mark of his early military years, with squared shoulders and rigid posture. Strict discipline, dignity at all times, and absolute obedience were her father's rules to live by. Age hadn't seemed to change that aspect of his personality.

Her parents had always seemed to her an odd couple—two people living at opposite ends of the spectrum. Her mother's opinions were forever changing at the whim of the ambiguous—"What would they think?"—and her father was decisive, sometimes stern and unyielding. Mallory longed to be close to him, but she often found it hard to confide in him.

"Whew! What a workout." Jake jarred the table when he flopped down beside her, and Mallory shifted away from the clammy arm that rested against hers. A distinct smell of maleness poured from him and the sweat-soaked shirt he had stripped off. He used it to wipe the perspiration from his forehead. "I need to grab a drink and a quick shower. If the others beat me to it, I guess I can wash off in the pond!"

"You sure couldn't smell any worse."

Jake snapped his wet T-shirt at her and sauntered toward the coolers for a can of soda. Muscles kept fit with pickup games of basketball and tennis rippled along his broad, bare shoulder and glistened in the sunlight. He joined Geoff and several of Mallory's male cousins.

Mallory cleared her dinner debris from the table, loath to join in any of the conversations going on around her. She dumped her trash and wandered down the lane toward the barn.

Huge, gray quarried stones made up the foundation of the ancient structure. She entered its cool darkness, and the echo of the children's laughter out in the paddock blended with phantom voices from her childhood.

She and Geoff had spent a lot of time in this barn. It was larger than her Grandpa Kaufman's, and she had always preferred its musty, deserted solitude to the livestock that crowded every corner of her mother's home place. Mallory frowned in the faint light and made her way to the hayloft. She hadn't been up here since she was a kid. She and her brothers used to come to her grandparents' home for weeks at a time. This farm held her best childhood memories.

She walked to the far corner of the empty haymow, avoiding the curled and rotting floorboards. Grandpa Kaufman's haymow had been filled with hay and had a high mound of straw below it. When they were kids, Eric had dared her to jump into it.

Almost without thinking, she traced the ridge of skin on her elbow.

Eric, help me! I'm bleeding!

Mallory's heart began to pound, beating out a horrible rhythm that took her to her knees. What was happening to her? She… couldn't…breathe. The dust rose from the wooden floor and clogged her nostrils; air couldn't get through the thickness in her throat. The pulse of her heart stabbed pain through to her backbone and echoed in her ears.

Was she having a heart attack? She wrapped her arms hard against her ribs and prayed. She had to keep the unseen, unknown evil at bay.

Breathe, Mallory, breathe.

Sudden, deep gulps of fresh air entered her lungs, and she pressed her hands to her head. *In, out, slow now.*

Mallory slumped against the floor. Whatever it was, it was over now. She looked around, thankful that no one had witnessed her foolishness. She stood and dusted herself off.

"Tie up the mothers and we'll scalp their babies!"

A sound like a banshee yell pierced the air and sent another jolt of adrenaline pumping through Mallory's veins. She leaned over the edge of the loft. Her cousin's son, Blair, and her nephew Marty had sneaked up on their sisters and jumped out to scare them.

"Go 'way!"

Bedlam erupted. Blair whooped an Indian war cry, and Marty snatched one of the girls' dolls and swung it around by its hair. He pulled out his pocketknife. Lindsay shrieked at Marty and reached for the doll in his outstretched arms. He laughed and threw the doll to Blair.

"Give it back!" The game of keep away enraged the girls further, and Mallory raced down the ladder of the loft.

"Leave me alone! Leave me 'lone, I'm telling!"

Marty advanced toward Lindsay. "How ya gonna tell if you're all tied up?"

Mallory's jaw ached from gritting her teeth, and a fury rose deep within. Marty held both of Lindsay's arms behind her back, while Blair twirled the doll by her dress. His sister, Kristin, crouched in the hay, sobbing and clutching the remaining dolls to her chest.

"Let her go. Now!" Mallory grabbed Marty by the back of the collar and yanked him away from Lindsay. Startled, Blair tossed the doll to Lindsay.

"Give me that knife."

Marty stuffed his pocketknife into his jeans and jerked his shirt from Mallory's hands, then straightened his clothing.

"We didn't do nothin'."

"Yeah, right. Just scared two little girls half to death by threatening to tie them up. Twisting your sister's arm doesn't sound like nothing to me."

Blair's eyes widened at the anger in her words, and he shifted from one foot to the other. "Aw, they aren't hurt."

Mallory knelt down in front of the girls.

"They're just dweebs." Marty's tone was still defiant.

She spun around. "And you're a bully, just like…" Mallory took a steadying breath, then turned to wrap an arm around both the girls. "I think you owe these two an apology."

Safe within the protection of Mallory's embrace, Lindsay's small tongue darted out. Marty charged forward, but stopped when Mallory moved in front of Lindsay.

"C'mon, Blair, they're not worth our time." Marty jerked his head at his cousin and turned to leave the barn.

"I think you forgot something, young man."

"Yeah, whatever," he mumbled and continued to stride toward the sliding doors.

Blair took one last look behind him, then hurried after Marty.

Mallory inhaled several deep breaths and then looked down at the girls. "You both okay?" They nodded. By this time they had recovered enough to look smug as their brothers were sent off in disgrace.

"Come on, let's find you a better place to play."

They left the barnyard and passed by the corral. Mallory called to her girls and then led them all back toward the swings, where the adults were still relaxing under the shade trees after their heavy meal.

Certain the girls were engaged in a new game of duck-duck-goose, Mallory searched the yard until she spotted Eric. His large frame was sprawled in a chair beside her parents. Heat still curled inside her belly as she marched over to him.

"Do you have any idea what your son was doing?"

"Hard to tell."

"I caught him terrifying the girls."

"Mal, you get too excited. He was just being a boy."

"Eric, are you aware that your son carries a knife?"

"Yeah, so? I had one when I was that age."

"I caught him threatening—"

"I'm sure he was only having a little fun."

"A little fun! Why do you always—"

Her mother put her hand on Mallory's arm. "Are the girls all right?"

Eric looked toward the swing set and took a swig from the can he held in his hand. "They look fine to me."

"They are now," Mallory managed between her clenched teeth.

Her mother put her arm around Mallory's back and drew her toward the picnic tables. "Mallory, let's not cause a scene."

Mallory shook her head and cast a dark look at her brother, then pulled away from her mother and went in search of Geoff and Jake.

"Hey, Mallory, wait up!" Holly sprinted off the porch to join her. "Where are you headed?"

"I was just going for a walk." Mallory paused at the corner of the back stoop. "Did you lose Geoff?"

"He said he and Jake were going to cool off in the pond. I guess it sounded more fun to them than a shower."

"More like the guys beat them out of the hot water, and they were stuck with the swimming hole."

"Where is this pond?"

"The path is behind the barn. We've always called it the swimming hole. Years ago, Gramps put in a short dock and a floating raft. It's a great place for kids on a hot summer's day. Although mine are a little young yet."

Mallory continued on the faint trail, which was still visible among the brambles and weeds, until she came to the opening in the hedge that grew around the pond. They spotted Geoff sprawled on the sun-warmed bank. Jake surged through the mud at the edge of the pond, shaking his head to rid it of the water still streaming down his body. He flopped beside Geoff on the grass.

"You two look like a couple of beached whales." Mallory sat down between them and laughed as they moaned without opening their eyes. She patted Jake's stomach. "You aren't protected from the sun the way this hairy beast next to you is. Maybe you'd better slip your shirt on."

Holly prodded Geoff with the toe of her tennis shoe. "Get up, you lazy bum!"

Geoff grabbed her ankles and tipped her on top of him. "I'm ready for some dessert. Want to help appease my appetite?" His exaggerated leer brought laughter and a sharp swat from Holly. She pulled Geoff to his feet. "Let's take a walk."

Mallory watched them stroll away, their arms around each other's waists, Geoff's dark head bent close to Holly's lighter one. He whispered in her ear, and Mallory heard Holly's low chuckle.

"Well, that takes care of the lovebirds, how 'bout a walk of our own?" Jake stood to help Mallory to her feet.

She shrugged and brushed the dirt off the back of her shorts, then followed Jake as he headed toward the wooded hillside. She looked back over her shoulder and saw Geoff draw Holly into his arms. She stumbled, and Jake reached for her hand. "Watch it. This is pretty rough in here."

Halfway up the hill they spied a stand of old birch, and they made their way to the shade of the towering trees. Jake grabbed a low-hanging limb and pulled himself up into the branches.

Mallory bent, reached for her ankles, and allowed her body to stretch the knotted muscles in her lower back. She bent in the opposite direction with a low moan.

"You okay?" Jake inquired from his perch several feet above her. She glanced up through the leaves. He had climbed even higher and leaned back against the trunk, his feet balanced on a branch.

Mallory turned to rest against the smooth bark of the tree and stare out over the valley floor. She took a deep breath. *Old Man Mullins must be spreading manure.* From this vantage point, her grandparents' farmhouse looked like a miniature, and the neighboring fields spread out like a patchwork quilt. "This was always one of my favorite spots to come to when I was a child."

With his free hand Jake gestured toward the valley, "I need to bring my camera and get some photos here. I wonder why I never thought of it before."

Lost in her own world of remembering, Mallory didn't respond. It was here that Geoff had challenged her to climb to the highest branches of the swaying trees. She smiled, hearing again Geoff's high-pitched voice of childhood.

"Honest, Mally, it's not that high up. I won't let you fall. Go up just one more branch, 'cause then you can see over the top of the hill. Uncle Mike's house is on the other side. Can you see it yet?"

Then, on the heels of her memory, other images came unbidden to her mind…

"Come on, Mally! The hill's not that steep. Dig your heels into her side and make her move."

"I can't, Geo. She won't!"

Geoff turned his horse back toward Mallory's. He nudged his horse alongside her stubborn mare and grabbed the bridle to pull the old nag along in the wake of the younger gelding. "Geo, my knight in shining armor." *She slapped her hand on her forehead in a dramatic pose.* "What would I ever do without you?"

A sudden movement in Mallory's peripheral vision jerked her from the memory, and when a hand slid around her waist, Mallory yelped.

Jake lifted his hands and backed away. "I didn't mean to scare you, I just wanted a hug." His eyes narrowed, and a frown formed in the center of his brow.

Mallory tugged at the bottom of her cotton top. "Well, just watch it, will you?"

Jake snorted and began to descend the trail; Mallory followed him in silence.

There's no sense being mad at him. He hadn't meant to scare her. He never did. And it was a stupid thing to get mad over anyway.

Mallory released a long-drawn breath and hurried to catch up with Jake. When they were in sight of the yard, Mallory moved up beside him and slid her arm around his waist.

Her eyes lifted and met the puzzled frown that displaced the disgruntled look in his hazel eyes. She hugged him as they approached the backyard, where the adults were lounging in the afternoon shade. Her smile felt brittle, and she wondered if anybody would notice.

Jake didn't say anything, but he didn't push her away either. She released her arm from his waist and asked if he wanted a soda. He gave her a swift nod and headed toward the ice chest. "I'll get it. You want one too?"

"Coke, please."

She joined her grandmother and aunts at the picnic table littered with plastic foam cups and aluminum cans. Jake handed her a can that dripped with cold water, then moved off to join the men.

"I like my music loud!"

Mallory turned to find the source of the angry voice and spotted Marty and her grandfather facing off.

"You call that music?" Gramps shook his head. "That's nothing but noise, boy. Play it that loud, and you'll be deaf before you're twenty."

"Whatever."

Marty's mouth will get him in trouble yet. Mallory popped the tab and took a swig of cola.

Aunt Patty's dark eyes appeared owl-like from behind her thick glasses. "I really don't know what Martin and Alecia are going to do with that boy."

"It's Eric that needs to take control of Marty. If he doesn't, there's going to be a heap of trouble in store for them, that's for sure." Liz set down her tall glass of iced tea with a thump.

Mallory took another gulp of her soda and stifled the impulse to voice her opinion. *Maybe somebody ought to take control of Eric.* It was no wonder Marty had problems.

"It's a little hard to do when Eric only sees him once in a blue moon." This from Patty, who reclined in a lawn chair near the table.

"Why Catherine had to up and move halfway across the country is beyond me," Liz continued.

"She went home. That's the first place I'd head if Mike and I ever split up," Aunt Patty retorted.

Gramps's voice carried across the yard, rising with his ire. "If I'd smarted off like that when I was a young un, my granddaddy woulda picked me up and thrown me against the nearest tree. In fact, that's just what happened. I can tell you, I never did it again."

"Aw, Gramps, that was a thousand years ago." Marty shoved a lock of sandy hair from his forehead.

"Marty,"—Eric's voice dripped with sarcasm—"show a little respect for your great-grandfather. I know it's hard, but give it a whirl."

Marty ignored his father and sauntered away.

Great job, Eric.

Gramps rose from the chair and headed with a slow, awkward gait toward the house. "Young generation! Bunch of upstarts. Need a leather strap applied to their backsides."

Yeah, Gramps—Mallory directed a baleful glare at her brother—*and I know who you should start with.*

September 29

O Father, something's wrong. I'm having trouble with my hands. They get numb and my wrists burn, like a rug burn, but deep inside. There aren't any marks. I know I didn't injure myself—it can't be anything serious. It can't!

I'm having trouble holding my drawing pencils and paintbrushes. God, You wouldn't punish me that way, would You?

Seven

"Come on, sweetie. We're home." Mallory turned to wake Angel, who was curled up in the backseat. She slipped her portfolio under her elbow and lifted her sleepy daughter into her arms.

The trip to Paxton's Publishing House in upper Cleveland had been accomplished with relative ease and quiet, despite lunch-hour traffic. The meeting there had been brief, and Angel had been as good as her name, but Mallory was glad to get home.

"Let's go meet Renee's school bus." Wide-awake now, Angel took off with a shout. Mallory followed with less enthusiasm. Her babies were growing up, and Mallory wasn't ready for that to happen. Angel was now four, and last week Renee had turned seven. No longer did she ask for her mother's help in getting dressed, picking out her clothes, or even fixing her hair. She insisted she could do it all by herself and grew adamant when Mallory offered to help. Life hadn't been this complicated when Renee was a baby.

Mallory helped Renee down from the bus, listened to her excited chatter about school with half an ear, and watched the two girls scamper toward their promised treat of milk and granola bars. She walked into the kitchen and found her husband's assistant raiding the refrigerator—a sight that had become commonplace in the last five years. She didn't mind. She liked Joey, and the girls adored him.

"Hi, Joey."

"Hey, Malo." Joey knelt on the kitchen floor to give the girls an exuberant hug. He picked up a girl in each arm and raced out into the backyard. Their giggles filled the air.

Mallory shut the back door and went in search of Jake. Maybe he was downstairs in his darkroom She called to the basement to see if he was there, "Jake?"

"What?"

"I'm home."

"Okay."

She walked back down the hall to her studio and dropped into her chair, then pulled a notepad within reach, tucked a pencil behind her ear and reached for the new manuscript.

It didn't take long for her to read through the children's book, and when she was done, she swiveled in her chair to lift her feet onto the two-drawer filing cabinet.

She loved her studio. When she and Jake built their house, he had helped her design it. The tiled floor, built-in cupboards along one full wall, and the stainless-steel sink in the corner made it an efficient place to work. She loved the faint hint of buttercup in the walls. Through the picture windows she could see Joey and the girls still roughhousing in the backyard. Her easel and paint box sat next to the stack of canvases piled in the corner. This was a place where her creativity flourished. Most of the time.

Mallory looked down at the manuscript she was holding. How was she going to illustrate this thing? She threw the book on the desk and swung her chair around to stare at the seascapes calendar on the wall above her drawing board.

Her meeting earlier today hadn't gone the way Mallory had

envisioned. To start with, she had been about ten minutes late. She'd nodded to the receptionist, left Angel sitting in a chair where she promised to stay, and knocked on the door to Dorothy Baker's office.

Rich, elegant, and sophisticated, the room was a reflection of its owner. "Mallory. Done with the illustrations already?" Dorothy removed her gold-rimmed glasses and allowed them to hang by the ornate chain around her neck. Her silver hair was curled back from her narrow face in a chic, modern style. Her tailored navy business suit clung to still feminine curves.

"Let me take a look at what you have." She slid her glasses back on her nose and led the way to the large layout counter.

Mallory spread the stiff illustration boards out over the marbled counter, then moved to the side, twisting her hands as the art director scrutinized her work. After several moments Dorothy looked up. "These are excellent, as always. I'll send them up to Beth, who'll consult with the author, but I see no problems." She gestured toward a chair. "Do you have a few minutes? There is another project that I think would be well suited to your style of work."

"I brought Angel with me today. She's with Gina."

"I'm sure she'll be fine long enough for us to have a short chat." Dorothy poured Mallory a cup of coffee and made herself some tea before returning to her desk for a manuscript. She settled into a chair near Mallory and handed her the sheaf of papers.

"We want a light touch for this project, and I thought of you. It's special to me. I've fought long and hard to get this children's book published. It's a book that will help teach children not to be afraid to tell if someone tries to hurt them.

"I really want you to do the illustrations on it, Mallory. It has your style written all over it. You do such a wonderful job of capturing the essence of children. We'll need the illustrations for it in four months. No later than five."

Mallory skimmed the title page of the book, then riffled through the pages as words and phrases caught her eye. A tremor ran down her back. She looked up. "That's not enough time. Besides, I don't think I'm right for this project, Dorothy."

"Nonsense. Your work is exactly right for it."

"I've never done anything like this." Mallory wrinkled her nose. "It's a...delicate subject. Perhaps you should get someone else."

"I have every confidence in your ability to produce what we need for this book, Mallory. Take it for a week and see what you might be able to do with it. If you think you can, we'll have the contract waiting for your signature. Please give it a try."

It was the financial offer Dorothy dangled in front of her that had convinced Mallory to look it over.

She turned back from the window and picked up the manuscript. She appreciated Dorothy Baker's faith in her abilities, but she wished she had told the other woman no. *Who am I kidding? I need the money.* Mallory went back to the first page, removed the pencil from behind her ear, and began to jot down notes as she reviewed the text.

She stood to take a break a short time later and went to check on the girls, who were playing with Barbie dolls in their room. Mallory didn't disturb them, but grabbed a drink from the refrigerator before returning to her project. She stretched her shoulders and rolled her neck, then she sat down again, determined to keep at it until she at least had some ideas on paper. She tried to concentrate on the words from the manuscript. Images bombarded her, and she began to sketch what her mind's eye was seeing. A groan escaped her lips as hot stabbing pain worked its way down into her fingers. She dropped her pencil and grabbed her wrist.

Joey leaned around the doorway of her studio. "Problems, Malo?"

She spun her stool to meet Joey's concerned stare and continued to massage her wrist. "I've had some pain in my hands lately. It's been driving me nuts because it comes at the worst times, like when I'm in the middle of delicate detail work. What are you doing anyway?"

The redhead moved further into Mallory's studio. "Mission of mercy. The boss man is about to dehydrate, so I volunteered to get some refreshments."

He set the beverages down on a stand and reached for Mallory's wrist. "Used to do this for my mama." His fingers prodded her flesh finding and loosening knotted muscles. "Does Jake know? Have you seen anyone about this?"

"No to both. Thanks, Joe, that's enough." She disengaged her wrist from his hands. "I think I've just been working too hard; it's probably a pinched nerve."

"You should have that wrist checked out." He leaned his jean-clad hip against her drawing board and looked at her preliminary sketches. "You are one radical artist." He picked up the first drawing—the face of a terrified child. "Whoa, who scared her? The devil? What's this book about?"

"Sexual abuse. Listen, I've got a deadline that's fast approaching—"

"Yeah, yeah, my cue to split. Besides, boss man will be roaring soon." He paused in the doorway, "I'll be praying for your hands."

"Thanks, Joey." She reached for her pencil again, but was interrupted by the light buzz of the cordless phone beside her. Jake didn't like to be disturbed when he was in the darkroom, so he had put the phone in her studio.

"Hello."

"Mally? It's Geoff. How are you doing, Sis?"

"Geoff! I didn't know you were home yet. I thought you were going to be in Columbus until next Tuesday."

"I finished up early and got back last night. Went by Mom and Dad's this morning. Uh, Mally—Mom said she hadn't talked to you this week. Eric didn't call you by any chance, did he?"

"Eric? Why would he call me? I mean, nothing's happened to him or anything, has it?" Mallory shifted the phone to her shoulder and began to sketch.

"No, Eric's fine. The guy could roll into a manure pile and wind up selling the stuff as perfume. It's not Eric. It's Marty."

"Marty? He's okay, isn't he? Not hurt or anything—"

"No, no, he's fine. That is, he isn't hurt or anything, just…" Mallory could picture Geoff rubbing his forehead. He always did that when he was agitated, and he certainly sounded that way right now.

"All right, Geoff, what's going on?"

"Look, I guess there's no other way to say it than flat out. The little twerp was caught molesting his six-year-old cousin. At a church social function, no less."

"He *what?* Who was it? Is she…" Panic swelled within her, and Mallory clutched the phone to her ear, trying to sort through the shock assaulting her. A rush of nausea rose to her throat, and she fought the urge to be ill right at her desk. *O Father God! That poor child...*

"Take it easy, Sis. It wasn't anybody on our side of the family. One of Catherine's sister's girls, I think. Why Eric hasn't done something about him before now is beyond me, except that the sorry so-and-so hasn't taken responsibility for anything in his life. Why should he start with his kid?"

"What did he say about it? What did Mom say? Never mind, I can just imagine what Mom said. Geoff, I can't believe—"

Mallory broke off, remembering Marty's out-of-control behavior at the family picnic. *"Leave me 'lone! I'm telling!"* She shivered. "I guess I can believe it. I told Eric in July he needed to do something about his son."

"Like that's ever worked before."

"You said Marty got caught. Does that mean they're going to charge him with anything?" Mallory snapped her drawing pencil in two. It jabbed her forefinger, and she stuck the finger in her mouth to soothe the pain.

"Already done. A Sunday school teacher caught him in the act and was required by law to turn him in. His court date is set for next Friday. He's in the detention center now. If he's convicted he could end up in juvenile hall."

Good. He can't hurt anybody else there.

Mallory shifted in her chair, suddenly uncomfortable. Was she being too hard on the kid? But what would make someone hurt somebody else like that? She closed her eyes. *I will not cry.* Sadness permeated her very soul. *God, help me. Help that sweet little girl.*

"Look, Mally, don't dwell on it. It'll work out all right. I told

Mom I would be the one to tell you, but I wouldn't call her for a day or two until she settles down."

"Thanks, Geoff." Mallory sat for a few moments holding the phone after the line had gone dead. She hit the Off button, replaced the phone on the desk, and stared at the drawing paper in front of her. Long black slashes had defaced the laughing little girl in the delicate draft she had been working on.

She ripped it into shreds and threw it in the wastebasket.

Only Renee's and Angel's plaintive cries for something to eat had drawn Mallory from her desk. She had just started frying hamburgers for them when Jake came into the kitchen. She stiffened when he wrapped his arms around her and pulled her against his chest. He kissed her hair, then released her and began to rummage in the refrigerator.

"Smells good. I'm starved. What else are we having?"

"Hamburgers aren't good enough for you?"

His eyes widened a fraction. "Hey, I was asking a question, not complaining. Hamburgers are fine."

"Just set the table. There's a new bottle of ketchup in the pantry if there isn't any in the fridge."

The girls came in then, clamoring they were hungry, and Jake began to make a game out of laying things on the table in alphabetical order. The girls' giggles filled the room, and Mallory's head began to pound. The simple meal took little time to eat, and when Jake offered to clean up, she agreed with relief.

"Girls, time for your baths. The Missions Fair at the church is tomorrow."

Jake snapped his wet dishtowel at a squealing Renee as she escaped through the doorway. "Count me out."

"You aren't going with us?"

"No, I thought I'd work in the yard. Wash the car, maybe find some time for a nap."

"Fine." She shoved away from the table, making the chair legs scrape in protest at the abrupt action. "Suit yourself, I've got laundry to put away."

Jake followed her up the stairs. "What are you so mad about?"

Mallory grabbed the laundry that lay on the bed, threw it into a dresser drawer, and slammed it shut. Did he have to ask? She strode to their bathroom and pulled a washcloth off the towel rack.

"You'd think it was the least you could do." She raised her voice over the sound of water running in the sink. "Is it so hard for you to do something for the girls? Just once it would be nice not to have to make excuses for you. Some people don't even believe I have a husband since they've never seen you."

"Hey—I go with you Christmas and Easter. Church is your thing. Why are you harping on me about going tomorrow? It hasn't been that big of a deal in the past. We'll do something in the afternoon when you get home. I'll take you out to dinner."

Mallory heard the thump of Jake's boots as he removed them and dropped them on the floor. She changed her clothes, still fuming when she heard him enter the bathroom doorway. She scrubbed her face with the washcloth. When she lifted her head, she saw him in the reflection of the mirror. He stared at the low-cut edge of her nightgown. She knew that warm, lazy look; it had worked on her more than once. She flung the washcloth into the sink and raked her hair from its constricting band.

Jake put his hands on Mallory's shoulders and turned her from the sink. "Sweetheart, what's eating you? You have been ticked all night long. The girls and I had some quality time this evening. Before supper I read to them for half an hour, and I played Candy Land at least three times. So what gives?"

Mallory stood unyielding in his arms, resisting his gentleness. He pressed her against his chest and kissed the top of her head.

"Jake, don't…"

"Come on, Mal." He coaxed her closer and began to whisper in her ear, persuading her to rest her full weight against him. Mallory forced her tense nerves to relax, and Jake enticed her into bed.

"Jake?" Mallory lifted her chin toward her shoulder.

An indistinct mumble answered her as he buried his face deeper into the back of her neck and tightened his arms around her. "Mmm."

With a slight protest from the now slumbering Jake, Mallory rolled to the side of the bed and made her way to the bathroom. She shut the door, then turned on the taps to the large whirlpool tub. Steam drifted from the water, and Mallory waited for the tub to fill. Despite its warmth and the central heating of the house, she couldn't stop shivering.

Mallory flinched as her aching body submerged in the hot water, and she closed her eyes. The whirlpool jets began their work. The day had been a long one, and she hadn't even told Jake about Marty.

She scooted down further into the water. She would tell him tomorrow…if the opportunity arose. Mallory struggled with her conscience and tried not to admit that she was afraid of how Jake would respond. What would he say? Would he be angry? Or worse, would he think it was no big deal? She turned off the jets and added more hot water.

Eric was the one at fault. She sank back down into the soapy water's comforting warmth. If Eric were any kind of a father—

Mallory cut off the bitter thought. In a strange way, she almost felt sorry for him. He was her brother, and, after all, she did love him. He just…annoyed her. It hadn't always been that way. She could remember him pushing her on the swing when she was a little girl, teaching her how to tie her shoes, even playing dolls with her.

Enough!

The last thing she wanted to think about was Eric. What she really wanted was to ease her throbbing body. Her toe nudged the button to turn on the whirlpool again.

The warm massage of the water began to make her sleepy, and her tense muscles relaxed. She wouldn't think about any of it now. Not Eric…not Marty…not even Jake. It felt too good just to lie here and think of nothing.

She yawned and closed her eyes.

"Mal?"

A gentle hand shook her shoulder.

"Honey, wake up. You fell asleep in the tub."

Mallory blinked to rouse herself. Jake held out a towel and helped her climb out. She forced herself to dry off, then put on her nightgown and sat on the edge of the bed to dry the back of her hair. Jake knelt in front of her, and the solemn look on his face halted her vigorous rubbing. Something was wrong.

"What?"

Jake's broad forehead was creased in a frown; his eyes were bright with unshed tears.

"What's wrong?"

He patted her leg and cleared his throat. "Your mom called. I have some bad news."

"What happened?" Mallory scrunched the wet towel in her fists.

His hands cupped her face. "Babe, I don't know how else to say it—Gramps is gone."

Gone? "Wh-what do you mean gone?" It came out in a hoarse whisper.

"He died this evening."

"No!" She didn't want to believe it. She wouldn't believe it. "Not Gramps."

"He had a massive heart attack."

"B-but I just saw him last week. He was here for Renee's party." Mallory grabbed Jake's shoulders and began to shake them. "No. Jake—no!"

October 2

God, I am so grateful that Gramps is in heaven, that I'll see him again, but it doesn't make the hurt go away. I loved his sense of humor and the way he always spoiled me. My happiest memories are of being with him and Gran.

How do I let him go? Who will comfort me now?

Eight

The smell of roses and the muted tones of music floated on the air as the Carlisles stepped through the door of the Taft Funeral Home. Jake took Mallory's arm, and she stiffened her back against the grief that threatened to overwhelm her. Calling hours hadn't begun, but the room was already filled with Benningtons.

She looked over the crowd and saw the stooped form of her grandmother at the head of the casket. Gran stroked her beloved husband's cheek, and Mallory swallowed past the lump in her throat. The tears that had been overflowing since the phone call two days ago fell once again.

Eric handed Mallory his handkerchief, and she looked up into his somber eyes. An instant later she found herself engulfed in his embrace as her tears drenched his striped tie. He stroked her hair and let her cry.

"This can't be happening."

He leaned back, took the hanky from her hand, and wiped her eyes with it. "Okay?"

She shook her head, "No, but I will be."

"You all right, Mally?"

Mallory flinched at the sound of the voice near her ear and jerked away from Eric. Why did she suddenly feel so ashamed of

Geoff's seeing her hugging Eric? *It doesn't make sense.* "Geoff! You startled me."

"Sorry, didn't mean to. How are you doing?"

She shrugged. "I want to see Gran."

"I'll take you." Geoff wrapped a protective arm around her and steered her past the small clusters of relatives.

She clung to her grandmother's frail shoulders. Arthritic hands patted Mallory's back and brought an onslaught of fresh grief. Mallory stared down at her grandfather's tanned, leathered face, remembering the way he used to wake from his afternoon nap, expecting him to yawn and stretch his arms wide. She shook her head. Gramps would never open his eyes again.

"Shush, child. The Lord gave us sixty-five wonderful years together, and I praise Him for every one."

Gran wrapped her arms around Mallory. Her steady heartbeat and loving arms enfolded Mallory with a sense of peace. She was amazing. "How can your faith be so strong? Aren't you angry? Don't you even want to ask God why?"

"I'm over eighty years old, child. Seventy-two of them I've been walking with my Lord, and He's never failed me, not once. Even now I feel His presence and His strength."

Mallory nodded, knowing Gran would want her to share that confidence in God. And she wanted to. But all she felt was sorrow. Deep, gut-wrenching sorrow that threatened to swallow her whole.

"Insomuch as it has pleased Almighty God to remove from this world the soul of our dear, departed friend, we now commit his body to the ground to await the resurrection of the dead as fore-told by the apostle Paul."

The pastor stepped back from the draped casket, and four elderly soldiers in worn uniforms moved forward to lift and fold the flag. They passed the three-cornered flag to Gran and saluted before taking their place in the crowd. A lone trumpeter stood on the hill above them, and the mournful sound of taps pierced the sultry air.

When Mallory's father buried his head in his hands, her mother wrapped her arms around him as a shuddering sob coursed through him. Mallory fought back her own tears.

I've never seen Daddy cry.

An explosion of sound rocked her back as seven rifles fired in unison. Once. Twice. Three times. Mallory turned into Jake's embrace and squeezed her eyes closed against the pain as the funeral director's calm voice announced the end of the committal service.

At the social hall one of her grandfather's American Legion bud-dies reached for Mallory's hand, gripped her fingers, and shared how much he had appreciated her grandfather's friendship in the years since they had served together. He shuffled toward her grand-mother to say his good-byes, and Jake set a plate of food down in front of her.

"You need to eat something, Mal. You haven't eaten for two days."

"I hate funeral food."

"I know, but at least try."

She tucked a napkin under Angel's chin. They had picked up the girls from the sitter after they left the graveside; Jake had been adamant that they were too young to attend the funeral.

When Jake turned to shake hands with a family friend, Mallory swapped her plate with an empty one nearby. She sipped her coffee and looked around the fellowship hall.

"How did Renee's birthday party go?"

Mallory turned to her aunt. "Okay." A glance to the other side of her confirmed that Jake had gone back to the food line. "There were ten girls squealing and running through our house. Of course, Jake wasn't anywhere to be found. He was working. If it hadn't been for Geoff coming to the rescue, I don't know what I would have done."

Aunt Patty followed Mallory's stare. "You and Jake not getting along?"

"Oh, you know how it is. Nothing major." She balled the napkin in her fist and pitched it onto her plate.

"Ruth, Liz, and I were wondering if one of the grandkids would want to spend a few days with Mom. I'm not far away, but Mike has an overnight business trip for the farm bureau and he wants me to go with him. I think we all would feel better if she had someone with her."

"The girls and I can go stay with Gran," Mallory volunteered. "I'll go suggest it to her now."

Gran was sitting with Uncle Mike in the far corner of the room. Mallory moved through the crowded tables, just missing a run-in with Lindsay and a heaping plate of dessert. The conversation at a nearby table caught her attention.

"Marty is still in the detention center. From what I understand, he has to go to counseling once a week and has to do three months of community service and pay his fines."

"Eric's furious. He has to take time away from his business every week. He has to go into counseling with Marty, and on the days of individual counseling, he has to take him."

Good! Eric needs it too. Maybe more than his son. Mallory hurried past her cousins to kneel next to her grandmother's chair. She laid a hand on the older woman's knee, and waited until Gran had finished her conversation.

Eleanor Bennington readjusted her glasses, then glanced down at her granddaughter.

"Gran, I was wondering if you would like some company for the rest of the week?"

"Child, don't you go fussing over me." The snow-white head bobbed. "I know where this is coming from. The girls are all concerned about me rattling around in that big old house by myself, aren't they?"

Mallory smiled at her insight. "Yes, but Gran, I need to get away for a while. Jake will be gone and I don't want to be alone. I need to spend some time at the farm. Can I, Gran?" Mallory's voice wobbled and she cleared her throat. "Would you mind if the girls and I came for the week?"

"Since you've put it that way..." Gran's smile soothed the ache in Mallory's heart. "Shall I just ride with you to your house while you get some things packed? Or shall I ride home with Mike and you come later?"

"Why don't you go home with Uncle Mike? It will take awhile to gather up what we need." Mallory stood and kissed her grandmother's soft cheek. "Thanks, Gran. I'll see you later tonight."

* * *

Jake threw the last of his things in his duffel bag, eager to be gone. He was tired of the arguments, the recriminations for things out of his control, the anger at offenses he didn't even know he'd committed. And this latest stunt, not telling him about the Visa card…

How could she max out two credit cards? What did she buy? Jake slammed his dresser drawer.

Only his shaving kit was left. He strode toward the bathroom. Mallory's reflection wavered in the mirror as he opened the door to the medicine cabinet. She was still in the dress she'd worn to the funeral. She shook her hair free from its confinement and fluffed the ends of the dark strands, then slipped off her shoes and tossed them into the closet. Her reddened nose and pale cheeks made her eyes appear even larger than usual. There was an ethereal fragility about her that unnerved him. She looked as though she would shatter at the slightest pressure.

Losing her grandfather had been a blow. Jake closed his eyes and winced as guilt assaulted him. He knew she was hurting. He also knew that whatever it was she needed, he didn't seem to be the one to give it to her.

He'd tried. He had taken time off from work to be with her, but it hadn't seemed to matter. She wouldn't eat, wasn't sleeping, and wanted no comfort, at least from him. But he was hurting too. He snapped his satchel closed. He couldn't do anything here anyway. Besides, he didn't have any choice. He had to work, didn't he? He moved to the bathroom and opened the door of the medicine cabinet and began to gather what he needed from the shelf.

He entered the bedroom but stopped when he saw Mallory

lying on her side with her hands tucked up under her head. She had drawn herself up into a tight little ball. His chest squeezed as if it were inside a hydraulic vise.

Mallory sat up on the edge of the bed when she saw him. Her hand trembled as she pushed her hair away from her face. "Are you leaving now?"

"The sooner I go, the sooner I can get back to you and the girls. When I talked to Joey, he said we could catch an early flight to New York. I left the number by the kitchen phone. I should only be gone a few days." He dropped his kit on the chair beside his bag and walked back toward her, wondering what he could say, how he could make her understand. "Besides, you and the girls are going to the farm to stay with Gran. It'll be good for all of you." She didn't respond. "Look, I wouldn't go if I didn't have to, you know that."

"Yeah, sure." Mallory slid from the bed and brushed past him to pick up her brush from the vanity.

"What's that supposed to mean? I don't want to leave you, but I do have to work."

"I understand." There was nothing wrong with the words she spoke, but the studied dullness of her tone made them sarcastic. She kept her back to him, brushing her hair with long, steady strokes. Anger flared hot and deep in the pit of Jake's abdomen.

"Why are you doing this?"

"Doing what?"

Jake raked his hands through his hair. "You know 'what'! Your coldness is like a block of ice between us." He and Mallory faced each other, squared off like fighters in a ring. What was happening to them?

He remembered his conversation with Geoff at the funeral dinner and clenched his fists. "Your brother told me about the money."

The hairbrush clattered into the sink. "He promised he wouldn't say anything."

"It just slipped out. He also told me about Marty." He watched her face but saw only a flicker of reaction. "Well?"

"Well, what? He's a little twerp."

"I'm not talking about your nephew, and you know it. How could you do this, Mallory? What did you spend nine thousand dollars on? And why didn't you tell me?" He shifted his weight and placed his hands in his back pockets, telling himself not to lose control, to be calm, rational. He needed some answers.

"Because I knew you'd overreact like you're doing right now."

"Overreact?" Jake swore. "I hate being in debt and especially to your brother."

"Geoff doesn't mind. Besides, what are you so uptight about? I have money due from my last project. We'll be able to cover it."

"All right, all right!" Jake threw up his hands. "So we can take care of it. That's not the real problem. The problem is you lied to me. Don't you get it, Mal? You're shutting me out. What's with you anyway? You won't let me get close to you. Not emotionally. And God forbid I should touch you physically!"

Mallory closed her eyes and wrapped her arms around herself. Two fat tears slipped down her cheeks. She began to rock herself back and forth, and Jake felt lower than the underside of a worm.

He hated it when he made her cry.

October 9

I can feel myself pulling inward. I want to lock all the doors and windows and withdraw to someplace safe. I feel my armor slipping.

Then what will protect me?

Nine

Mallory's thoughts scampered through her mind as her feet scattered leaves from the path. It was Friday. The swiftness of the week at the farm had been bittersweet. She and Gran had laughed and cried, sometimes at the same time. Saying good-bye was hard. Mallory leaned against the bark of her favorite climbing tree and allowed the memories to engulf her.

Everywhere she looked brought flashes from her past. The fields where she and her brothers had followed the tractor and wagon picking up rocks, the abandoned chicken house, the corncrib where they helped shuck corn, the farmhouse. Looking at the house now, Mallory realized it needed painting and some work done on the porch. She hadn't noticed that during their reunion.

It was hard to believe that just months ago everybody had been together, celebrating. Mallory's gaze passed over the place that had been her haven in an often-hostile world. No, it wasn't the place…it was the people. And it would never be the same without Gramps. She closed her eyes and drew in a deep, painful breath.

Blinking back tears, her eyes skimmed over the old homestead. Seeing the TV antenna brought a smile in spite of the tears as she recalled the only time Gramps had paddled her. She had been climbing the forbidden tower when he had stormed out of the house, carrying a newspaper. She hadn't been able to get higher than the fifth rung. Upon seeing his approach she hastened down as fast as she could, but hadn't been fast enough. He grabbed her arm and smacked her bottom with the rolled paper. It made a loud noise and little else, but it had done the trick. Mallory had run into the house crying her eyes out. She flung herself into Gran's waiting arms and sobbed against the worn apron. "Gramps doesn't love me anymore. Gran, he hit me!"

"Sweetie, you were doing something Gramps forbade you to do. He paddled you because you disobeyed him and because that tower is right next to the lane. If you'd fallen when a car was coming, you would have been hit, and Gramps and I would be so sad if you got hurt while visiting us."

Mallory shook her head at the memory. *I never told Gramps what an impact he'd had on my life. Now it's too late. I'll never get to tell him. God, could You tell him for me?*

Mallory turned her thoughts back to the present as her eyes scanned the vista before her. Autumn had painted the hillside in vivid colors of red, gold, and orange. The last of the colored leaves contrasted with the endless blue sky. The rich farmlands were at rest now, except for the last of the corn.

She hugged her grandfather's Bible against her chest as she moved deeper into the woods behind the farmhouse. Tears burned her eyes as she paused to thumb through the well-worn book. On the cover page was an inscription that read, "To my sweet Paul, Merry Christmas! Your beloved Eleanor, 1932." And just below that was another inscription, in the same elegant script: "To Mallory, Gramps loved you exceedingly, and so do I. Gran."

She stared down at the soft, worn leather. Every evening Gramps would read from his Bible as they gathered in the living room for devotions before going to bed. His big, booming voice brought the stories from the Bible to life. The next day she and Geoff often played games based on the Bible characters. Mallory was always David, Geoff was Goliath. Or Daniel in the lions' den.

Now, as she thought back on it, she realized Gramps had been planting the seeds of her faith. *Oh, Gramps, I took you for granted.*

She reached for a grapevine. Running her hand down the rough bark, she tipped her head to scan the monolith rock formation crowding against the towering oak tree supporting the vine swing. *It was right here that Gramps taught me about trust.* How old had she been...five? Scared of her own shadow, but wanting to do everything the boys were doing. She remembered being so terrified of heights and of falling that she would have nightmares about it. The dreams lost their hold on her the summer they spent several weeks here.

I think it happened when Gramps taught me to conquer my fear by facing it head-on.

Gramps' voice from yesteryear echoed in her mind, along with her own.

"Grab the vine, Mally."

"I'm scared! What if I fall and get hurt?"

"Mally, my Mally, I won't let you fall. I won't let anything hurt you. Trust me. Let's swing out together. You hold my neck, and I'll hold the rope. Ready?"

The cawing of a crow dissipated the images of the past. Mallory tried to fight down the lump in her throat. "Oh, Gramps!" Fresh tears made their way down her cheeks. "You taught me to trust, to have fun, to be me. Whenever I needed you, you were always there. Through all my years you supported me, helped me, loved me—even when I was at my worst, rebellious and wild, you always loved me."

Mallory had thought she knew what it was like to be alone with Jake gone so much, but nothing compared to the abandonment she felt at that moment. *O God, please, please help me. I feel so hollow, so full of emptiness.* She sank into the leaves, pulled her legs to her chest, and buried her head in her arms.

Jake was late. He was more than two hours behind schedule, and the last thing he wanted to do was tangle with the Benningtons, but he didn't have much choice. He had promised Mallory he would work a half-day so he could be there to help the crew that had assembled at Gran's. Uncle Mike farmed the land and took care of some of the upkeep of the house, but there were a number of jobs that needed doing. The family workday had been scheduled long before Gramps had passed away, and Gran told the family it would be okay to keep the date.

Jake slowed his vehicle and turned down the farm lane. He saw Angel's red sweatshirt streak across the backyard. Renee stuffed an armful of leaves in a garbage bag, dropping most of them on the ground, while her grandfather and great-uncles raked the large yard. Jake shut off the car engine.

"Daddy!"

His girls' greeting drew him from the car. Angel caught him around the knees, and he swung her up into his arms. "Hi, sweetheart." He kissed her hair, and the pungent smell of smoke assaulted his nose.

"I been helpin'."

"She can't rake or put them leaves in the bag like me."

Jake reached down to hug Renee. "I know Grampa Martin and Uncle Mike are thankful for your help, honey."

Jake set Angel on the ground, and the girls ran back to the yard. He waved to the men and headed for the kitchen door.

"Jake, you darling boy, you missed lunch. Can I get you something?"

"No thanks, Aunt Patty. I've already eaten." He turned to Eleanor Bennington who was seated at the table. "How are you, Gran?"

"Making it just fine, with the Good Lord's help." She patted his hand where it rested on her shoulder. "I'm thankful for the good care I've received from my children and grandchildren."

"Looks like they've been working hard."

"You haven't seen the half!" Liz came in from the front parlor, carrying a duster in one hand and adjusting the bandanna on her head with the other. "We've cleaned, dusted, sorted, torn up, and thrown out more things than I even knew Mom and Dad owned!"

"Maybe I spoke too soon." Gran looked at her daughter and daughter-in-law. "They've all been after me for a while to get things in order around here."

"Where's Mallory?" Jake turned as his mother-in-law entered the room. The lights flickered off, then on again.

"That Eric!"

"Oh my, I do hope the dear knows what he's doing."

"He *is* an electrician, Patty." Alecia looked at Jake. "He was in the attic checking the wiring, then said something about checking the fuse box. Mallory was up there doing some sorting, I think."

"I'll check it out." Jake took the narrow stairs two at a time, glad to leave the confines of the kitchen. He was uncomfortable around that many women. "Mal!"

"Up here." The muffled voice came from the dark hole above him. "Eric went to fix the lights."

Jake started up the ladder, and light dispelled the gloom just as he reached the top step. He sneezed. "This place is a mess. What are you doing?"

Particles of dust hung suspended in a channel of daylight that streamed through the clouded window. Mallory sat beside an open steamer trunk. A mound of clothes and shoes were heaped beside her, and stacks of books and papers were strewn in a haphazard pile on the floor. A lopsided antique dressmaker's dummy, yellowed with age, stood behind her. There was a long, black streak on her forehead. She looked as if she had come in from a hard day at play and was ready to try dressing up in her mother's clothes. Or her grandmother's clothes.

Mallory shoved the hair out of her face, leaving another smudge of dirt across her cheek. "It was Aunt Liz's idea. Notice I'm the one doing this. I think we should just pitch this stuff, but there are a lot of memories up here. Made a great hideout when we played cops and robbers." She rolled onto her knees. "What time is it?"

"It's quarter to four. Why?" Eric's work boots shook the old wooden planking as he stepped around the ladder and ducked to avoid the slanted ceiling. "Hey, Jake! You made it now that the work's all done."

"I had a meeting." Jake walked to the far wall. Dozens of boxes were piled in the corner.

Mallory looked at him. "What meeting?"

Bits and pieces of electrical tape and wire lay scattered among the tools on the floor. "Looks like you've been busy," Jake commented to Eric.

"Got it licked now, I think." Eric picked up a length of electrical cord and began to coil it around his elbow and hand.

"You didn't tell me about any meeting, Jake. You were supposed to be here to help us at twelve." Mallory stood and brushed the dirt off her hands. She rubbed them together and stroked the length of her fingers.

"Must have been a blonde." Eric chuckled at his own joke and yanked on the last of the wiring. It slithered from beneath a cardboard box, and he stepped over it to avoid getting tangled, then began to wrap it around his arm again.

"You had a meeting that took three hours?" Mallory kicked aside the pile of books and clothes, making a path to walk through.

"I had lunch with a colleague."

"Like I said, a blonde."

"Oh shut up, Eric." Mallory started down the ladder. "This was a waste of time."

Eric stared after Mallory, then shook his head at Jake. "What's with her?"

"She's your sister. You tell me." Jake followed his wife downstairs and caught up with her at the front door. "Mallory, where are you going?"

"I wanted to wave good-bye to Daddy and Mother. They're leaving." Laughter rumbled down the hallway. "Everybody else is in the kitchen. Let's get the girls."

"Martin and I were down by Digger Creek, skinny dippin', and just as the train came by, we stood up." Uncle Mike rested his arms against the kitchen sink and faced his audience seated around the table. "What we didn't know was that Pa was on that train coming home on leave."

Jake sat down next to Aunt Patty, and Mallory scooted a chair next to Gran. When Angel saw her mother, she pulled her thumb out of her mouth and scrambled off of Gran's lap and onto her mother's.

"What's *skinny dippin'?*" Renee looked at Jake from across the table.

"Never mind."

"Don't you even *think* about telling her," Mallory warned her uncle. "We'll discuss it later, Renee."

"Anyway, we were happy to see Pa when he got home, but he grabbed us both by the arms and hauled us out behind the barn, tugged our britches down, and whipped us to within an inch of our lives. It was five years later before I ever found out why."

Liz laughed. "You were always making Daddy mad about something. Remember the day Daddy caught Martin drag racing down on Bender's Road?"

Uncle Mike groaned, then laughed. "Pa took a pound of skin off his back. I think that's when he decided to run away and join the military, but Martin was only fifteen."

"Gramps did that to Daddy?" Mallory's eyes widened.

"I believe Paul saw an awful lot of himself in Martin and didn't want him to grow up to be just like him. Your grandfather was a different man, though, once he found the Lord."

Eric came through the doorway. "Of course he was. After all, according to you, Gran, God takes care of everything."

"He does, Eric. I wish you believed that, honey."

Eric looked at Jake and rolled his eyes, and Jake winked back at him. Gran was worse than Mallory at trying to get everyone to buy into the whole God thing.

"I tied off that line above the attic stairs, but it will need to be replaced." Eric dumped a bright orange electrical cord at Renee's feet. The end of the cord caught on her shoe. She giggled and swung her feet out at her uncle. "Watch it, rug rat, or I'll tie your legs to the chair."

"Let's go, Jake."

Mallory's abruptness caught him off guard. He looked at her and was startled to see how pale she was. "Are you all right, Mally?"

"We need to get the girls home." Her words were impassive as she stood Angel on the floor, but Jake saw her hand tremble when she reached for Renee and pulled her from her seat.

"Mommy!"

"Get your coats, girls."

"Can't we stay?"

"I said let's go. Now."

Jake followed his wife and daughters out of the house amid calls of farewell from her bewildered family.

Eric stopped him just outside the door. "What was that all about?"

Jake shrugged his shoulders and lifted his hands. "I haven't got a clue." *But I intend to find out.* Jake followed his wife to the car.

He needed some answers.

November 11

Angel wet the bed again last night. She woke up screaming and crying over and over, "A bad man wants to hurt me; a bad man wants to hurt me, Mommy."

I don't know how to keep her safe.

Ten

Mallory closed her journal at the sound of approaching footsteps. Confused by a sudden rush of guilt, she hid the book in the bottom drawer of her nightstand underneath a stack of lingerie. A door closed with a soft thud. Water began to run, and Mallory let out her breath.

It's just one of the girls going to the bathroom.

Silence once more settled over the household, and Mallory relaxed. Jake had called from the office earlier; he'd be home late. *Of course.* His work consumed him.

She went to her vanity table and grabbed up her brush. She and the girls should be the center of his life, not his work. The stiff bristles of the brush scraped against her tender scalp and brought tears to her eyes. She dropped the offending object on her dresser and stared into the mirror. Maybe she should cut her hair.

It was the same shade as Geoff's, and when she was younger she had bemoaned the fact that he had gotten the curls, not her. He had reassured her that he liked her hair straight. It was Geoff who had begun the nightly ritual of brushing her hair. She'd been six, and her hair had fallen to the middle of her shoulder blades. It tangled so when she slept that getting ready for school had been a nightmare. He had convinced her she needed to braid it and had started combing it for her at bedtime.

Mallory picked up her hairbrush again. *One, two, three, four…* She made herself do the requisite hundred strokes, then went to the sink to remove her makeup. The heat from the washcloth eased the tension throbbing at her temples, and Mallory pressed it against her skin, then paused. Was that a sound? Had she just heard a slight thump over the sound of the water rushing from the faucet? Her hands stilled against her face, and she cocked her head. Maybe the girls were up again. She searched for the knob to shut off the water. Silence. She turned the water back on and rinsed her face.

Mallory pressed the towel against her eyes, then stopped. Somebody was in the house! She could feel it. What if someone was breaking in? Should she call the police? She leaned toward the open door, straining to hear, but there was only silence. She looked down at the goose bumps rippling her skin and clenched her fingers into fists. *This is silly! It's just my imagination.* She patted the last of the drops of moisture from her cheek.

Strong arms reached around her from behind, and a deep chuckle rippled down her spine. Mallory screamed and twisted her shoulders, jerking her body out of her attacker's reach. Her head slammed against the corner of the doorway, and searing pain sliced through her.

"Babe, are you all right?"

Mallory's eyes flew open. Sweet relief coursed through her. *Jake!* She rubbed the side of her head and sagged against the wall. "Don't *do* that!"

"Mallory, I'm sorry. I thought you heard me."

Jake had been upstairs long enough to undress. She *should* have heard him. What was the matter with her? She was still trembling when he reached for her, and she spun away from him. "I tell you time and time again not to terrify me, and what do you do? You sneak up on—"

"I called out when I came in the door! I know how jumpy you've been, and I didn't want to frighten—"

"Sure you did."

Her snort of disbelief earned a lift of his eyebrows, and he crossed his arms. "I said I was sorry."

"If you really were, you would try harder." She brushed past him and stalked to the bedroom.

He followed hot on her heels. "How about if I yell at the top of my lungs every time I come in the d—"

"There are times when I wonder if you love me at all."

"What the devil is that supposed to mean?" He spun her toward him, his eyes as cold as glacial ice. Shivers of fear scurried down her spine. "What do you want, Mal? I try, God knows I try, and nothing satisfies you."

The closet door crashed shut as Jake's foot smashed against it. "Why do women always use that line, *if you loved me,* just to manipulate things and get their own way?" She winced as his hand slammed against the wall before he paced around their room. "I don't care? I don't love you?" He grabbed his pants off the chair and thrust his legs into them.

"I work my tail off for you and the girls." He yanked his belt through the loops. "And all I ever get from you is 'Don't, Jake,' 'I'm tired, Jake,' 'Don't touch me, Jake.'" He turned on her. "I am sick to death of paying for your mistakes. We got another credit card bill today. Do you know how long it's going to take to get those things back under control? What did you buy anyway?" He pivoted on his heel, eyes scanning the room as if trying to figure out what she had bought and why he'd never even seen it.

She shrank back. "Jake?" Where had her mild, easygoing, even-tempered husband gone? And who was this ranting madman deposited in his place?

Jake continued to drag on his clothes. "I can't believe this. You're the one night after night who says, 'Not now, Jake.'" His mocking falsetto made Mallory wince, but she said nothing. He had reason to complain about the physical side of their relationship. If only she could explain it wasn't him. It was—

Mallory jerked as his heavy work boot collided with a bang against the wall. *He threw his boot!* She stared at her husband. His shirt was unbuttoned, his hair a mess from hands that swept through the thick strands.

"What, Mal? Is it somebody else?" His glare was hard. "If you're having an affair, just tell me straight out."

"Jake, *no!*" Mallory couldn't help it. Her laughter rang out. How ridiculous! It was all she could do to manage her relationship with him. "I would nev—"

The change on Jake's face was immediate. His jaw tightened, the shutters went down, and his walls went up. He didn't wait to hear her denial, but strode from the room, slamming the bedroom door as he went.

The reverberations left Mallory stunned. If she didn't feel so devastated, it would almost be funny. She sank onto the bed. Her husband had left barefoot! She heard the car engine rev and the tires screech in the drive.

Had he at least found a coat to put on before going out in the brisk November air?

With that absurd thought, Mallory dropped her head into her hands and wept.

Early morning, November 12

He's still not home. I'm getting scared now.
  Jake, where are you?

Eleven

The grandfather clock bonged the hour. Three A.M. Mallory grabbed for the telephone on its first, shrill ring, knocking the receiver off its base before bringing it to her ear.

"Jake?"

"Malo?"

"Oh, Joey." Mallory slumped back against the sofa cushions.

"Yeah, it's me. Jake's here. He showed up beating on my door a little while ago. I just got him to bed. Man, is he tanked! I don't know what happened, but I figured you'd be worried."

"Did you say Jake was tanked? Do you mean drunk?"

"Yeah, soused, tight, looped, way past three sheets to the wind—"

"Jake? Joey, he doesn't drink." Mallory sat erect on the edge of the couch. "His father is an—"

"I know. I've met the old geezer. I've never seen Jake take even a sip of alcohol, let alone get plastered. I know things haven't been good between you two... that is, I mean if you want to talk or anything..."

"Joey..." Mallory didn't know whether to laugh with relief or cry with anger. *Of all the irresponsible—*

She caught her lip, remembering too well the harsh words that had started all this.

"Did he—did Jake say anything?"

"Nothing coherent, only a badly sung, off-key version of 'I Love You Truly.' Then he hugged the toilet and passed out. I'll try to revive him in the morning and send him home."

Mallory replaced the receiver. "If he'll come home."

Jake came to, second by agonizing second.

He was alive—maybe.

What had run him over? A semi? He rolled over, and his head began to pound with the force of a jackhammer against concrete. He groaned. Even that hurt and caused him to groan again. He sat at the side of the bed and glanced around the unfamiliar bedroom. Where was he? The memory of the night before slapped him full force, and he wanted to swear but held back, considering the pain it would bring.

Drunk. He'd been drunk. He never drank. He'd promised himself long ago he would not be like his father. Self-loathing supplied him with the energy he needed to make it through the nearby bathroom door. When he returned, he found Joey waiting for him.

"Whoa, boss man, you look bad."

Jake grimaced. "Keen eye, Peterson. Just what I need… someone to point out the obvious." With an effort, Jake tucked in his shirt.

"It's what I'm here for. You going to talk about it?"

"Nope." Jake touched his temples and cringed before the weight of his pain bowed his head into his hands. "If you really want to be helpful, quit trying to psychoanalyze me, keep your voice down, and get me something that will do some good. Like about six aspirin."

Jake was thankful when Joey left the room. He tried to piece together the last several hours. He had blown his cool with Mallory—

"Oh, Mal…I'm sorry." He groaned, then made his way to the kitchen, where he found coffee brewing and Joey shaking several aspirin onto the counter beside a small glass of orange juice.

"I should call Mallory."

"Already done. 'Course it was sometime in the wee hours this morning, so I'm not sure how pleased she was to get my call. Or how pleased she was to hear you tied one on, but someone had to do the dirty deed."

"Uh, thanks." Jake tipped his head back and swallowed the pills, trying to hide his embarrassment. Joey knew his feelings toward booze…but there was no condemnation from his friend.

Seated at the kitchen table, Jake took a swallow of the hot, strong coffee. "I blew it, Joey." He closed his eyes and continued. "I got angry and stormed out." With a sudden realization, he opened his eyes and looked at his bare feet. "I left without my shoes and bought a cheap pair of canvas tennies."

"They're in the living room."

It didn't matter. Nothing mattered, except things couldn't continue as they had. He dreaded the thought of going home.

He managed to choke down a little of the scrambled eggs Joey fixed for him, then decided he'd better get the worst over with.

"Jake?"

He paused in the doorway at the seriousness of Joey's voice. Maybe he hadn't managed to escape the sermon after all.

"Whatever you need—I'm here."

Jake's throat thickened, and he tried to swallow past the lump that formed there. It took several tries before any words came out. "Thanks, Joey."

He didn't have the courage to call Mallory before he left Joey's. What could he say? "I've had it, Mal. I don't want to be here anymore"? Or how about, "I need some space"? Well, space was what he needed. Distance. Time to sort everything out. He thought about his friend's parting words…

Would Joey put him up for a while? Just until he got things figured out…

He sighed. As if he could ever figure Mal out. Who knew what he would find when he got home. Would she be angry? Sorry? Indifferent? Would she even be there?

Jake's heart began to race, then settled as his common sense took over. She wouldn't leave the girls—

The girls! What was he going to tell them? He clenched his jaw. Nothing, if he could help it. He drummed the steering wheel and readjusted the mirror for the sixth time. *Home.* Just a few more miles, and then what? What should he do? What could he say?

Mal, I don't want to hurt you, but we're destroying each other. You refuse to let me get close to you, and it's killing me…

Maybe staying at Joey's was a good idea. Just until they worked some things out. He needed some space, and she needed…what? He wished he knew. All he was sure of was that they both needed time.

He pulled into the driveway, turned off the ignition, and sat for several moments staring at the back of their minivan. The rehearsal of what to say to Mallory continued in his mind. Guilty relief mingled with trepidation. *God…if You're there like Joey says You are…*

Jake drew a deep breath and stepped from the car.

He found Mallory in the kitchen, seated at the table, sipping a cup of coffee. She acknowledged his presence with a slight nod. "Coffee's still hot. Looks like you could use it."

"Thanks." He reached to get a cup, more to give him something to do with his hands than anything else. He couldn't read the expression on her face. It was closed. Cold. Was she still angry with him? Or did she even care anymore? Frustration at his own stupidity washed over him. The fact that she had already seen him was all that kept him from bolting back out the door. He set his cup on the table, turned a kitchen chair to straddle it, and looked around. "Where are the girls?" *Do they know I got drunk?*

"Staying with friends. I thought we might need the time to talk." Mallory continued to sip her coffee. At least she was speaking to him, though she had yet to allow any eye contact between them. Jake took a deep breath and began to speak at the same time Mallory did.

"Look, Mal…"

"Jake…"

"You go first." Jake was relieved to have even a moment's respite from the uncertainty of what to say. What could he say?

"Jake." Mallory put her cup down and turned toward him. "Last night…" She hesitated. With an audible release of pent-up breath, she began again, "I'm sorry. I know I'm partly to blame for the fight." Her downcast eyes rose to meet his. Pure, unadulterated anger brewed in the depths of her green eyes.

She was furious.

"But do you think running off to some bar was the answer? Do you even remember where you were?"

"Of course I remember." *I think.* "I drove around awhile. Went to Kmart and bought a cheap pair of shoes. I went to Stan's Tavern and then…" Jake stopped, unable to go on.

"Then you got drunk. Drunk, Jake. I couldn't believe it when Joey called this morning. Do you have any idea how out of my mind I was with worry? And the girls! What was I supposed to tell them?"

Jake shoved the chair away from him. It rattled against the table, and their cups tilted. Two puddles of brown liquid spread and merged into a large stain on the flowered fabric of the table-cloth. He heard Mallory's cluck of disapproval and folded his arms and walked toward the kitchen door. It would be so easy to open it, to just leave.

"Mal, I don't know what to say. I'm sorry. I don't have any excuse for last night. But if you think you've been out of your mind with worry, that only begins to describe the way I've felt trying to please you. Your mood swings first one way, then another. You've changed. I just don't know what you want anymore."

He couldn't look at her, but he wouldn't back down from saying what needed to be said.

"Me?" The shrill word made him cringe. "You're the one that's changed. You're gone so much I feel like a single parent. You used to take the girls and me places. Now you just take us for granted."

At the hurt in Mallory's voice, he shoved his hands in his pockets and turned around. "My work is just what it's always been. It's what helps put bread on the table. You knew about the traveling I'd have to do when I took the job. You said go for it. In fact, you were as excited as I was." Jake strode to one end of the kitchen and back, trying to think through the words churning inside him before they spilled out in a fury. "It's just not the same around here. We fight constantly. You're angry or upset all the time, about me or my job. I don't know what to do anymore, how to please you."

Mallory sat at the table, pulling apart the napkin that was still stained with coffee. She shredded one small strip after another and laid them in a pile before her. Jake watched her demolish one napkin, then reach for the napkin holder and start on another.

"Did you even hear what I just said?"

"I heard."

"Well?"

"Well, what? What do you want me to say? That it's what I expected of you? That you're just li—" Mallory lips clamped shut tight.

Go ahead and say it, Mal; you're just like your old man. He slammed his fist against the nearest cupboard. Mallory's head snapped up, and her shoulders flinched in startled response.

He had her full attention now. "You sure you even want me around? You haven't let me near you in weeks, and when we are intimate, there's this—this distance between us. What happened?" The ache in his heart grew as he saw the tears on the tips of her lashes. "What's happened to us?" His last words were said on the trail of the deep breath that he had to draw to fight his own tears.

Mallory dropped her head on her arms and began to weep. Bits of torn napkin scattered across the table. Her shoulders shook, and Jake felt more helpless than he could ever remember. He stood there, wanting to comfort her, but unable to scale the walls that stood between them now. *I just want out. I don't know what to do.*

Mallory's tears caused a hot burning in the pit of his stomach, and as her sobs continued to rip at his insides, a sense of déjà vu filled him.

Just like with Mom…

He could no more stop her pain than he could his own. And now…now Mallory was hurting, and he was just as useless.

Jake moved to lay a tentative hand on Mal's shoulder, and she jumped. "Don't do that!" He snatched his hand back and thrust it into his pocket. He couldn't do anything right. Not even comfort his wife. He was only making things worse.

He strode toward the kitchen door. "I can't take this anymore, Mal. I can't do or be whatever it is you want." He stopped and turned toward her. "I've tried—God knows I've tried. It's best if I just leave for a while. We both need some space."

Surprise and horror inched across her red-splotched face. "L-leave? But, Jake, what will people think? What will we tell my folks?" Mallory's voice rose to a shrill wail. "What will we tell the girls?"

The girls. The hot burning of his insides turned into a flaming ball of fire that raged toward his throat. "I…I'll talk to the girls. It's only for a little while."

"You're really going to leave?" She jumped to her feet. "Just like that?"

Just like that? No, not just like that. My gut's wrenching, my heart's being ripped out—but I can't do anything right. I'm only hurting you. "I'm done. I'm out of here."

"You can't!"

Jake yanked open the kitchen door. "Watch me."

November 25

Jake is gone.

    I am numb. Mentally. Physically. Spiritually. I am empty and overwhelmed at the same time. It doesn't make sense, but that's the only way I can describe it.

    This morning's devotional verse was Isaiah 7:4: "Take heed, and be quiet; do not fear or be fainthearted…"

    But how? How do I stay quiet? And how on earth am I supposed to not be afraid?

Twelve

Mallory dangled her arm over the roan's broad back and leaned her weight against the warm side of the gentle horse. She sighed. Not even the prospect of a long horseback ride on this warm November day lifted her aching soul. She caught herself sighing again and glanced at Heather to see if she noticed. "I hope the girls are okay."

"Move." Heather shoved her weight against her palomino to get the stubborn horse to lift its hoof. She grasped the fetlock, cocked the hoof, and began to pick it clean. "Why wouldn't the girls be okay? They're with Uncle Geoff."

"I just want them to be safe."

"Stop worrying. They'll have a great time with Geoff. He loves those munchkins almost as much as you do. He would never let anything happen to them."

"I know." A circus was scheduled at the indoor amusement park and convention center. Geoff wanted to introduce his nieces to the world of the big top and then spoil them the rest of the day with junk food and rides. She twirled the currycomb in her hand and stared out the open barn door.

"You're supposed to be grooming her so we can ride sometime today." Heather's words—and her pointed stare at the comb—propelled Mallory back to her work. She flicked the animal's mane, and Heather moved to the front of her horse.

"It's just that amusement parks can be overwhelming, and they've never been anywhere with Geoff *and* Holly before."

Heather rose from her awkward position and crossed her arms while making sure that the grimy pick remained well away from her body. "Are you jealous?"

"No! They just don't know Holly, that's all."

Heather raised an eyebrow.

"I am not jealous." *Am I? This is ridiculous. Why in the world would I be jealous of Geo having a girlfriend?* Mallory moved to the other side of the horse to hide her heated face from Heather's scrutiny.

"You told me she was a nice person. This is a good way for them to get to know her. Who knows, this outing with your children just may inspire that playboy brother of yours to settle down with a family of his own."

Mallory laid her grooming tools aside and reached for the saddle blanket. She didn't want to talk about Geoff and Holly. She didn't want to talk about anything. She just wanted to forget...so many things. Maybe this ride would help her. But she knew that regardless of how much she enjoyed today, the relief would be short-lived. She lifted the heavy saddle onto the roan's back and tightened the cinch. A huge sigh rent the air.

"Will you quit that?"

"It wasn't me this time!"

"Sure."

"It wasn't! I don't think Tekoa likes the tight girdle I just put on her, but then what woman does?"

"That was the horse?" Heather chuckled. "You two sound an awful lot alike today." Heather slipped a silver-studded bridle over Seba's head.

"Oh, thank you very much for comparing me with a horse." Mallory led Tekoa outside to the white fence where she could mount. She pulled a pair of gloves from the pocket of her sweatshirt while she waited for Heather. She'd used every legitimate reason she could think of to avoid Heather these last few weeks. *But she's going to find out about Jake...I've got to tell her or she'll be hurt. But how?*

She reined in her runaway thoughts when Heather and Seba exited the white building. Two short hops, and Heather was in the saddle.

"Ready?"

Mallory nodded.

"Then let's go have some fun." Heather nudged the palomino into a fast trot down the lane and past the row of outbuildings. The farm where Heather stabled her horses was tucked among gentle, rolling hills and acres of furrowed land. The fields lay barren, as the last of the crops had been harvested. Though the sun was warm, the wind held a faint chill, and the sky's deep, rich, endless blue reminded Mallory of God's vastness. Even that thought was overwhelming, so she shifted her focus to the scent of fallen leaves and the sounds of acorns dropping in beds of lifeless dried leaves.

Mallory gathered the reins and shifted forward, directing her horse to follow in Seba's trail of dust. Heather slowed her mount to a walk as they approached tangled meadowland, and Mallory reined Tekoa to a slower walk, trying to avoid conversation as long as possible. She tagged along behind Heather as the horses picked their way through fields of brown grass. They left the open field and bright blue sky for a stand of naked trees. In the distance

Mallory heard water gurgling and nudged Tekoa toward the sooth-ing sound.

"So what's going on? You missed Bible study this week."

What do I say now? Mallory kept her eyes straight ahead.

Heather turned in her saddle. "Hey! Wait for me." She circled Seba back toward Mallory, then nudged Seba closer to Tekoa. "It's hard to talk with you that far away. All I heard was the air whistling in my ears. So? Catch me up. I've missed talking to my best friend."

Here it comes. "Not much, I guess. Work and the girls." *Liar.*

"What's up with Jake? Did that assignment in Malaysia get him the promotion he was looking for?"

"I haven't heard."

"Why not?"

Mallory squeezed her eyes shut and gripped the reins tighter. "He left."

"Again? Where'd he go this time?"

"No, Heather, I mean he left. As in gone, walked out of my life, abandoned me and the girls." As though she could escape the words she'd just spoken, Mallory kicked Tekoa into a trot.

"What? Mallory, wait a minute! Stop that stinking horse." Heather caught up to Mallory and grabbed Tekoa's reins to slow her down. "What do you mean he left? What happened?"

Mallory clutched the saddle horn and refused to look up. "I don't know."

"You had to have some clue. He'd never leave you without…"

"A reason?"

"Well, yes."

Mallory dropped her head. "The day he…" She couldn't say it

again. "We had a huge fight. Over something stupid, I guess." *Jake didn't think those two credit cards were stupid.* "I laughed. He left." *Please don't ask me to reveal the rest, Heather. It's just too humiliating.*

Heather's smooth forehead creased at the bridge of her narrow nose. "That doesn't make any sense."

"I know." Mallory reached down to adjust her stirrup, and silence filled the air. She peeked through her lashes to gauge Heather's reaction. Her friend's expectant look spoke volumes. She wanted more information.

Mallory's words were measured and slow. "He got drunk."

"What? Wait. Let me get this straight. Jake, the man who adores you, got mad because you laughed. Jake, the man who doesn't drink alcohol, went out and got drunk because…?"

Warm tears filled Mallory's eyes and began to fall. She simply shrugged. She couldn't understand it herself, so how could she explain it to Heather?

"Let's tie the horses up and walk down by the creek." Heather's voice was compassionate—and almost unbearable.

The silence stretched between the two women as they pushed past the dead underbrush and low hanging limbs. Their boots shuffled the fallen leaves, scattering them in all directions. A faint breeze kicked up, stirring the pungent odor of decaying foliage.

Heather didn't say any more until they were beside the narrow rush of water. "Let's sit here." She settled on a moss-covered rock.

Mallory sat down beside her and scooted forward to dangle her feet over the splashing water. She had a childlike urge to jump into the middle of the creek and let its cleansing flow wash all her cares away. The knowledge that the water would be frigid kept her from following through on her impulse. Instead, she reached down for a handful of pebbles and began to toss them into the sparkling depths. *Plop. Plurp.* She tossed each stone with increasing force, watching with an almost morbid satisfaction as the pebbles settled into their chilly grave.

Heather's hand on her forearm halted her. "Mallory, there's more to this than you've told me."

A branch creaked as the wind caught it and set it swaying. A crow sent out a raucous call. Chipmunks chattered as they scrambled for the last of fall's provisions. It should have been a perfect, peaceful moment.

But all Mallory felt was chaos. She studied the toe of her scuffed boot and balled her hands into fists to keep them from shaking. "I overspent on the credit cards. There was an emergency and I…I maxed out the card." Mallory closed her eyes. *You just lied to your best friend.* But she couldn't tell Heather the truth. If she did, Heather would never go shopping with her again. "I forgot to tell him." Another lie. It just kept getting worse. "He has every right to be mad, I guess. I just never expected him to walk out on me." She heaved the rest of the stones into creek.

"But, Mallory, if it was an emergency, surely he understood. You guys have been in financial straits before and have pulled through. I can't believe this."

Mallory's heart tightened its hold. She couldn't catch her breath and leaned forward to push the feeling away. She wrapped her arms around her bent knees and buried her head against them. "I don't know what's happening, but I'm scared to death."

Heather's strong arms went around her. "First you need to talk to God, then you need to talk to your husband."

"I don't know how to talk to either of them anymore." Mallory shifted in Heather's arms and leaned her head against her friend's shoulder. "I try to talk to God. I do…but it's as if there's this glass ceiling that my prayers just bounce off of and God never receives them."

"Honey, you know that's not true." Heather's gentle chide pricked Mallory's pain and hooked her anger.

She shifted away and rolled to her feet. "Of course I know that it isn't true, but that's how it feels."

"I'm sorry. I didn't mean to offend you. I just wanted to remind you that God does care about you, He does want to help you, and He doesn't want you and Jake to be living like this." Heather stood and reached out a hand to Mallory. "Maybe you need someone to stand in prayer with you."

I really don't know how much prayer will help. God, I'm sorry. I just feel so alone—so isolated, even from you. Despite her feelings, Mallory nodded. Maybe Heather was right. Maybe she just needed someone to pray with her. After all, Scripture did say that if two or more agree on anything, it will be done. Mallory gripped Heather's hands, listening as she prayed, hoping against hope it would make a difference.

But when Heather finished, though Mallory didn't feel quite so alone, there still wasn't much peace in her heart, and her world was still turned upside down. It hurt to think that God was leaving her all alone in this.

No, she corrected herself, looking at her friend. *Not all alone.* Heather was here. So was God, even if she couldn't feel Him.

Swallowing the hardness in her throat, Mallory tried to lighten the tone. After all, Heather had planned this outing to be a fun time for both of them. "I suppose we should go get the horses before they think we abandoned them."

"Mal?" Heather took the lead back through the woods. "Could I make a suggestion?"

Mallory's back stiffened as her defenses switched on. "I guess."

"Talk to Jake, and the two of you go see Pastor James together."

Mallory stopped. "Jake doesn't want to see me. Besides you know he doesn't have much use for religion."

"I know, but he does like James. I've heard him say that." Heather turned around and came back to Mallory. "You can't keep living like this. It's going to destroy you and your marriage. Your relationship is too good to let something small and silly destroy it."

Mallory forced herself to nod, but as Heather turned away again, she had to bite her lip to keep from crying out, *Small and silly? What's happened isn't small and silly at all! And if you think it is, you just don't understand!*

"I don't think it's silly at all, Jake Carlisle!"

Mallory's voice rose an octave, and Jake spun around from watching the girls plow through the first snow of winter, then disappear around the side of the house, throwing snowballs as they went.

"Keep your voice down. The girls had a good day with me, and they don't need it ruined by their mother's shrieking at their father." Jake rested his foot on the bottom step of the long, narrow porch.

"Shrieking?" Mallory hissed. She stepped down so that her

flashing green eyes were level with his. She was way beyond mad. "I ask you to help save this marriage by going to see Pastor Gates. You call it silly and nonproductive, and then you have the unmitigated gall to tell me that I'm shrieking?"

Jake gritted his teeth and shoved his hands deeper into his pockets to keep from shaking her. If Renee acted this way, she would end up across his knee. Once again the reasons for leaving were slapping him in the face. He didn't want to be away from his family, but by all that was holy, he didn't want to have an irate woman screaming at him twenty-four hours a day either.

"I don't need to talk to James Gates. I'm not the one who can't say no to a sale. I'm not the one who tossed our household budget down the toilet. I'm not the one who pushed away first." How could she blame him for this mess? He stomped down the steps, then turned at the corner of the house to look at his wife. She had her head turned away from him, her arms crossed like some kind of shield in front of her. The sight did nothing to cool his anger. *What do you want from me?*

Even as the words flitted through his mind, the answer came. He knew what she wanted. She'd made it painfully clear. "You got what you wanted, Mallory!" It felt good to yell. "I'm out of your bed and out of your life."

December 9

Gramps is gone. Jake left me. My body is rebelling in ways I can't even describe. The nightmare has come back with a vengeance. Every night the same theme plays itself over and over in my head...

I'm out of control. My world is crumbling. I think I'm going insane. I don't know what to do! Please, Jesus, please tell me what to do!

Thirteen

"Mallory, my dear! How are you?" Eleanor Bennington smiled when she heard the sound of her granddaughter's voice on the other end of the phone line.

"I don't really know. Oh, Gran, I wish I could be with you right now! I know it's hard on you without Gramps."

"Yes, it is, but the Lord is getting me through." Eleanor wiped her hands on a dishtowel. Mallory sounded close to tears. Had something else happened? Two weeks ago Mallory told her that Jake had moved out. Just for a while, her granddaughter had assured her, but Eleanor had been burdened with the weight of the news ever since. She eased into the bentwood rocker in the corner of her kitchen. "I suspect this phone call is more about you than it is about me. What is it, sweetie? Missing Jake?"

"Yeah, I guess…maybe…" Mallory's voice trailed off, and Eleanor heard the threat of tears.

"I thought so." Her words were cautious, "Have you talked to Jake?"

"No. I doubt he wants to speak to me."

Gran chuckled at the little girl voice that met her ears. She had heard that tone so many times before. "How do you know if you haven't even tried to talk to him?"

"Because he sent a check to the house with a tiny note that

said, 'For the regular bills.'" A sob broke over the line, and silence blanketed the conversation for several long moments. "Gran, he's the one that left." The words were clipped and harsh, revealing the hurt of his betrayal far more than Mallory's tears.

Eleanor wanted more than anything at that moment to pull her granddaughter onto her lap and wipe away her tears and her pain. But Mallory wasn't a child with a skinned elbow or tormenting brothers to cry about. This was something even a loving grandmother couldn't heal.

"Oh, sweetie, I know how hard this is, but just because Jake left doesn't mean he doesn't love you. You said yourself that he needed time to work through his confusion. Besides, you know as well as I do that it takes two in a marriage to make it work…or to ruin it. You have to work together on this."

"Well, it's a little hard to work together when he won't come around. I'm not about to pack the kids up and trail after him."

Eleanor moved toward the counter. She needed some tea. *Dear Lord, how do I say this?* "Have you thought about talking to someone who is a little more clearheaded than the two of you?"

"I'm talking to you, Gran."

Eleanor laughed. "You need someone more clearheaded than I am, I'm afraid. I was thinking more along the lines of a counselor."

"I don't want to talk to some stranger about our personal problems. Besides, Jake—"

"What about your pastor? You seem to like him." She turned the flame on beneath the old copper teakettle.

"I don't know."

Eleanor frowned at the hesitancy in Mallory's voice. "There are times in all our lives when we need someone who is objective to help us out, dear. I've even been known to go talk to my pastor on occasion. Just think about it." When the teakettle whistled, she filled her cup and carried it to the table, enjoying the warmth seeping into her hand.

"I'll promise to think about it if you'll promise not to push me on it."

"Done." Eleanor waited, fairly certain there was something else on Mallory's mind. She started to take a sip of her tea.

"Gran? Would you…could you tell Mom and Dad about Jake and me?"

She froze, her cup stopping just beneath her lips. "You mean they don't know?"

"No. I just couldn't work up the courage to tell them. I tried! But you know how they are. I don't think I can handle the lecture from Mom and the silent disapproval from Daddy."

Eleanor traced the pattern in her lace tablecloth and pictured her daughter-in-law's displeasure. She'd seen it often enough—Alecia's lips set in a tight line, the creases around her mouth emphasizing her disapproval. *I see what you mean.*

"Your mom may be upset at first, but I am sure she'll handle it. She hurts when her family hurts. She just has an unusual way of showing it."

"I know. I just don't think I can face her way of dealing with my pain. I don't want to hear them rag on Jake either. So please, Gran, will you tell them?"

Eleanor smiled. "Now how can I possibly say no? I'll call them tonight. Why don't you head off to bed and try to rest? And leave all of this in God's hands."

"Thanks, Gran. I love you."

"Love you too, sweetheart. Good night."

Eleanor hung up, then rose from her seat and moved to pour another cup of tea. She returned to the table, studying the rich, brown liquid as though she'd find some kind of answer there. But she knew there was only one place for the answers she—and Mallory—needed.

"Okay, Lord, now what? What am I supposed to say to them?" She sipped her tea and looked toward the ceiling. "Yes, I know that You will supply the words when I need them, but this is going to be tricky."

Eleanor reached for the phone before she could change her mind.

Alecia hung up the phone, then reached over and straightened the family portrait she had insisted on getting three years ago. She stared at it...

Where had the years gone? And just where had she failed as a mother that so many awful things could be happening in her family? Things like this happened to other people's children, not to hers. Alecia sniffed back a tear as her hand fluttered to the collar of her blouse.

She heard the rattle of Martin's paper. "Who was that?"

She turned to face him, even as she tried to make sense of the phone conversation. "Your mother."

"Is she okay? Did she need something?" He turned the page, rattling the paper again as he folded it back. He looked beyond his half-moon reading glasses.

"You won't believe what's happened now."

Martin lowered the paper onto his lap. "What's the matter?"

"First Eric and Catherine, then Marty, and now this. What's happening to our family?" She twisted her wedding rings and paced back and forth in front of him.

"Now, Alecia, it can't be—"

"Martin, don't you "now, Alecia" me. This is serious! Jake left Mallory and the girls weeks ago, and she never even told us!"

"He left?"

"*Left*, Martin. He walked out on our daughter and those two precious babies. How could he do that, and why is it that a mother is always the last to know these things?" She sniffed back another tear. "She couldn't even confide in me. She told your mother and now—"

"I can't believe it." Martin dropped the footrest on his recliner. "Why in the world would Jake leave?"

"I don't know. Your mother was given the details, not I." She sat down on the couch and tucked her skirt around her legs. Her tears fell. "Martin, what are we going to do?"

"There isn't much we can do, dear, except be here for them."

"I can't believe your mother is trying to talk Mallory into seeing someone about her marriage. What will your sisters say about this?"

"What can they say? They didn't have anything to do with it."

"You know how your family likes to talk." Alecia gripped her hands together. "We can't tell anyone about this."

"Alecia, the boys need to know. Of course, Geoff must know already—"

"Martin, we can't tell *anyone* about this. What will it look like?"

"At least let Eric know. He is her brother."

"But, Martin…"

"Sweetheart, Eric should be told. He may be able to help her. After all, Catherine left him."

Alecia stood to her feet. "I don't know why I always end up making these calls. I'll look like a busybody."

Martin snagged her hand as she walked passed him and kissed her fingertips. "Alecia, I let you call because you have a way with words."

She pulled her hand away. "Just once in your life, Martin Bennington, I don't know why you can't make a phone call to your own son."

"I don't know what you want me to do, Mom. Mal's a big girl now. Let her handle her own problems."

"Eric!"

He jerked the phone away as his mother screeched in his ear. He stroked his beard and leaned against the headboard, then punched the volume on the television remote.

"Are you listening to me? Did you hear what I said?"

"Yes, Mother, I heard you. Jake left. Well, Mallory's marriage isn't the first one to hit bumps in the road." Pain knifed his heart, and the knot that formed in his throat moved to his stomach. He knew that pain so well. Betrayal. Humiliation. Abandonment.

And the questions. A million questions with no answers.

He upped the volume on the television another notch. Better not to think about it. Mallory was a Bennington. She was tough; she would make it through. "So what do you want me to do about it?"

"Well! Your father and I thought you might want to know what's happening in your own family. We thought that you might be able to talk to her."

"What could I possibly say to her?"

"Aren't you at all concerned?"

"Yes, Mother, I'm concerned, but spreading gossip through the family isn't helping. When Mal wants our help, she'll ask for it. Then I'll get involved." He thumped his pillow. "Ma, I've had a long day. Please hang up and let me go to bed." He began to channel-surf.

"Eric, I just can't understand why this family won't tell me anything. After all a mother goes through, I deserve a little more respect."

Because you whine. Because you gossip. Because it always ends up being about you.

Eric slid down beneath the covers and cradled the phone against his pillow, watching the pictures flash across the screen.

"Your father and I have always tried to do our best, and what do we get for it? Nobody gives us a second thought. I just don't know what to do!"

Just give it a rest will you, Mother? "Let them work it out. Just go to bed, Ma."

"But, Eric—"

"Good night, Mother." He rolled over and dropped the phone into its cradle, then jerked the sheet up to his chest. An adult rating appeared on the left corner of the screen and theme music began to play.

Eric smiled as all thoughts of sleep vanished from his mind.

December 24

I hate holidays.

Fourteen

Jake shivered, huddled against the wall near the front door, and tugged the fleece collar of his jacket around his ears. His and Mallory's relationship was almost as cold as the freezing air, but at least they had called a truce and were on speaking terms now.

He looked up at the second-story window to see if the light had come on in their bedroom. Not for the first time, he regretted leaving Mallory and the girls. The separation was even harder during the holidays.

If he heard "I'll Be Home for Christmas" one more time, he would smash his radio.

He snuggled deeper into the meager warmth of his coat and decided being home sounded pretty good. *I could be up there right now, instead of out here freezing my tail off.* The thought of his wife in a snug, dry bed was making his vigil out in the falling snow even more miserable.

Everyone wanted snow on Christmas Day, but right now Jake could do with a little less of it. He'd had the bright idea of being here when the girls woke up, but now he wasn't so sure. He wanted so much for this to be a day when they could be a family again.

He brushed the big, feathery flakes off the packages piled at his feet. He had delivered several presents to Mallory earlier in the week, but had found himself shopping for more things last evening.

Jake shifted his position on the stoop of his house, and his thoughts grew as uncomfortable as his position. Leaving Mallory had been difficult; leaving the girls, next to impossible. He saw them as often as he could, which was more than before he moved out, but it wasn't the same. He knew it, and they knew it. The memory of the conversation he had with Renee and Angel to try to explain why he didn't live with them anymore still hurt. How could he explain it? The situation wasn't the way he wanted it to be.

The way he had it figured, it was up to Mal. He couldn't believe she wanted him to go see the pastor. Just what he needed, more religion being shoved at him.

No, that was unfair. Living with Joey had not been the constant Bible-thumping he had feared. Joey had remained neutral in the matter, going about his business, but being available to listen when Jake needed to vent.

As for Mallory, well, things hadn't changed that much, and anyone she wanted to see who could help her get her head on straight was fine with him.

Jake fidgeted on the cold cement. It wasn't that he didn't want to work things out. He just didn't agree with the idea of some pious preacher telling him what to do. And anyway, it was Mal that needed help, not him.

Things had once been so good between them. How did it all fall apart? Here in the shadowy darkness, the times of laughter and closeness with his wife seemed further away than ever, but Jake longed for it more than he longed for the heat of a blazing fire and the protection of a roof to shelter him from the snow.

He loved his wife; he just couldn't live with her anymore. *I wanna come home, Mal.* Jake wanted it all to be over, to be like it used to be. He just couldn't comprehend her mood swings and unreasonable demands. She shut him out and didn't want him near her.

Jake pulled back on his runaway thoughts. This wasn't the day to dwell on such things. *It's Christmas.* He and Mallory had vowed to give the girls a good memory. They had suffered enough; it wasn't their fault their parents couldn't seem to get along. When he and Mallory decided to spend Christmas morning together, they had agreed not to argue. Nothing controversial was to be discussed or brought up. *"For the girls' sake."* Jake hoped it happened that way for his sake, too. He ached to be back in the center of his family. With Mal. With the girls. All the time, not just to visit like some stranger.

That's what had brought him here early this morning. He couldn't wait any longer. He wanted to be there when the girls first woke up and came downstairs, excited to see what Santa had brought them. He hadn't felt right about using the key to the house, but if Mal didn't wake up soon…

Jake fingered the key in his pocket. *Come on, Mal, it's cold out here.*

He burrowed his icy nose into the heat emanating from his jacket and stomped his feet. Maybe he should use his key. Just as he stood and reached for the door, the downstairs hall light came on. Jake peered through the door and saw Mallory heading for the kitchen.

He rapped on the door several times, then turned to gather up the bright-papered gifts. Over the tops of the bows he peeked at Mallory, giving her a smile stiffened by the brittle air.

"Hi. I'm a little earlier than what we'd planned, but I couldn't wait." Jake was having difficulty focusing on what he was saying. Mallory looked like a hesitant little girl. She was wearing her ratty bathrobe over his old football jersey, and he braced himself against the onslaught of memories...

Even with her thick hair rumpled and no trace of makeup, she could still make his heart beat double time.

Mallory's breathing quickened as the frigid draft of air swirled snow through the open doorway. In the early morning light Jake's eyes held a hint of mischief. The crushing weight of loneliness and a longing for the times when there had been no discord between them descended over her.

He forgot to comb his hair again. And shave. Even the faint stubble of blond beard couldn't hide the heightened color on his cheeks. Must be from the cold, she decided. His expression held a hint of uncertainty beneath the firm smile fixed on his face. She felt her own smile waver and fought the urge to smooth the rebellious strands of hair that fell across his forehead. She stepped back to allow him entrance into the warmth of the house and shut the door on the bitter morning air.

Mallory attempted to relieve Jake of the packages in his arms, but he shifted them out of her reach. "No fair trying to peek."

"I wasn't peeking. I was trying to keep them from crashing to the floor during your attack of shivers." She led the way to the living room. "Haven't you bought enough stuff already?"

She flipped on the lights to the tree, and the glow bathed dawn's shadows with soft color. The limbs of the Douglas fir were laden with twinkling lights, popcorn strings, paper chains, crayon-colored angel cutouts, Popsicle-stick stars, and an assortment of their daughters' other creative efforts.

"You should talk." His pointed stare at the cascade of colorfully decorated gifts spilling into the open area of the living room made her squirm. Her defenses snapped into place, and it took a moment to tear them back down. *No arguments.* She would not let her precarious emotions spoil the day for the girls. She could hear them even now as they tumbled down the stairs in their haste to see Jake.

"Daddy! Daddy!"

"You're here!" Renee's excited voice rose over Angel's as they flung themselves at their father. They'd seen him just a few days ago, but Mallory's heart squeezed at the sight of Jake with his daughters. Somehow he had managed to catch one in each arm. The girls clutched his neck in an unbreakable hold. After a moment, he began to tickle their cheeks with his bristled chin. The girls' delighted squeals and Jake's deep laugh filled the room.

"All right, move it out of here." Mallory cleared her throat. "You know the rules, no wrestling in the living room. Do you want to knock the tree down? How about some breakfast?"

"Aw, Mommy, can't we open presents first?"

"Yeah, can't we see what Santa brought us, Mom?"

"Yeah, please?" At Jake's little boy appeal, Mallory knew she had lost the battle. She looked at the hopeful expressions of the three most important people in her life and caved in, "Oh, why not. We'll eat when we get hungry."

With a move that startled her family, she dove toward the

mountain of presents, reaching for a package that had her name written on it. Laughter rang out as the girls and Jake followed suit. Ribbons and bits of wrapping paper flew like colorful snow.

As one, Jake and Mallory settled back against the end of the couch, both content to watch as the mayhem continued around them. She and Jake had gone overboard on the presents, trying to compensate for the girls' hurt and confusion.

As if anything could compensate for Jake being gone.

His gaze captured hers in a lingering look, and Mallory's mouth went dry. Was he any closer to understanding what her needs were? Was *she*?

"I think I'll go make some coffee. Maybe work on breakfast." The words broke the gossamer thread that held them bound together.

"Daddy, look at this!" Angel's gleeful words followed Mallory into the kitchen. Mallory smiled past the pain. It was good to hear the laughter in her daughters' voices.

After their traditional Christmas breakfast of homemade hot chocolate and blueberry pancakes, Mallory sent the girls to dress while she cleaned the kitchen. Jake volunteered to get rid of the mounds of crumpled wrapping paper still strewn about the living room. She could almost convince herself that they were once again a family.

"You can take two," Mallory replied to the girls' pleas to take their presents with them to her parents' house. "Grandma will have something for you there."

The girls' attention was diverted at the thought of yet more packages to open, and they rushed to the other room to choose their favorite toy.

"That ought to take them awhile." Jake shifted his feet. "Uh, anything else I can do for you here?"

Come home. Mallory turned to the sink before Jake could read her thoughts and folded the wet dishrag before saying anything aloud. *No pressure, Mal. If he doesn't want to live with us, that's his choice.* She twisted back to him. "No, thanks. I'm done."

"Well, I, uh…guess I'd better be going. I told Mom I wouldn't be late." Jake paused in the living room door where the girls were arguing about what to take with them. He called to them and knelt down on the floor. When they ran to him, he crushed them to his chest and kissed them, then he rose.

"Daddy? Aren't you coming too?" Renee's voice wobbled as he reached for his coat.

"Love bug, I promised Grandma Carlisle I'd spend Christmas with her."

"But, Daddy…"

Jake knelt before Renee and pulled her into his arms. He brushed the hair out of her face. "Honey, I made a promise to Grandma, and you don't want me to break it, do you?"

Mallory's vision blurred. More pain. When would it ever end? She wanted to destroy the demon that was killing her family…if only she knew what that demon was.

Jake pulled his sobbing daughters into another hug and kissed the tears from their faces. His smile was forced as he continued, "Besides, you'll be with Uncle Eric, Lindsay, Uncle Geoff, and Grandma and Grandpa. You won't even miss me. And even if I was there, I'd just be snoring on the couch and you'd be playing."

He looked up, misery etched his face. Mallory refused to help him out. This was his doing.

His pained glance returned to the girls. "Please don't cry anymore. I'll see you tomorrow."

Renee's sobs began to ebb. "Promise?"

"Cross my heart." Jake ran a finger over his chest and looked up at Mallory. "Walk me to the car?"

She threw a jacket around her shoulders and followed Jake out the door. As he leaned back against the hood of his car, his eyes searched hers, and in that moment Mallory thought she saw both regret and longing.

"I've missed you." He reached out a gloved hand and lifted her chin to study her face.

Mallory bit her lip. *I didn't kick you out, Jake. You left us, not the other way around. I want you back, but I won't beg.* Were those tears collecting at the corners of his eyes? The tips of his lashes were wet. Probably from the light snow still drifting down.

"I love you, Mallory. That has never stopped. I had a wonderful time today with the girls and with you." His eyes slid away. She shivered, and he pulled her close. It felt so right that she didn't even think of stopping him. "I hate it that I hurt you so bad. But I didn't… I still don't know how to handle this situation. I don't know how to respond to you, how to connect with you the way I used to. I wish I could. I wish…" His voice trailed off.

Mallory pulled herself from his embrace. Was there any solution? Tears were close to the surface again. Nothing had changed. She and Jake were as far apart as they had been for months, yet she still needed him.

He stepped back. Her longing must have been on her face, because he shook his head. "I'm sorry, Mal, but I can't…I can't come home yet."

Her chin jutted forward, and she raised her head. She slid her hair back behind her ear, then folded her arms across her chest. "I didn't ask you to, did I?"

The muscle in Jake's jaw twitched, and his lips thinned into narrow lines as a cold, brittle look erased his loving expression. He shoved his hands in his pockets, raked his eyes over her, then muttered, "I gotta go."

She refused to watch him drive away, and she shivered as the cold draft followed her through the door and into her thoughts. She closed the door tight—then leaned against it and allowed her tears to fall.

Mallory wiped the last dish and put it in the china cupboard. She peeked around the doorframe of her mother's formal dining room into the immaculate living room. A gigantic white artificial Christmas tree decorated in silver and gold sat in the corner. Her father was tipped back in his La-Z-Boy recliner while Eric sprawled on the couch next to him.

Her mother was on the floor with Renee and Angel, next to the Christmas tree. Geoff knelt down beside Angel and shook a package next to her ear. Mallory's mother handed a small gift to each of the girls and dared them to guess what was in them. Mallory stared. Had her mother ever been that lighthearted with her or her brothers?

"Cleanup's done. Want to go outside and get some air?" Holly's husky voice startled Mallory.

Mallory turned to her. "I'd love to."

"Let's see if anyone else wants to come." Holly stepped into the living room. "Mallory and I are going to get some fresh air. Anyone want to come?"

"Yeah. Where you headed?" Geoff rolled to his feet, and Renee and Angel jumped up behind him.

"I saw some inner tubes in the garage on our way into the house." Holly pointed over her shoulder. "Have you ever used them for sledding?"

Sledding. Mallory stopped just short of running into Holly. *Cold. Wet. Loud wails of grief.* Everything associated with sledding was a forbidden topic in Mallory's family. Her every nerve was taut, waiting for a reaction from her father and mother.

The flash of a little girl's image filled her mind. Cold stiff lips…lifeless skin beneath her fingers…

"Kiss your sister good-bye, Mallory."

"No!"

The loud chorus came from every adult in the room. The word echoed in the room's sudden silence.

Mallory saw her mother's face blanch and her lips pinch together. She looked down at her hands curled together in her lap. Mallory's father opened his mouth, then closed it. Renee and Angel huddled together, sensing the strain but not able to understand the sudden emotional upheaval. Eric's face darkened in a scowl, but he, too, said nothing.

"We don't go sleddin'. We're not allowed." Angel's innocent remark broke the awkward tension.

Mallory swallowed hard and tried to think of some way to ease Holly's discomfort. Her eyes were half-closed, her face a bright red. Mallory could tell she was mortified.

Geoff stepped behind Holly and slid his hands onto her

shoulders, pulling her back against his broad chest. "How about a walk instead?" With that, he drew her toward the hall closet.

Mallory was close on their heels. "Girls, why don't you stay and play with Grandma and Grandpa and Uncle Eric?" Their solemn nods indicated that they understood that the walk was for adults.

Mallory, Geoff, and Holly slipped out of the still-quiet house, and Geoff took Holly's gloved hand. Mallory fell into step beside her brother.

"I'm sorry, I didn't realize—"

"Our sister was killed in a sledding accident."

Geoff's low voice bought Holly to an abrupt stop. Her eyes widened. "I'm sorry. I had no idea. When? I mean, how long ago did it happen?"

Their footsteps crunched in the snow as the story came out in frozen breaths. "My sister Shelly was seven. Mally was four, almost five. I was nine."

Holly stopped and pulled Geoff back beside her. "But that was over twenty-five years ago. Are you telling me that no one in this family has gone sledding for twenty years? Surely, Geoff, your family has healed by now."

"You don't understand. It was a painful thing. I think we all blame ourselves for her death. Sledding is dangerous."

"So is driving fast, but you do that."

Mallory intervened. "But no one in our family was ever killed in a car accident. I don't remember Shelly." Just stern commands to never mention the word *sled* or her sister's name again. "I don't even remember much of what happened."

"She was killed. Her neck was broken." Geoff began to walk

once more. "There was no school that day because of the snow, and we were out with a bunch of neighborhood kids."

Mallory held her breath. She'd tried for years to get information about the accident, about her sister, but she had always been ignored or told to be quiet. Even Geoff wouldn't tell her anything. She had been afraid to ask, afraid she would be reprimanded for being thoughtless and cruel to bring up such a painful time.

No one talked about the accident.

Until now. The dam of silence had been broken, and it was as though Geoff couldn't stop the flow of words from spilling out.

"I got cold, so I told Eric that I was going in. Shelly had begged me for one more ride. We had been riding double on Jaggerman's Hill. You know where that is, Mal." She nodded, and Geoff continued. "She got mad at me, but I didn't give in. I heard Eric promise to take her clear to the top if she'd let him go down once on his own.

"When I got home, Mom wasn't back from Grandma and Grandpa Kaufman's, so I let Dad know that the others were still out playing. I remember Mally was asleep on the couch with her head in Dad's lap. I can still see him stroking her hair as he watched a game on TV. I think you had cried yourself to sleep because Dad wouldn't let you go with the rest of us."

Mallory blinked away sudden tears. "I don't remember any of that."

Geoff pulled the collar of his coat up around his ears. His voice was thick with grief, and moisture sparkled in his eyes. "Eric came running home terrified. He was screaming at the top of his lungs, something about Shelly not waking up. Dad went on the run once he made sense of Eric's babbling, but it was too late."

Mallory swallowed around the lump in her throat. "What happened, Geoff?"

He didn't answer. He turned into the entrance of Willow Hill and made his way toward the deserted playground. Mallory shivered. It was near here the police had found that little girl last summer…the girl who'd been murdered…

Geoff's boots scrunched in the snow. He hugged the pole of the swings. The vulnerability in his wide eyes made him look like a lost little boy. Mallory remembered that look from childhood. Holly wrapped her arms around his waist. "What happened, sweetie?"

Mallory reached for the chain of the swing, brushed the seat off, and sank onto it. "Geoff?"

He rubbed his eyes and stared at the stark, barren trees at the edge of the park. "Allen Morgan told me about it later. Eric talked Shelly into climbing on his back. He took her almost to the top, and then they started their ride. They hit the first dip, gained momentum…then hit the second dip and lost control. Eric was going too fast, and when he shifted his body to steer, Shelly was thrown off. She hit a tree and broke her neck. Eric broke his arm." He closed his eyes. "The rest of us were broken too. Nothing was the same after that."

He looked at Mallory. "I remember at the funeral that Aunt Patty made you kiss Shelly good-bye. You didn't understand and when you touched Shelly, you just started screaming. You had nightmares for months. But then, I think we all did."

Mallory's throat constricted, and a fist-size lump formed in her stomach. She shoved her toe into the snow and set the swing in motion. The family that Geoff had described was hers, but it was one she couldn't remember. Her sister's death had changed every-thing, changed everyone.

She locked her arms around the chains and began to pump the swing with her legs, stretching and pulling until the swing's momentum had reached a peak far above Geoff and Holly's heads. The swing jerked and started its downward arc, but Mallory kept pumping, trying to drive away the image that flooded her mind.

The image of a tiny, broken girl lying in the cold, unfeeling snow.

December 30

I can't tell anyone. I can't let anyone know. They'll think I'm crazy. The dreams or visions or whatever they are—they're too ugly, too terrible, too BAD. I keep hearing that in my head. "Mallory's a bad girl."

I have to get myself together. Please, Father God, help me. I'm tired of being a single parent. I'm tired of being alone. I'm tired...of being afraid.

Fifteen

"May I have your driver's license, please?"

Mallory couldn't find her wallet. Checkbook, credit card holder, Angel's toy from McDonald's—it *had* to be in her purse somewhere. She lifted out her keys and sunglasses and shuffled past the mail she had stuffed there earlier. She smiled at the bank teller. "Don't you hate this?"

"Mine's a mess. I can never find anything."

"Here it is."

"Thank you. I just need to make a credit check, and your account will be ready to go."

Mallory swallowed, forcing her tone to stay upbeat. "Is that necessary?"

The teller smiled. "It's just standard procedure for opening a new account. It will only take a moment."

"Mommy, can we go now?"

"Just a second, Angel." Mallory's head started to pound. Why was this taking so long? What would the credit check show—?

"But I'm thirsty."

"I said *wait!*" Mallory bit her lip, then glanced down at Angel. Fat tears pooled at the corner of her daughter's eyes. "Honey, I promise we'll get a treat when we're done, okay?"

"All set." The teller came back to her window and handed Mallory her driver's license and cash.

"Thank you." She lifted Angel into her arms and swung her around in a circle. "That wasn't so bad, now was it? Let's go pick up Aunt Heather and we'll go to the mall. We'll get you your very own drink, how about that?"

The cold blast of air caught Mallory in the face, and she tucked her chin into her muffler and shifted Angel to a better position on her hip. Wood smoke wafted down on the heavy air and burned her nasal passages. Mallory shuddered against the chill that ran up her spine.

An arm snaked around her waist and pinned her arms to her side. Something cold, round, and hard pressed against her temple. "Don't scream and don't move." His warm, moist breath moved the hair at her ear—

"Mommy!"

Angel's scream was followed by the blast of a horn and the squeal of tires. Mallory jerked backward. A rush of air swirled the snow at her feet as a car roared past. She hugged Angel's trembling body close. "It's okay, honey. It's okay."

By the time she reached Heather's, the incident in the bank parking lot had receded. Angel slurped on her Dr Pepper while Mallory waited for Heather to open the door of her apartment.

"All right, mis amigas are here. What took you so long anyway?"

"Errands." Mallory's smile felt stiff. "But I'm here now, so let's go do some serious damage at the mall."

Heather chuckled. "Somehow that thought scares me."

Mallory grinned. "And well it should. Let's go."

The mall looked desolate, forlorn since the mad rush of after-Christmas shoppers had desecrated its shops. Sale posters declaring 75% off hung in the store windows. Mallory nudged Heather's arm. "I want to check out this place." She pointed to Jasmine's Art Supplies. "This is new. When did they open?"

"I don't know." Heather leaned close to Angel. "Do we want to tag along with Mommy, or would you like to help Aunt Heather pick out a toy for her very best niece?"

"Go with *you*." Angel almost shouted it.

Heather grinned at Mallory. "See you later. We'll be at Toys 4 U."

Mallory nodded and entered the store. She fingered the fine hair of the sable brushes as she went down the aisle. A dark mahogany case stopped her. Its satin finish was smooth against her hand. She thumbed the sterling silver latches. With a soft *click* they snapped open. She lifted the lid to find brushes nestled in lined compartments. Turpentine and tubes of oil paints filled the bottom of the case.

It was beautiful.

Mallory closed the lid and lifted the red tag. An artist case of this quality for that price was a steal. She tucked it under her arm and turned toward the cash register.

February 5

Dear God, the very fabric of my soul is being consumed by a black hole. I'm hanging on to my sanity by a single thread. It's coming. I know it's coming. But what?

Sixteen

Mallory laid out the illustrations on her drawing table. They were done.

Please, please let them be right.

All she wanted to do was deliver this project and move on to something else. She worked her left thumb into the palm of her right hand and down her wrist, then gathered up the set of drawings and placed them in her portfolio. She would drop them off at Paxton's, then go to the Bible study at Heather's.

She didn't want to, but she had missed several of the meetings already, and she'd run out of excuses. It wasn't that the study wasn't interesting—Yvonne Gates was an excellent teacher. And it wasn't the people—Mallory enjoyed the women who attended. Most of them were from her church. It was just…

Mallory walked to the window and looked out at the desolate yard. Without snow to cover its bleakness, it was rather depressing. The house was deserted and too quiet. The girls were at her mother's.

She moved to the bronze eagle that stood on a three-foot pedestal in the corner of her studio. Wings outstretched and talons reaching for its prey, it was majestic. Her hands ran over the rough texture of its feathers. It was an exquisite piece; she hadn't been able to resist it. Her one regret was that it wasn't her creation.

She had never done anything in bronze or other metals. She did illustrations for the money they brought in, but her paintings in oils and acrylics were for her own enjoyment.

Mallory studied the unfinished painting on her easel and wanted to weep. Dark storm clouds rolled in from the sea and were ready to crash upon the as yet unpainted shore. A partial lighthouse beckoned a wind-tossed sailboat. The boat's spinnaker billowed; its keel leaned almost horizontal to the water.

It was hopeless. She couldn't paint. She tucked her hands into the pockets of her khakis. She'd tried. It had been hard enough to finish the work for Dorothy. Now even her pleasure had been taken from her.

Was it over? Was she losing even this—her livelihood, her joy, her escape from the pain?

She needed to keep drawing, but she knew her work lacked the passion, the depth, it once possessed. Everything had changed. When Jake left he took a vital piece of her with him. She was dried up. *Old.* And pain was everywhere. Her physical body screamed at her; her mind was in torment; even her faith seemed futile.

Had her creativity shriveled up as well?

Perhaps it wasn't something she could blame on Jake. Maybe what was wrong was something within her. Something she didn't know how to change. Something even God couldn't change.

O Father! Help me.

"Anyone have any prayer requests before we close?"

Mallory watched as Heather scanned the group of women seated in her living room. There were six other ladies from the

Shiloh Hills Community Church, plus the pastor's wife, Yvonne, who taught the study. Mallory pressed into the corner of the sofa. She had tried to concentrate but felt disjointed, her thoughts fractured. They were studying the book of Philippians, and tonight their topic had been contentment.

A little tough to relate to…

The women had been kind to her, but it bothered Mallory that they knew about her marital separation. *What are they thinking? That she and Jake needed help?* Well, they did, didn't they? She doodled on the side of her study book, taking notes as the ladies listed their prayer concerns.

"We need to remember the family of the little girl they found strangled and beaten in Willow Hill Park."

Mallory trembled. *Another child. Dear God, no!* She bent her head to her Bible, struggling against tears.

"At least they caught the guy. The thought of anyone torturing and raping a ten-year-old—"

No—no! Mallory's vision tunneled. Blackness was closing in. *Please don't let me faint.* Her chest squeezed; she struggled to force air through her lungs.

The women's conversation dwindled into a constrained silence. Mallory kept her head bowed, her eyes focused on her pen and paper, battling the swirling sensation in her head.

Heather started to pray, but Mallory couldn't hear the words. All she could hear, over and over, was *little girl…strangled and beaten…little girl…strangled and beaten…*

She hadn't heard about another child being found. *Willow Hill.* She and Geoff and Holly had been there on Christmas Day.

Mallory's hands were shaking, and she gripped the edge of her Bible to still them.

She managed a weak smile at the group of ladies, who seemed to be leaving Heather's apartment en masse. She stood and gathered glasses and plates from Heather's elegant glass coffee table, willing the images in her mind to flee.

But split-second pictures of a small girl's terrified face swam before her. She could almost hear the screams of absolute panic. Had he tied her and gagged her like…like…

Like me. Like I was tied and gagged.

Mallory's hands went slack. She watched the stack of plates and glassware crash at her feet on the tiled floor, then awareness was blocked out as terror flooded her.

She could smell the pungent odor of burning leaves. Burning, searing pain ripped through her. The darkness was overpowering. Oppressive…closing in.

It was coming. And, God help her, she couldn't stop it.

Heather jumped at the sound of breaking glass. She sprinted to the kitchen doorway and found Mallory, unmoving, standing among broken china and slivered crystal. Her friend's eyes were wide and glazed…as if she were looking into another dimension. Her fists were pressed against her trembling mouth. She turned dark, haunted eyes toward Heather, and recognition flickered in them.

"Mallory, are you okay?" Fear shimmied up Heather's spine. What had happened? *Precious Lord, she's terrified.* "Mallory what is it?"

"I…the plates." Mallory's dazed eyes went to the plates scattered on the floor. "I'm sorry, Heather, I'm so sorry. I broke your plates. The mess. I have to get a rag." Mallory's whole body shook as she took a step over the broken dishes.

"Don't worry about that." Heather ignored the mess and picked her way through the rubble on the floor. "You're shaking."

Mallory stiffened and backed away, staring at a point past Heather's shoulder. Prickles of fear raised the flesh on Heather's arm, and she looked behind her. Nothing was there. Whatever Mallory saw was happening in the recesses of her mind.

"Mallory, are you all right?" Heather took another step, and Mallory slid further into the kitchen.

"Did something break?" At the sound of Yvonne's voice, Heather flinched and Mallory bolted to the far corner of the kitchen. "What's going on?"

"I don't know. Something has terrified her." Panic rose within Heather. *I don't know what to do.* Heather reached out to touch her, but Mallory jerked backward and cowered away from her.

"Mal?"

Mallory retreated. Her eyes darted about the kitchen, like a frightened rabbit looking for a place to bolt.

"Mal? It's okay." Heather dropped her voice to a soft pitch. At her tentative step, Mallory pushed against the wall. *God, what is going on? Please help her.*

"No. No. No," Mallory's words were barely audible. Mallory shook her head from side to side and massaged her wrists.

If she backs up any further, she'll disappear into the wall. "Yvonne, what should we do?" *Dear God, please help us.* Heather looked behind her to Yvonne.

"Mallory." Yvonne's voice was firm. "You're safe. Heather and I are here with you. Whatever is frightening you can't hurt you here. You're at Heather's house, in Heather's kitchen. There's nobody else here. The other ladies left. Do you remember? The Bible study, Mallory, it ended, and everyone's gone except us. No one here will hurt you. I promise."

With every word Yvonne spoke, Heather inched closer to Mallory. Like someone trying to coax a jumper off a high-rise ledge, Heather eased her hand to her friend's rigid shoulders. The tension pulsing through Mallory radiated up Heather's arm. Mallory's eyes made contact with her, and Heather saw recognition, then confusion. *Please tell me I'm doing the right thing.*

She wrapped her arms around Mallory's still trembling body and pulled her close. Yvonne laid her hand on Mallory's shoulder, and Mallory turned into Heather's embrace Yvonne's voice lifted above the sobs racking Mallory's body. "Father God, You are powerful. More powerful than anything happening right now inside Mallory. Calm her. Give her peace. Through the power and blood of Your Son, Jesus Christ, please, God, help us."

Yvonne's prayer continued, and Heather could feel the tension ebbing from Mallory. Her friend was like a delicate piece of glass that the mere hint of pressure would shatter. Heather's fear intensified. What if they said the wrong thing? Did the wrong thing? It could push her right over the edge. No, prayer was the only thing that would help Mallory.

Heather and Yvonne guided the now sobbing Mallory to the couch in the living room. Before long, Mallory's convulsive weeping slowed into hiccuping gulps of air, and Heather reached for the box of tissues she kept on the stand beside the couch.

Mallory mopped her eyes and nose and then began to laugh through her tears at the sight of the mound of used tissues on the floor. Relief, then bewilderment swept through Heather. What on earth was going on?

Mallory seemed to regain control and mumbled a thank-you, followed by a soft "I'm sorry."

Heather took a deep breath and sat down beside her. Thank God, she seemed to be returning to normal. "Mal, it's okay." Heather wiped the tears away from her friend's drenched eyes. The deep green pools were haunted, but Heather was thankful to see the worst of the crisis seemed to be over. "You have nothing to be sorry for. Can you talk about it yet?"

Fresh tears began as Mallory's halting words came out. "He kept hitting me. He hurt me. He hurt me."

Heather's stomach lurched. Bile rose, and she swallowed it back. *Dear Jesus, I never knew this happened to her. When? Who?*

Mallory buried her head in her arms.

"Who hit you, Mallory?" Yvonne's voice was gentle.

Mallory rocked herself. "I was seven. He raped me, and I was only seven." Horror flooded through Heather. *Dear Father in heaven.* Her stomach plunged as she struggled to comprehend her friend's words. *How could anyone do that to a child?*

She couldn't imagine the terror and pain Mallory must have gone through. Wrapping her arms around Mallory, she looked into Yvonne's compassionate face. *What do we do now?* Heather's tears flowed with Mallory's, and she pulled her wounded friend closer.

"Oh, sweetheart"—Yvonne knelt down on the floor at Mallory's feet—"I'm so sorry."

Mallory's sobs slowed. "I'm so…tired." She curled up in the corner of the sofa and tipped her head back against the cushion. Her eyes fluttered shut, and Yvonne took the cotton afghan from the chair and spread it across her still shaking form.

"Rest." Heather reached out and stroked the thick, silky hair away from Mallory's ashen face.

"Can I use your phone, Heather?"

Heather looked up and nodded. Yvonne touched her arm on the way out. "I'll be right back."

Lord, what are we going to do? I promise I will do whatever I can to help my friend. Just show me what to do.

Heather's hand stilled at the sound of Mallory's heavy, even breathing. She dried her own tears on her sleeve and slipped off the couch. Mallory didn't move, and Heather tiptoed into the kitchen. Yvonne was still on the phone.

"James, I'm really concerned. She's quiet now, but it looks like a flashback of childhood abuse." She turned away from the doorway to the living room and lowered her voice. "Honey, she told us she was raped when she was seven." Her voice broke. "Do you think Jennifer Price could see her?"

Heather frowned. *Who is Jennifer Price?*

"Okay. I'm going to stay awhile. Call me if you get hold of her." Yvonne hung up and turned to Heather. "James is going to try to get Mallory in to talk to a psychologist who deals with this sort of thing."

"A psychologist?" Heather sagged against the wall. This couldn't be happening. "Maybe she needs to see a doctor. Should we take her to the hospital?" *How could anybody suffer this sort of—what? Breakdown?—and not need a doctor?*

Yvonne leaned around the door. "Looks like she's sleeping. Let's wait for her to wake up and see how she's doing."

"I've never seen anything like it before. It was like she went off the deep end." Fresh horror swept over Heather as she recalled the look on Mallory's face. What if it happened again?

"I'm no expert, but James and I have done some counseling and have seen this kind of thing a few times." Yvonne sat down on a kitchen chair and massaged her temple with a fingertip. "I think Mallory was reliving a traumatic event from her childhood."

"I...I don't understand." Heather pulled out a chair opposite Yvonne. "Couldn't you and James talk with her?"

Yvonne looked her in the eye. "Heather, this goes way beyond what James and I are qualified to deal with. Jennifer is better equipped to handle this crisis."

Heather nodded but wasn't convinced. "But all she needs is God." *Right, Lord? You're all she needs.*

"I can't fault your theology on that"—Yvonne leaned forward—"but sometimes there are deep issues in our lives that become a jumbled mess, and we need someone to help us sift through that debris."

But Dad always said psychology was the world's thinking and the devil's inroad into today's society. Even as her thoughts assaulted her, Heather's spirit was convicted by the promise she had made in the living room.

She *would* do whatever it took to help Mallory—but just the thought of her friend seeing a psychologist made her tremble.

February 6

My mind is in such torment—arguing back and forth—what's real, what's not?

And what if I remember more, something worse, something—unthinkable.

I don't want to believe it. I don't want to see or feel the pain and the ugliness all over again, but if I don't face it now, I will go mad.

In a strange, convoluted way, it all makes sense. And there is great relief in knowing there's a reason for my fears, but I need to know why it happened. And more important—who?

Seventeen

"I wanna go home! Why can't we go home?"

Angel's sobs stabbed into Martin's heart. He tried to turn a deaf ear to his granddaughter's distress as he reached for his work coat. He checked the living room. Alecia knelt down in front of Angel and tried to gather the stiff body into her arms. "I know, sweet pea. I told you that Mommy's not feeling very well today, so that's why you get to stay an extra day with Grandma."

"Grandpa could take us home. We'd be real quiet!" Renee's voice wobbled just a little. "I'd take care of my sister."

"Grandpa has to go, and you are too young to have to take care of Angel all by yourself." Amazing how Alecia's voice was both calm and accusing at the same time.

Martin's vision blurred, and he cleared his throat against the gathering pain. He patted his pockets, checking for his gloves. He needed to go. Geoff had called earlier with a problem of his own and needed Martin's help. Guilt and relief vied for position. Well, what could he do here? He'd never been good with women in tears—not even when they stood under four feet tall and had big, round eyes filled with pools of water just waiting to spill over. Geoff's call had been a godsend, though self-reproach over leaving nudged once more against his conscience.

"I want Mommy!" Angel wailed as tears spilled over her

chubby cheeks. Martin shrugged into his coat and pulled on his gloves. He wouldn't be gone long. Just until the tears had been dried and the girls distracted by his wife's ingenuity.

"I want your mommy too. But she's not here right now. Let's go make some cookies. Okay?"

"Daddy could come get us." Renee lost the battle with bravery. "Please!"

"I don't know where Daddy is today." Martin heard his wife's voice take on the texture of granite. How well he knew that tone…just as he knew the girls didn't stand a chance against it. He shook his head. They had been through so much. Still, Alecia was much better at this than he was. He reached for the doorknob.

"Martin!"

His back stiffened and he gripped the knob, waiting in silence for her to continue.

"Find out what Geoff knows, and see if you can pull him away from whatever is consuming all his time. His family needs him."

He turned to watch Alecia lift Angel to her hip. "Come on, girls, please quit crying! If you do, Grandma will let you play with her dollhouse! Before you know it, Mommy will be here." She turned to Martin. "Wait until I see her!"

"Wait until you see her, Dad. She's a beauty."

Geoff wiped his hand on a greasy rag and stuffed it into the back pocket of his coveralls. He laid a hand on Martin's shoulder and guided him around the New England–style home to the four-car garage at the back.

Martin yanked upward on his coat zipper in an attempt to

ward off February's biting wind. The weather pattern coming off Lake Erie had created lake-effect snow, which was wreaking havoc further south into Ohio than normal. Claybourn and its surrounding areas were taking the brunt of old man winter. Martin stepped through the side door and reversed his zipper. It was at least forty degrees warmer in here. Geoff's garage was filled with clutter, and at its center sat the current apple of the boy's eye: a rusted, bulky piece of metal on worn-out rubber wheels.

Cars and computers had always been Geoff's passion. Martin remembered the way Geoff's eyes had glowed when he came home from high school and related in great detail how they had to rebuild a car in shop class. He'd been hooked ever since.

"Well?" Geoff's hand caressed the rusted fender. "What do you think?"

"A Nash wagon, huh?"

Geoff nodded. The motion caused a strand of hair to fall across his forehead. At that moment he looked like a teenager again. "A 1957 Rambler Rebel. She'll be a beauty once she's restored. I've already ordered the paint. I found a solid wood console panel and have ordered the upholstery for the seats. Carpet is next on the list."

Martin turned to study the other cars lined in the garage—a '64 Corvette, the Triumph Geoff had driven to the Fourth of July picnic, and a Mercedes.

"So what did you want my help on?" He pulled a pipe from his shirt pocket and clamped it between his teeth. He fished in his pockets for the tobacco pouch and filled the bowl. Soon the calming scent of burning tobacco curled around his head.

"I'm having trouble with the carburetor and wondered if you

could give me a little help." Geoff reached for a socket wrench. "I figured you would know more about these cars. After all, you lived in that era."

Martin laughed and moved toward the space heater. He rubbed his hands before the warm air. "I know some. Let your old man get his hands heated up first. I can't believe you would get an ugly old Nash Rambler. A wagon, no less."

"I like them. It reminds me of the car you used to have."

Martin rolled Geoff's toolbox closer to the car. Maybe this would be the best place to pick his son's brain. Geoff had always been close to Mallory. He'd stood up for her when Eric teased her. He defended her from the bullies in school. He'd been a good kid, really…kept to himself, did what he was supposed to do, got good grades, and moved on to a successful career.

His son. Martin was proud of him.

Geoff spoke over the sound of the ratchet wrench. "How's Mom?"

"None too happy with me when I left the house."

Geoff chuckled. "Wanted to come, did she?"

"No. The girls were wailing at the top of their lungs. Why is it that kids always want Mommy when Mommy isn't well? I just hope after the session with that counselor she'll feel like—"

"Counselor? What counselor? Dad, are we talking about Mal?"

"Of course we're talking about Mal."

"What's going on?" Geoff set the carburetor aside and looked him full in the eye. Martin started when he saw his son's wide, confused eyes and rigid back.

Martin rubbed his jaw.. "You don't know?"

"Know what? Dad, what's going on?"

"Mallory went to see a counselor today. Her pastor didn't know how long it would—"

"Mal's seeing a shrink? What for?" The wrench clattered into the toolbox.

"She had… an episode at Heather's two nights ago. This psychologist wanted—"

Geoff's stiff hand rose to cut Martin off. "Episode? What kind of episode?"

"If you'd just keep quiet, I'd tell you." Martin chuffed on his pipe, sending up waves of smoke around his head.

Geoff groped for a stool, dragged it nearer, and eased down on it. *He didn't know. Mallory didn't tell him.* Martin thought Mallory and Geoff talked about everything. He paced the floor and recounted his own sketchy version of the incident.

All he knew was that Mallory had been at a prayer meeting and had gone berserk. The following morning her friend Heather took Mallory to the doctor for some tests, which apparently had checked out okay. So now she was at a session with a psychologist. Martin shook his head. "Jake's leaving must have hit her harder than any of us realized."

"This is stupid! Mallory doesn't need to see a shrink." Geoff jerked to his feet, his hands balled in fists at his side. He looked as if he were squaring off for a battle. But with whom? "There is absolutely nothing wrong with her."

"Mom said she hasn't looked good for a long time. We hoped it was something physical. Mom thought maybe it was a female thing, but the doctor couldn't find anything."

"She always tells me her problems. Why hasn't she discussed any of this with me?"

"I'm as stunned as you are."

Geoff reached for the phone. "I'm calling her. Whatever it is, it's a family matter and needs to be kept there. She's not going to spill her guts to some stranger. "

Do I have the courage to spill my guts to a stranger?

Mallory chewed at a stubborn hangnail. The skin on her finger gave way and started to bleed, and she popped the finger in her mouth.

Relax...

Right. The worst that could happen was they would put her in a straitjacket and take her to the funny farm. She ripped off another piece of skin on a different finger, then gripped her hands in her lap. If she didn't stop, she wouldn't have any fingers left.

She slapped her hand against her thigh to stop the sudden tingling.

The canned music coming through the ceiling speakers irritated more than it soothed. It didn't seem to have that effect on Yvonne, who sat reading a magazine beside her, but then she wasn't the one who was crazy.

"Hello, Yvonne." Mallory turned to see that the door to the inner office had opened and a woman stood, hand outstretched. "Mallory?" At Mallory's nod, the woman continued. "I'm Jennifer Price." A short cap of dark brown curls framed her face. Only the fine laugh lines etched around her dark brown eyes and narrow lips marred her creamy complexion. "Come on in and let's get acquainted."

Jennifer held the door while Mallory bent to pick up her purse and stuff her unread magazine in the rack. She took one last look at Yvonne. *Don't make me do this.* It felt a little too much like being sent to the principal.

Jennifer's office was light and airy, with pure white walls and accents of sea-foam green pillows on the couch and chairs. It looked more like someone's living room than a shrink's office.

To keep the invisible voices calm, no doubt.

"Have a seat wherever you're comfortable." Jennifer walked to her desk, leaned against the reflective top, and reached for her yellow legal pad. Mallory Carlisle had the classic look of a woman in torment.

Jennifer closed her eyes for a moment. *Father, help me hear her through Your ears, and see her through Your eyes, because only You can help her to full restoration and healing.*

Mallory sat in the plush corner chair. Corners always seemed to draw her clients: There was no way someone could sneak up on you when you were in a corner. Mallory set her purse on the floor next to her feet and crossed her legs.

"Would you like some coffee or tea?"

Mallory's slender brow lifted, but her reply was neutral. "Tea, please."

"Sugar or cream?"

"Sugar."

"How was the trip in?"

"Fine."

Jennifer made the tea, then handed it to Mallory. "I usually sit here"—she pointed to the chair opposite Mallory—"but if you would be more comfortable with me sitting elsewhere, I can do that."

Mallory shook her head. "That's fine."

Jennifer settled in the chair and sipped her tea. Her heart went out to the other woman. So much pain and confusion were etched on her face.

Mallory was studying the office with interest. Her gaze slid across the walls, taking in the pictures and eclectic bric-a-brac Jennifer had collected from clients over the years.

"I didn't expect it to look like this."

"My office?"

Mallory nodded. She was beginning to relax. That was good.

"I spend a lot of time here, and I like working in a space that feels more like a living room. My clients seem to like it better as well."

Some of the women who passed through Jennifer's doors found sitting on the floor much easier, more comforting. Whatever worked to help them feel safe was what Jennifer strove for.

Mallory twisted one finger at a time, sending a faint popping sound through the room as she cracked each knuckle in turn.

"What can I do to make you more comfortable?"

Mallory shrugged. "Can I take my shoes off?"

The question came out in a little-girl voice. Jennifer nodded. "Please do whatever helps you to relax." *Except leave.*

Mallory reached down and slid off her shoes, then studied Jennifer for a brief moment. Her eyes were big and dark.

Jennifer leaned closer. "What is it, Mallory?"

"I don't know how to do this." The threat of tears was in her voice.

"That's okay. We'll start out slow and easy." Jennifer settled back in her chair and smiled. "Why don't you just share some things about yourself, and I'll jump in with any questions that need clarification, or if you get stuck I can prompt you with some questions and you can respond to them."

Mallory nodded but said nothing; instead she nibbled on the edge of her thumbnail. *She'll need some prompting.* Most clients did at first. It was amazing, though, how soon they opened up, often revealing things they weren't even aware they were revealing.

"Let's start with a brief history, okay?"

"Okay." She sounded like a frightened four-year-old.

"Yvonne tells me you're married and have children. Two girls?"

Those eyes got bigger; she'd hit another nerve. Jennifer jotted a note to herself while Mallory began to talk about her two girls, then about her miscarriage before Renee. Her husband had begun traveling more then, working longer hours. Jennifer scribbled another note. *Have they worked through this tragedy?* Though Mallory and her husband were separated, Jennifer was glad to hear they were on speaking terms. And it was apparent that she loved her husband. *That's good. Reconciliation may be a viable option.*

Jennifer listed Mallory's family history: Parents both alive. Two older brothers, Eric and Geoff; Mallory was the youngest. She had a sister, Shelly, who died at the age of seven. Jennifer wrote a comment beside Shelly's name: *Family ghost. Family dynamic probably changed with the sister's death.* Next to that she wrote, *Grief. Family dealt with? Mallory?* Each piece of the puzzle of Mallory's life would become clearer as they began dealing with the surface problems.

Jennifer flipped back a page and caught Mallory craning her

neck to see what was written there. Jennifer smiled. Mallory watched her like a truant schoolgirl who had just been caught. She tapped her yellow pad. "It's just to help me keep the facts straight. I jotted down a few notes last night when I talked to Yvonne, and I need to refresh my memory."

She glanced down at the scribbled page. *Resurfacing events—prayer requests for a seven-year-old beaten and strangled at Willow Hill Park.* She scrawled, *Daughter—seven years old. Other daughter, Angel, age Mallory was when sister died.* That might be enough to trigger the episode. Both her girls being the same age as Mallory when traumatic events happened in her life would be like an emotional bomb exploding.

Jennifer was pretty sure that once they began to sift through the debris in Mallory's soul she would see how the suppressed memory had manifested itself in other ways. The trick was helping her believe she wasn't crazy or stupid, and wasn't making it up…and to help her accept that what had happened to her was not her fault. The biggest undertaking was going to be getting her back to emotional balance where she would be willing to look at her memories and perceptions through the eyes of truth. Because perception had a way of being much more powerful than reality.

According to Yvonne, Mallory had a solid spiritual foundation. That was a good start; faith in God was a stronger remedy than all the counseling Jennifer could give.

"Mallory, would you be willing to meet with a small group of women and go through a three-month session in tandem with your individual therapy?"

The young woman's head snapped up; her expression was

guarded. "Group therapy? Talk to people I don't know about this?" Her walls and defenses were clearly in place, but Jennifer would have been more concerned had they been down. New environments and situations called for protection of the vulnerable places. The goal was to get Mallory comfortable enough to risk. No easy task. Some clients never got there and years later were still in therapy.

"A group of six to eight women. They each have their own stories, but each is similar in some ways. All of you have suffered great pain, mentally, physically, sexually, and emotionally. You will be able to help each other in ways you never dreamed of."

"I don't know."

"Fair enough. I think it would help, but the decision is yours. I won't ever make you do anything you don't want to do, but once we have made an agreement I would expect you to follow through with it. So just think about it and tell me next week what you decide."

Jennifer leaned back in her chair. "Now, can you tell me about what happened at your friend's home?"

Mallory pushed against the chair back and rubbed her thumb over her wrist as, in disjointed words, she recalled what happened. Most of what she remembered was feelings interspersed with a few vivid, powerful images.

"Is this the first time anything like this has happened?"

"Yes. It feels like some kind of nightmare. What if I imagined it?" Mallory twisted her interlocked fingers and hunched further into the chair. Jennifer expected her at any moment to curl up in the chair and wrap her arms over her neck. She didn't.

Jennifer crossed her arms over her notepad. "Mallory, can you look at me?" She shook her head, but finally, with painful slowness, did so—though only for a heartbeat.

"I don't think you're making this up."

Mallory scraped her finger across the ragged edge of her thumbnail. "But I can't remember everything…only bits and pieces."

"Give it time. It's amazing the way God made us. Our mind has an awesome way of dealing with traumatic events that happen to us."

"Things like losing your memory?" Mallory's gaze focused on a painting of a mountain scene, and Jennifer noted with interest the way her stiff shoulders relaxed a bit.

Jennifer laid her pencil down and rested her chin on her hand. "Yes. That and a multitude of other ways. The body and the mind learn to cope. However, the memory is not so much lost as buried. It's our job to see if we can't help you feel safe enough to allow those memories to rise to the surface so we can deal with them."

Mallory shuddered and pulled her legs up into the chair, curling up in a ball. "I don't think I can let the memory come back. It's so…it's too… Jennifer, I can't do this! Please don't make me do this."

Jennifer slipped out of her seat and knelt next to Mallory. "I'd like to touch you, to comfort you. May I?" Mallory's nod was abrupt, quick, and Jennifer laid her hand on Mallory's knee. She lowered her voice to a soothing drone. "It's okay, you can relax, Mallory. I promise that you're safe. No one will hurt you here."

Jennifer would do everything she could to make sure no one would ever hurt Mallory again. Her years of experience told her there was something more that Mallory didn't want to face.

Obviously, since she'd buried memories of the abuse. What happened to Mallory was so horrific she was too frightened to reveal who it was. But with God's help, and in His timing, they would figure it out.

The perpetrator couldn't hide forever.

April 27

I am not a child anymore. He can't hurt me now. Then why am I still afraid? And why can't I remember it all? If only I could rewind the video of my mind—just to see what happened, to see that I'm not crazy, I didn't make it up.

I know it happened.

Eighteen

Mallory's hand slammed against the ball tethered to the pole by the thick rope. Unanswerable questions screamed in her mind. What had she ever done to deserve this?

"Nothing, Mallory," Jennifer had told her. So easy to say, so hard to believe. She hit the ball again. She didn't want to think about it anymore—not the pain and not the confusion. The ball came at her from the other direction. She lashed out, her knuckles colliding with the metal ring attached to the rope. She welcomed the stinging pain of her bruised and bleeding knuckles.

She shook out her hands, then pressed the heels of her palms against her forehead.

For the last several sessions Jennifer had been working hard to get her to release some of the anger that was consuming her soul. She knew Jennifer would be disappointed that she took her revenge out on the tetherball without some kind of protection on her hands.

"We want to keep you safe, Mallory," Jennifer had told her at their last meeting.

But it feels so much better without the protection. I want to feel the physical pain. Then she didn't have to deal with the emotional pain.

Jennifer's words came back to Mallory. "Why won't you let your anger out?"

"I'm afraid once I do, it will never stop."

"I promise you, Mallory, that the anger won't last forever. But you have to let it out."

Mallory shivered at the memory. Jennifer had hugged her, and Mallory had wished she could stay forever in the safety of her therapist's embrace.

A month ago Jennifer had her do a Bible study and look at how many times Scripture mentioned anger or the wrath of the Lord. Mallory had been relieved. Finally, an easy assignment, one she could enjoy doing. Too bad her relief had been short-lived. That study had been a catalyst for her brewing rage. It had boiled to the surface and bubbled into every area of her life. The only way she could handle it was in some sort of physical release.

Every visit, Jennifer reassured Mallory that the rage would end, but that she needed to let it all go. Once she did so, she would experience peace in a way she never had before. It was a promise Mallory clung to.

Now here she was, four sessions later and with yet another hard assignment.

"Mallory, you've been in sessions for over two months. When are you going to tell Jake that you're in therapy and why you're here?"

With one simple question, Jennifer had knocked out from under Mallory the facade of normality that it had taken weeks to build. By pretending everything was under control, Mallory had managed to make it through her day-to-day responsibilities. If the girls had noticed their mother's distraction or mood swings punctuated with bouts of weeping, well, what else was new?

Where were they? Panic clawed through her, and she spun around, then relaxed. Renee was swinging her way across the monkey bars, while Angel cheered her on. Other children played in the early spring sunshine.

Mallory drew in a deep breath. *This isn't Willow Hill...* At the reminder, Mallory's heart settled back to an even rhythm, only to give way to another onslaught of anger and confusion. How anyone could brutalize an innocent child was beyond her comprehension. She pounded the ball until sweat was dripping from her and her hands were numb. She left the tetherball swinging and hopped up onto a picnic table, then slumped backward to lie, knees bent, staring into the hazy blue sky.

Jake's eyes sometimes turned that color...

Jake. She avoided him and had very little trouble doing so. The ironic twist of her sudden gratefulness for his out-of-town trips made her laugh. The few times she had seen Jake, it just hadn't seemed the appropriate time to tell him.

Who am I kidding? There won't ever be an appropriate time.

What was she going to do? How could she tell him? How could she tell anyone? The secret had been buried for twenty years. It wasn't something she could simply bring out, dust off and say, "Oh, by the way..."

Mallory groaned out loud. She rubbed her aching knuckles again and played out several scenarios in her mind as to how she could approach the subject. *It has to be away from the girls. Should I go to Joey's? No, I don't want Joey to hear this. Maybe I should just call him at work and we could meet somewhere.* They needed someplace neutral, but also someplace private.

How was she ever going to tell him?

* * *

He had to tell her. But tell her what? He wasn't even sure yet what he was going to do.

Jake flipped the thick envelope over and over in his hands, as if that simple gesture could provide him with the solution. All he knew was he couldn't continue to live his life the way he had been living it, in limbo, day to day. Regardless of the consequences, he had to make a decision. It had to be today, and he had to tell her soon.

Joey came out of bathroom wiping his face on a towel. He looked up, took a fast step back, and held up his hands. "Whoa, dude. Don't shoot. 'Cause whatever it is, I didn't do it."

"What?"

"The look on your face could have melted steel."

"Thinking about my life has a way of doing that." Jake thrust the envelope in his briefcase and slammed it shut. Man! How had everything gotten so messed up? He slid his cell phone into its holder and looked at Joey's still-cautious face. "It's okay. I wasn't gunning for anyone."

Joey returned his look, scrutinizing him until he apparently decided Jake wasn't about to blow up at him. He tossed his towel back into his bedroom, closed the door, and reached for his boots. "Pays to be careful, y'know? I don't like wearing bruises that aren't mine."

Jake grinned. "I guess I haven't been the most congenial room-mate in the world."

"S'alright, boss. Life's put you in the squeeze."

Jake blew out an imprecation and paced around the small living room. "Yeah, like a garbage compactor. Now I know what an aluminum can feels like."

Joey moved closer to Jake before he asked, "Could I make a suggestion, boss?"

"What?"

"Talk to someone."

Jake folded his arms across his chest. "I am. You."

"Naw. I ain't the dude to help you. I'm a little too close to you and Malo. Sometimes talking to a neutral third person helps you talk to the one you love."

"Learn that in your counseling class, did you?"

"Nope. Learned it through life. Just think about it, okay?" Silence filled the room, but Joey continued to study him. "What else is going on?"

Jake turned away and leaned against the bookcase, careful not to dislodge Joey's prized possessions from his travels around the world. A colorful mask from Africa was displayed next to a rock taken from Germany when Jake had photographed the Berlin Wall and a jar of sand from the photo shoot of the troops in Desert Storm.

"I got a letter in the mail…" Jake fingered another stone, remembering the day Joey took it from the base of the Wailing Wall in Israel. His gaze wandered to the black-and-white photo he had taken of Joey listening to an ancient rabbi.

His attention skimmed across the variety of pictures he had taken of Joey—the young man had made friends with someone from every country they'd ever been in. He fingered the frame and studied the image of Joey with his arms around the Malaysian boy who had become their guide. Jake smiled. It was one of his favorite pictures. In one eternal moment, it had captured the very essence of Joey's compassionate spirit.

"Boss? What kind of letter?"

A letter that could change everything. Jake reached for the envelope that held the possible key to his future—to all their futures. Jake turned to his friend. "It's a job offer." He tapped the letter against his palm. "I need to make a decision, Joey. It's going to affect us all." Pain lanced through him, and he turned to Joey, fighting the desperation that threatened to engulf him. "And...I don't know what to do."

June 3

"For the enemy has persecuted my soul; he has crushed my life to the ground; he has made me dwell in darkness, like those who have been long dead. Therefore my spirit is overwhelmed within me; my heart within me is distressed" (Psalm 143:3-4).

How much worse does it have to get before it gets better? So much pain. So many conflicting emotions. So many lives twisted and destroyed. Warped.

Nineteen

Mallory watched Renee scurry up the porch steps after her little sister. She had reason to hurry—she was fleeing her mother's wrath.

Mallory backed her car out of her parents' driveway, peeling the tires as she went. It had been an excruciating day, and she had a headache to match it. What's more, she still had a therapy session to get through this afternoon.

Wonderful.

Renee's teacher had called and asked that Mallory and Jake come to the school to see the principal before taking Renee home. Jake, of course, was unavailable, so Mallory had to face the ordeal alone. She couldn't believe Renee had been in a fight! She slammed on her brakes just as the amber traffic light turned red.

Perfect. All she needed was a ticket to top off her day.

Fighting! It's so unlike my little girl. When she had talked to Renee, her daughter confessed to having pushed another child. Renee had been tearful and repentant, and when the whole story came out Mallory realized there might have been some provocation, but…fighting! Not only had Mallory lost a grip on her life, she was failing as a mother.

She tried so hard to hide her turmoil from the girls, but they both knew something was wrong. These last months had been devastating. They were her babies; how could they understand? Every day they asked when their daddy would be coming home, and Mallory had no answer for them.

Therapy had been good—and bad. Some days Mallory thought she was doing better, that she was stronger. But most of the time she just struggled to survive the pain. Maybe it would have been better to keep it all buried. Even now she grappled with hazy images, incomplete memories. It was right there…if only she could remember! But the memory was like words on the tip of her tongue that she just couldn't spit out.

Maybe she wasn't so sure she wanted to recall it.

What had surfaced so far had been agonizing, terrifying. She had started group therapy with five other women. Jennifer had been right—going through the process with others who understood, often without words, had helped. It would be almost impossible to explain to anyone else what she was feeling.

She drew a steadying breath. How could these women share at all? Their stories of multiple offenders sometimes made her pain seem insignificant. She found she had to deal with a sense of guilt that she seemed to be the exception and not the rule. Jennifer set her guilt to rest, telling her no person's story is more traumatic than another's. Pain is pain. They each had their own journey of betrayal and woundedness, their own story of survival, and somehow in sharing they helped each other.

The seminar that Jennifer had sent Mallory to had helped as well.

"I have a colleague who teaches a course at Ashland University." Jennifer had riffled through a pile on her desk until she found a business card. "It's a four-day training seminar for professionals—police officers, teachers, social workers, clergy—but I urge all my clients to go. It's an excellent course that will give you more information and help than I could in months of therapy."

Mallory had debated going, but decided she needed to. Good thing, too. Those four days had been both enlightening and grueling. Fear, rage, pain, overwhelming sadness, relief that what she was experiencing was "normal"—myriad feelings had pierced her soul. The abuse had impacted every area of her life. So much made sense now.

The whole thing was such a roller-coaster ride. One minute she'd tell herself to trust God, to forgive, to put the past behind her, then the next she'd end up sobbing her heart out because of the pain she couldn't seem to eradicate. Everything hurt—her body, her mind, her spirit. All she wanted was to get beyond this, to be a good mother to her precious girls, to somehow find a way back to a relationship with her husband…to just have this whole nightmare over with.

Can that ever happen, Lord?

Mallory rested her head on the steering wheel. She couldn't sit out in the parking lot in front of Jennifer's office forever. Best to go in and get it over with.

"How have you been?"

Mallory stared at the ground. "Tired. Anxious." She raised her eyes to meet Jennifer's gaze. "I feel like I'm waiting for the other shoe to drop. Empty. Scared."

Terrified. Out of control. The list is endless.

Mallory picked up the pillow from the couch and hugged it to her chest.

Jennifer scribbled on her ever-present legal pad, and Mallory wondered what she was writing. Despite Jennifer's explanation that the notes were just to help keep her mind fresh and help to guide Mallory's recovery, it was unnerving to hear Jennifer's pen scratch away as Mallory unfolded the details of her life.

"Those are normal feelings for what you've just been through. It will take time."

"I'm still having the migraines."

Jennifer's pen kept pace with her questions and Mallory's responses. "What about the anxiety attacks? Are you still having those?"

"Yes, sometimes."

"Will you tell me if they intensify?"

Mallory picked at the tassel of the pillow and promised nothing.

Jennifer stopped writing and studied her. "I really need to know, Mallory. The emotional, as well as physical and spiritual, are all pieces of the same quilt." She tapped the pen against her chin. "Recovery is much like an onion—layers of other issues have built up around the core. So we begin by peeling away one layer at a time. The first layer is easy to talk about, and while it's important, it's not the real issue. What you find impossible to talk about is what we're digging for."

Mallory swallowed hard and fought back the tears. The tingling was back. *Darn it!* She kneaded her knuckles with her other hand. *You can handle this. You can get through it with your self-respect still intact. I think.*

I hope.

Jennifer leaned closer. "I may be wrong, and it may not fit for you, but I notice that every time I mention what happened that night at Heather's or we talk about the memory you have, you begin to massage your hands."

Mallory's hands stilled. It was true. Her hands had started tingling at those times.

"What does it feel like?"

"My hands go numb. Just like that. I lose the feeling in them, or they start tingling, or sharp pain shoots through them. At the craziest times." *This is weird.*

"Such as?"

"I don't know. When I've had a fight with Jake. Watching TV. Drawing. Several months ago my publishing company gave me an assignment, and my hands hurt the entire time I was working on it."

Jennifer tilted her head, and Mallory had to drop her eyes.

"What were you working on?"

Mallory swallowed, almost choking on her suddenly desert-dry throat. "It was a children's book on protecting themselves from abuse—oh!"

"It makes sense, doesn't it? Your body responds to those things that trigger your memory and fear. Our bodies have a way of remembering what the mind forgets. It's called tissue memory. Your tissue will actually store the memory, and then your body responds to similar stimuli as it is being triggered." Jennifer reached for her coffee and took a sip, studying Mallory above the rim. Her voice grew softer. "What were you just thinking?"

Mallory lifted her shoulders. The sound of the clock intensified in the sudden silence. It was loud and obnoxious. "I'm not sure."

Jennifer's momentary silence was as disconcerting to Mallory as her fixed focus on Mallory's face. *Does she believe me?*

"That's okay, Mallory. We'll dig through the rubble together. And then you'll find an even greater dignity from having walked through this, the true dignity that comes from knowing that you are wrapped in God's abiding love. No matter how ugly or how painful it is to look at your past, that's right where God wants you to look."

Mallory stared at the empty grate in the fieldstone fireplace. "I don't think I can face my past, Jennifer. There is something... something horrible. But it's like it has been locked away for so long that even if we get the room open, I don't think I have enough energy or will power to face what's inside."

"I came across a verse this week." Jennifer flipped through her notebook. "I put it in here somewhere." She pulled out a slip of paper and handed it to Mallory.

Instead of your shame you shall have double honor, and instead of confusion they shall rejoice in their portion. Therefore in their land they shall possess double; everlasting joy shall be theirs (Isaiah 61:7).

Mallory read the verse again, aloud. She looked up to find Jennifer watching her.

"I kept thinking about you when I read it, and I felt the Spirit urge me to give it to you. It's a promise to God's chosen nation, Israel." Jennifer's smile crinkled the corners of her eyes. "You are just as precious to Him, you know. Shame and confusion often go hand in hand with abuse. God wants to set you free from all of that. He wants to heal that area of your life."

Mallory blinked to clear her blurring vision. "I'm not sure I can face this. What if I find out...what if I can't handle this?"

"One step at a time, Mallory. With God's help, you'll make it. Scripture says, 'You shall know the truth, and the truth shall make you free.' You are at the starting point of recovery. You, your husband, and your children will benefit from your liberation."

"I'm so scared."

"Of what? Can you tell me?'

"Everything." At the whispered confession, Mallory realized her guard was slipping. Fear compressed her stomach in a knot. She twisted her hands in the folds of her blouse and refused to meet Jennifer's gaze.

"Whoever hurt you took away your power and control, but you've begun fighting back. You're regaining control, and that will strengthen you in the days ahead as we unravel the mystery of who hurt you." Jennifer pulled several Kleenex out of the box on the stand beside them and placed them in Mallory's lap. "Mallory, can you look at me?"

She lifted her face but wasn't able to maintain eye contact. Jennifer's voice was unyielding. "You were the victim."

Mallory shook her head. Jennifer's hand came into her line of vision and touched her fingers. "Yes, you were. Someone injured you. You were the victim." Jennifer's intensity was palpable. "In the last several months you have come so far in dealing with so many things. I would never have asked this before, but I feel that now is the time to deal with the memory that you had at your friend's apartment."

Mallory trembled. *Here it comes. Please, Jennifer, I can't think about it. It will destroy everything inside of me.*

"Can we do this?"

No. Mallory hunched her shoulders. "If we have to."

"In those moments before you broke, you told me you had a memory of someone hurting you. Do you remember who it was?"

Mallory began to shake her head but halted midswing as images flashed in her mind.

No. Don't make me remember. I can't remember. I can't tell. He will—I hear him! He's coming!

She could feel herself pulling inward. He would put her in that dark place again. He would tie her hands.

He tied my hands! They went numb from the wrist down. And my ankles.

Scooting back into the corner of the sofa as far as she could, Mallory willed herself to become small, to fade into the couch itself so no one could see her.

No! Don't hurt me!

The room faded around her, but she could hear Jennifer's voice. "Mallory, I'm going to push you. But you've grown so strong over the last few months that you are ready for this. Who hurt you, Mallory?"

Don't. Please don't!

"Who put you in the dark?"

The light was cut off as the door closed with an echoing bang.

"Who tied your wrists?"

Bailer twine dug into her wrists. Her arms were stretched above her.

"Can you see him?"

He laughed. Rough and hard. His hand skimmed around her neck. She could hear the loud tick of his watch. He slid around in front of her.

"It's dark. But you know who it is, don't you, Mallory?" Jennifer's relentless questions beat at Mallory. She could feel the answer surfacing and shook her head, jerking the pillow in front of her eyes. She had to hide. She couldn't tell. She couldn't. If she told—

She hadn't realized she voiced her thoughts until Jennifer spoke. "What will happen if you tell, Mallory? Who told you not to tell? Who hurt you?"

She closed her eyes. *"I'll hurt Geoff. You want to keep Geoff safe, don't you?"*

"You know, don't you? Who was it, Mallory?" The gentle words pummeled her, and she almost choked on the upsurge of emotions that built as the knowledge strained to break free.

His face pressed against hers.

Sudden sobs racked her body as she tried to force the knowledge back into the hole from which it had burst. But it was too late.

Like a tidal wave, the truth erupted, and Mallory gasped for breath. "He told me not to tell. He said he would hurt Geoff. He said I would never see him again. He said he would lock him in a dark place too, and that Geoff would never come out again. He hurt me. He hurt me." She buried her face in her hands, torn between relief and agony. She knew…she finally knew. It was real. It was horrible. And…

"It was Eric."

Jennifer knelt by the couch as Mallory wept. The years of buried pain raged through her like a river flooding its banks, and Mallory had no recourse but to let it take her.

When the storm had eased, Mallory took the proffered Kleenex box from Jennifer's hand. At Jennifer's soft "Are you all right?" Mallory could only nod her head. Jennifer shifted back to her chair.

Mallory wiped her nose and eyes and leaned back against the couch. "Is it always this painful? I feel worse than after twenty hours of labor with Renee and no anesthesia."

"The birthing process is rough, but how did you feel afterward? How do you feel now?"

Mallory started to answer, then paused. She lifted her head and looked at the woman opposite her. "I feel…better. I'm exhausted, like I've run a marathon, and every part of my body hurts, but it's…it's a good hurt. Like it accomplished something."

"You have accomplished something, Mallory. Something very positive and something that took a great deal of courage and strength."

Anger coursed through Mallory and landed in the pit of her stomach. "And I'm angry. Very angry. How could he? *Why* would he?" The cry seemed to explode from the very deepest part of her. "What did I ever do to him?"

"You did nothing to him, Mallory, and you have every right to be angry because what happened to you shouldn't have happened."

"Then why do I feel so guilty? Terrified…and *guilty*. I've spent my life feeling every bad thing that happens is my fault. I'm so tired of feeling this way."

"Mallory, that's a normal response. But you have nothing to feel guilty about. It wasn't your fault."

The Kleenex Mallory was twisting broke in half, and she scrunched the soggy tissue into the palm of her hand. Why did she struggle with the horrible thought that there was something more she couldn't remember? Something terrible.

Something I did?

Mallory shivered. What if she didn't know the whole truth?

July 10

It's not my fault.
    If only writing the words could make me believe them.

Twenty

Pray, Joey said.

"Prayer works, Jake. Just try it."

Yeah, well, it might work for Joey. God did seem to care for Joey, but God never paid much attention to Jake Edward Carlisle. God didn't listen when Jake asked Him to stop his father from drinking or when he asked God to keep his mother from being beaten up. God didn't listen when he asked for the football scholarship or when Mallory miscarried with their first child.

God might be out there, but He sure didn't care.

That's okay. I've made my decision, and I didn't need God to make it for me. Now he just needed the courage to tell Mallory.

Jake swallowed hard as he straightened his tie and looked toward the door of the restaurant. He was more nervous than the first time he'd gone out on a date. *Shock* didn't come close to describing what he had felt when Mallory asked him to meet her here. He was glad she had called him, because he hadn't had the nerve to phone her.

He had just returned to his desk from a meeting with Karl when she called. Meeting? Shouting match was more like it. Jake wasn't sure who had scored more verbal points, but the final blow had been delivered, and he had held victorious in the end.

Then Mallory had called. She startled him in more ways than one. She sounded aloof, even careful, when she spoke to him. But beneath the cool exterior he sensed a vulnerability. Anxiety coiled through him. What did she want to talk about? Was she ready to call it quits? Would she understand the changes he was making in his life?

Jake stood when he caught sight of Mallory weaving her way through the tables toward him. She was gorgeous. Her dark hair, pulled back in a French braid, shimmered in the dim light. A smile eased the usual somberness of her face.

Longing coursed through him as he pulled out the chair for her, and the scent of her perfume drifted over him. "You look beautiful." The words were out before he could consider the wisdom of saying them. He didn't care. She was his wife, and he missed her. He would take whatever tonight brought and go with it.

"Thanks." She smiled as she settled in the chair. "You look very handsome."

The waiter came for their drink order, and Jake studied Mallory. He had never seen her wear that color, nor, come to think of it, had he ever seen that dress before. He loved it. The deep copper brought out the auburn highlights in her hair. Her skin appeared translucent in the dim light from the sconces on the wall next to their table.

Mallory's slender fingers reached for her glass of water. Gone were the stubby, bitten nails. Her nails were long now and manicured, with the same metallic color as her dress.

Still, not all the changes were positive. She had lost unnecessary weight, making her appear more fragile than before. He noticed her hands tremble when she lifted her glass to sip her drink. Her eyes were haunted. The look flickered, and then was gone.

"Mal, are you okay?"

"I'm doing okay. It's hard—"

The waiter interrupted her as he set their drinks before them and took their dinner orders. Silence descended between them; Jake fidgeted with his napkin.

"How's work? I saw your shots in Daddy's *World Graphics*. They were exquisite."

"Thanks." *What a perfect opening*. He opened and closed his mouth several times. The words wouldn't come. He reached for his water. "How are the girls?"

"They miss you, but they seem to be adjusting."

Jake leaned back as his salad was placed before him. He said nothing until the waiter set Mallory's plate down and disappeared. "Is Heather watching them?"

"No, Mom. She's been taking care of them quite a bit. They like being with her and Daddy."

Jake reached for his fork and stabbed at his salad. *What do I ask now?* He remembered a time when the conversation flowed between them, when even the periods of silence were comfortable, peaceful...warm.

"Is that a new dress?"

Mallory's head snapped up. A fire ignited in her eyes.

"It's a beautiful color on you." His sincere words doused the flames of her emotions. He wanted to wipe away the beads of perspiration that popped up on the back of his neck, but he refused to let her see his anxiety.

"Thank you. I picked it up at Goodwill." She laughed. "It cost all of three dollars."

He chewed on his salad, refusing to say anything else about money, and pushed the plate back when he was done.

"How's Joey?" Mallory picked up her fork and played with her lettuce.

The small talk was getting on his nerves. "Fine." They were treating each other like strangers. Worse than strangers.

Neither of them seemed to have much appetite. The main course was served, and their conversation faltered once more. Jake shifted in his chair to study the room full of laughing, conversing people. Couples with their heads bent close together. Families enjoying being together.

He wanted to cry.

Pasano's had always been their favorite Italian restaurant, and when Mallory had asked to meet him here, Jake wasn't sure if that was a good sign or a bad one. It was looking more and more like a very bad sign. The tension between them was thicker than the hunk of beef he couldn't finish. Jake set his dinner plate at the edge of the table and sipped his coffee.

Mallory did the same with her almost full plate of veal parmigiana. No wonder she had lost weight if she wasn't eating any more than that.

Jake ran out of conversational gambits, and the suspense of not knowing what she had to say was gnawing at his insides. Maybe he should just say what he had to say…but she was the one who had called for this date.

"So are you going to tell me what this dinner is all about? It has to be more than your overwhelming desire to see me or because you were hungry." Jake watched Mallory over the brim of his cup, but she didn't reply. She leaned one elbow on the table and played with the back of her hair. "That bad, huh?"

Mallory's eyes flashed at him. "This is hard enough, Jake, don't make it any harder. I'm not sure I can even say what I need to. I don't know where to start." She took a deep breath. "Okay, I'll just get it over with."

Jake's stomach tightened at her words. Was this it? He balled his napkin and pitched it onto his plate, swallowing hard. "Just say it, Mallory. Whatever it is that has you tied up in knots, just say it. I'm a big boy. I can handle it."

"Jake..."

Here it comes. She wants out of the marriage.

"I...had...While you were on assignment...I had..."

An affair? His steak threatened to come back up. His fingers turned icy, and he curled them in a fist. *Anything but that!*

The haunted look was back in her eyes with a vengeance. He felt his heart rip in two and closed his eyes against the pain.

"I had a breakdown while you were away on assignment."

It took several moments for the meaning of her words to sink into his numb brain. He almost laughed in relief. *She doesn't want a divorce. She didn't have an affair. It'll be okay.* They could work things out.

"I was at a prayer meeting at Heather's, and all of a sudden I felt as if I were standing at the edge of a bottomless pit and the ledge I was standing on just gave way. I was falling. It was so terrifying. I didn't even know where I was for the longest time. Then Heather's voice was reassuring me that things would be okay. But things aren't okay."

He leaned against the edge of the table, listening to the low pitch of her voice. Whatever she had to say, it was almost destroying her to get the words out. Why was she so terrified?

"Jake, I've been in therapy ever since, because…because I was sexually abused when I was a child. No…raped." She refused to meet his gaze as she whispered the rest. "By Eric. He…raped me when I was a child."

Raped. A sledgehammer seemed to hit his stomach—but at the same time, all the pieces of the puzzle snapped into place. It all made such perfect sense that he sagged in visible relief. Silence stretched between them.

"Jake, say something."

He wished he knew what to do or say to help her, but the words wouldn't come. She needed him to be strong. He could do this for her. He lifted his eyes to search her face. It was flushed, and her eyes refused to meet his. She was twisting her napkin into a thin rope. Was the sudden heat in her face from embarrassment or shame? Or was it from anger? Was there more? *God, no!*

His teeth ground together. "Is that all?"

Her head jerked up, and the fire surged into her eyes. "Is that all?" she hissed at him. "Isn't that enough? What else do I need to go through? I just told you that my older brother raped me, and all you can say is 'Is that all?' Thanks, Jake. Thanks a lot. I just thought you might want to know what kind of hell your wife has been going through in the last few months and that perhaps you love me enough to want to help, but I was wrong. Seems I've been wrong most of my life about everything and everyone. Thanks for meeting me." She stood, scraping her chair on the wooden floor, and fled toward the exit.

Jake threw some money down on the table and sprinted after her. He caught up with her in the parking lot. "Mal!" He grabbed her arm and spun her toward him. She flinched in his grasp. "Mallory, wait. Listen to me. I didn't mean—"

She tugged her arm free and stood glaring at him, daring him to go on. What had he meant? He expelled a long breath of air before trying again. "I wasn't trying to imply that what you went through wasn't a horrible thing for a little girl to go through." He paused, willing her to meet his gaze. He wanted her to understand. "I didn't mean to be heartless or flippant. I was just relieved."

"Relieved!"

He winced at her scathing tone and put a finger over her lips to halt any further tirade. "Please, let me try again." At her stiff nod, he dropped his hand and shoved it deep into the front pocket of his pants. "I thought you were going to tell me you wanted a divorce." He stared at the toe of his leather shoe. "That you'd had an affair."

"Jake!"

"Don't get mad again. That was just my first thought."

"Do you want a divorce?" She sounded hurt, angry, scared.

"No!" Jake shook his head. "I don't want a divorce. That's why I was so relieved." He tried to gauge her mood. Was he getting through? "And I'm sorry for even thinking you had an affair."

Mallory bowed her head.

Now what? Jake was at a loss. He had already proved that he lacked any tact or sensitivity. He didn't want to make it worse. He ran his finger against her soft cheek. "Mal, I'm so sorry."

His finger came away damp, and he wiped her tears on his suit coat, wishing he could wipe them from her heart as easily. "Are you going to be okay?"

Her reply was muffled, but he saw a slight movement of her head, which he took as a yes. He held his hand out to her. She took it and the weight pressing on his heart lifted. With deliberate slowness he drew her into his arms and felt her hands move to the small of his back. "It's going to be all right, honey."

She sagged against him, and Jake braced himself against her weight. "We'll get beyond it. After all, that was a long time ago. You're an adult now."

Mallory tensed. "You don't understand!"

I said the wrong thing—again. "Honest, Mal, I'm trying."

She pushed against his embrace, and his arms dropped to his side. He turned, looked up, and searched the sky. "What did I say now?"

"Forget it, Jake." Her words held abject weariness, and she backed several steps away. "I know you're trying. I just have some things to work out yet. Maybe we could finish this discussion another time."

She turned from him before he could make a reply and got into her car. She slammed the car door and revved the engine. The taillights of her car had long disappeared when Jake finally moved to his own vehicle. He hadn't even gotten the chance to tell her his decision. He suddenly felt an overwhelming fear that it didn't really matter. Nothing mattered.

Not anymore.

July 21

I want to be whole, Lord Jesus, I want to forgive…but I can't.

Nothing is as it appears. My perfect family…at least to outside appearances. All the years I buried this. Why didn't someone else know? Could they have known? Why didn't I tell?

I was afraid.

How could he hurt me like that? I loved him! He was my big brother. He should have protected me, not hurt me.

And why? Why? What did I do to him? I'm so angry and full of rage—it rips through my body from the top of my head right to my toes. Father, I'm so scared I'll get lost in the anger.

I know You want me to forgive. I know You forgive…but how do I get past it? How do I move beyond the pain, the devastation, the loss—the ugliness.

Oh, God…the shame.

Twenty~One

The steady slap of Mallory's feet against the pavement calmed her frazzled nerves. As she ran, she took little heed of the rain that plastered her hair against her head.

Years of grief and loss washed over her as the memories played unbidden in her mind. Confusion and bitterness followed hard on their heels. The ever-present *why?* chased around in her head like a dog after its tail. It was so hard to deal with all the chaos in her life when there was no one to share her pain.

She slowed to a walk when she reached her mile marker and stopped to grasp her ankles and stretch. Mallory rested against the Sanborn Village Limit sign and watched the rain in the muted light of the gray afternoon. It fell in a shimmering curtain, blurring the edges of the trees that lined the highway…just like her past—gray and blurred, difficult to see through.

Mallory pushed herself away from the post and began a rapid walk homeward.

How could she tell anyone else? There was such overwhelming shame, she just couldn't imagine telling her parents, maybe not even Gran. Could she have told Gramps? She doubted it. She wouldn't even let herself think what Geoff might say if he ever found out.

"Instead of your shame, you shall have double honor…"

How could that even begin to be possible? The shame ran too deep. *What could be honorable about my past?* Her furious thoughts drove her pace faster.

Each time she worked through one area of her life, another would rise up and smack her in the face. What had Jennifer called it? The onion effect? She'd said that each layer peeled away would bring her that much closer to healing.

"Mallory, you can be the key to unlocking more than just your own painful past. You can help unlock the painful past of your entire family. Imagine your family freed from generations of secrets. And not just the past, Mallory, but think of the future, think of your girls. Abuse is a cycle, often passed from one generation to another. The cycle can be broken with you." Mallory grimaced against the memory of their conversation.

"Do you think your family will come in for a session?"

"No!" *No way.*

"Then perhaps you could start by writing them a letter. It's time to tell your family what happened."

"I can't."

"Yes, you can."

Easy for you to say, Jennifer! It was so hard. This was harder than anything she had ever tried to do. It would shatter all the barriers of her childhood. What would her mother say? What would Daddy do?

She had never been able to talk to her parents, and now she was supposed just to go up to them and say, "Your elder son is a sadistic rapist. I know because I was his victim"? What if they didn't believe her? What if...

Stop it! Just...stop it! Mallory began to run again, splashing in

221

every puddle she passed. All right. She'd admit it—she was terrified. But that didn't resolve the problem of telling her family. Telling Jake had been hard enough. She shook her head and felt the heavy tug of wet hair against her cheek. What had she expected? That he would weep for her as she had wept? That he'd shed tears for the little girl she had been? It amazed her that he didn't want to blow Eric away with a shotgun.

She did.

She grimaced again. *I didn't mean that, Lord!* The hardest part of all this was her confusion. She loved her brother, but she hated him as well. At least now all those years of contention between them began to make sense.

Jennifer seemed convinced that once Mallory released her own pain and recognized Eric's, forgiveness would come. But it was so hard to get to where she knew God wanted her to be.

Pastor Gates's sermon the previous Sunday came back with haunting clarity: "No one has offended us more than we ourselves have offended Jesus Christ, and we have His complete forgiveness, if we'll only accept it." She agreed with him on a mental level, but at gut level…it was much, much tougher.

She pulled off her sodden shoes and clothes in the garage and dropped them in the laundry room on her way upstairs to shower and change. The girls were with Jake, and the house was quiet. She didn't like days like this. There was too much time to think. Nowhere to run and hide.

She was tired of her thoughts, tired of the unanswered questions, and sick of her own defeated attitude. If she wanted any kind of life, any kind of future, she was the one who had to deal with it. No one could go through healing for her.

Mallory had written a letter to her parents—her assignment for therapy. Jennifer would say she was proud of her, but Mallory was just angry at herself for being such a wimp. *What am I so afraid of? They can't whip me or send me to my room!*

Jennifer's words rang in her head: "God is a God of truth, Mallory. 'God is light and in Him is no darkness at all.' Satan is the father of all lies, and he uses them to destroy. Truth is your only weapon. By dealing with the truth in love and helping your family deal with that truth, you will see God begin the process of restoration for all of you."

Father, I don't want to be a wimp anymore. I want to take back control of my life—I don't want to be ruled by fear.

She wouldn't mail the letter to her parents. She wouldn't even take it to show Jennifer. She would go over and see her parents and tell them in person.

Today. It has to be today. Or I'll chicken out. She longed to call Gran, but for once in her life she was not going to rely on somebody else to help her deal with her parents. She had to handle this one all by herself, if it killed her.

It probably would.

Jake was going to keep the girls overnight, and she would call and tell her mom she would be over, that she wanted to talk to both her and Daddy. Some way, somehow, she had to do this thing.

What if I rip this family apart? How do I deal with that guilt?

No, truth was the only way. Look what all the years of secret keeping had done to her, and how could Eric find hope and healing if they continued in deceptions and lies? She had to do it.

God help her, she had to do it.

* * *

It was almost dark by the time Mallory reached her parents' home. It took most of her courage to stay headed south on the road and not tuck her tail and run back home.

C'mon, Mal! God hasn't given you a spirit of fear, but of power and of love and of a sound mind.

"A sound mind, Lord—now there's a promise I need to hang on to." She pulled into the driveway of her parents' home and got out as soon as she shut off the engine. If she hesitated, her courage would fail. She took a deep breath and marched to the front door. "Remember, no fear."

Her mother lifted a cheek for her customary kiss as Mallory entered the living room. Mallory had never considered herself very tall, but she towered over her mother by three inches. How could such a tiny woman be so intimidating?

She turned to kiss the top of her father's head. He had settled for the evening in his favorite chair. The TV flickered in the corner of the room. The volume was turned down so that the background noise was like a persistent, pesky bug. He laid a finger between the pages of the book he held and smiled up at her.

Mallory took a seat on the couch opposite her parents' chairs and watched her mother's slim figure move to pick up the remote to shut off the offending noise. "Now, dear. You said you needed to talk to us. What about?"

Her father studied her. "You look pale, are you feeling all right, honey?"

Mallory cleared her throat. *Lord, help me.* "Well, I…uh…

wanted to talk to you both because, as you know, I've been having some…some problems."

Her mother's brows lifted a notch. "You mean the situation with Jake. Are you any closer to getting back together?"

"No, not really, Mom, but there are some other things I need to discuss." Mallory shifted her position on the couch. "I guess you know I've been seeing a therapist." She saw her mother's head tilt down, though whether in disapproval or acknowledgment, she wasn't sure. "The…the reason is because I have to deal with some things from my childhood. Things you may not be aware of."

Mallory's eyes were fixed on a small spot on the carpet where Renee had spilled red Kool-Aid. She could still hear her mother fussing that she never could get that stain out.

Just like the stain on her own life.

Her dread and fear threatened to shut off her vocal cords. *Just say it.* "Mom, Daddy…I was raped when I was seven, and it was Eric who did it."

She held her breath in the ensuing silence. The tick of the clock on the mantel grew loud and oppressive. Afraid to look at either parent, she kept her eyes glued to the spot on the carpet.

Wash me and I will be whiter than snow… Please, God…

They had to respond. They had to say something. Long moments passed, and each one seemed to stretch to infinity. Finally, the thump of her father's book closing broke the constricting silence, and Mallory dared a look at him. The broad lines across his forehead deepened. A tremor passed through her body. Was he angry? At her, or Eric? Did he believe her?

"Mallory."

In one, single word, her mother seemed to convey disbelief, horror, disapproval, and rebuke all at the same time. Mallory watched her mother's long fingers twist together in her lap as she wrung her hands. Her horrified glance flitted to her husband, then back to Mallory. "Are you sure?"

Mallory tried to keep her expression neutral, but it was hard considering the absurdity of the question. *No, Mom, I'm not sure. I just thought I'd spit it out and see how it sounded!* "Yes. I'm sure."

"I'm not saying that we don't believe you, but is it possible this therapist put this into your head?"

"No, Mom! No one put anything into my head."

She looked to her father. *Oh, Daddy, please…say something!* He removed his glasses and rubbed the bridge of his nose.

"Daddy, I know it was a long time ago, but the pain is still real. I've never dealt with it until now. I think it's time, don't you? Twenty-five years is a long time to carry that kind of secret."

"But why? Why didn't you come and tell us?"

Her mother's quivering voice rose, and Mallory realized the enormity of what her son had done was just sinking in.

"I-I tried…" Mallory frowned. She had? When?

Suddenly a stern male voice drilled through her head: *"Mallory Elaine Bennington! Only bad, wicked, little girls would say a thing like that! Being mad at your brother is no reason to tell lies. Go to your room now, young lady."*

Mallory jumped up from the couch. The harsh voice ringing in her mind put flight to her small reservoir of courage. *What have I done? I should never have come here!*

"I…I know this is a shock. I'm sorry. I don't want to hurt you; I just…" She knew if she didn't leave right that moment, she would dissolve into a mass of hysteria. "I'm sorry." With that, she fled from the house.

Her hands shook so she missed putting the key in the ignition twice. But that was nothing compared to the shaking going on inside her...

She had to get out of there. Fast.

Geoff tightened his grip around his sobbing sister. Something terrible had happened—something about Eric and their parents and the secret. But that was as much as he'd been able to get from her.

"Mal. Mally, honey. Shh. It's okay. I've got you. Geoff's here. Shh. Come on, come over to the couch." He stumbled toward the couch with Mallory clinging to his neck. He decided carrying her would be easier and lifted her in his arms, then sat down in the nearest chair. He drew her close and rocked her against his chest. His insides churned. Something had devastated her. Over the top of her head, he nodded to Holly. "Get a warm washcloth, will you?"

Geoff was still holding Mallory when Holly knelt beside them and placed her hand on Mallory's back. He eased her away from him and wiped her tears and the strands of hair that clung to her wet cheeks. "Mally, please quit crying."

"Mallory?" Holly's ministrations were tender. "Let me wash your face. You need to quit crying so we can understand what you're trying to tell us." Geoff slid his arm higher to support Mallory's shaking shoulders, and her hiccuping sobs began to subside. She shifted and moved her head from beneath his chin to rest her cheek against his heart.

"Think you can talk now, Mally?" *Please, tell me what's going on.*

Mallory sniffled and nodded. "I'm...I'm okay." She took the washcloth from Holly and pressed it against her face. "I went to see Mom and Dad."

"Are they all right?" Mallory seemed to droop in his arms, and her voice slurred. Geoff tried to put quell the panic shimmying up his spine. "Mally?"

"They're okay. I think."

He wanted to shake an answer out of her, but forced his voice to stay soft. "Mallory, what happened?"

"I went to see them."

"We already know that." Geoff rubbed his forehead. "What happened? Was there an accident? Is anybody hurt?"

"No. At least not physically." Mallory seemed to rouse herself. "I went there to tell them that... I went to say... I had to say... Oh, Geo!" She began to shake in his arms as she buried her face against his chest.

"Mally. Listen to me." He pulled her away from his chest. "We need to know what is going on. What happened?"

Holly put a hand on his arm and mouthed, *Let me try.* "Mallory, are you saying there was no accident? That no one is ill, no one is hurt?" At Mallory's nod, she pressed on. "Can you tell us what happened? What upset you so much?"

Mallory refused to turn her head, but began to explain, her words muffled by the fabric of Geoff's shirt. Rage built with every pump of his heart, and with every painful syllable the blood pounded in his veins. His arm lashed out and sent the lamp beside the chair flying across the room. Like a terrified animal, Mallory bolted from him and took refuge behind the love seat. Her wild eyes darted across the room as if to seek safety.

His knuckles turned white as he gripped the arm of his chair to keep from venting any more of the fury that ripped through him. All he permitted himself was one low, fierce obscenity.

He's mine. I swear, he's mine. And he's dead.

July 22

I feel it. Hear it. See it. It's a wonder the girls don't sense it too.

I don't want to feel it, but the rage seethes beneath the surface like molten lava. Building up pressure, waiting to explode.

I'm afraid, Father. Afraid to admit that…

Dear God, I want to kill someone.

Twenty-Two

Eric opened the door to his dark house and tossed his keys on the bookshelf in the hall. He was mentally and physically fatigued. This therapy session with his son had been less productive than last week's, and that one had been useless.

The hallway, bathed in a dim, ominous red, went to darkness and back to red in a rhythmic pattern as the indicator light on the answering machine flashed. Eric jabbed the button. The machine went through its obligatory rewind before a customer's voice explained the reason for the call. Next was a message from his wife. Ex-wife. She wanted to know where the child support check was. She didn't have the guts to ask him when she saw him at the counselor's office? He swore.

"When I get paid, lady, you get paid," Eric muttered as he scribbled a note on the pad before him.

Then Geoff's voice met his ears. The message was to the point. "I'm coming over. You'd better be there."

Eric stared at the machine. "Or what? You'll tell on me? Beat me up?" Who did Geoff think he was? He snorted as the machine clicked off, then went to the refrigerator for a beer. "Little Brother, I could care less what you want. You're one of the last people I want to see right now."

He popped the top of the beer can and downed the contents.

He squashed the container like a bug, tossed it in the trash, and reached for another.

"Go easy on those," he warned himself. "The last thing you need is a hangover when you place your contracting bid for that housing development."

He kicked off his shoes and fell backward onto the sofa, holding his can away from him to keep it from spilling.

Marty.

The court had ordered him to stay with Catherine after he got out of the detention center. He shook his head. *Where did I go wrong with you?*

"What were you thinking? Your cousin? In a church, no less." He slugged down another swallow. "Did I teach you nothing? Do you hate me and your mom that much?"

Eric smashed a pillow beneath his head. Four hours of wasted time. He could think of a half-dozen different things he could be doing instead. Making money to hand over to Catherine came to the forefront of his mind.

Psychologists! Pains, all of them. Talking about where the blame should be laid. Why is it always tossed back into the parents' laps?

Too bad kids didn't come with an owner's manual. Eric stared at the family portrait that still hung on the wall. The one Catherine had taken only three weeks before she had walked out. The somber eyes of his daughter's laughing face gazed back at him. What a contradiction. Her mouth might be smiling, but her eyes weren't.

He was glad she was staying at his parents' this weekend.

Was this home that bad a place to grow up in? Yeah, well, it was better than the one I...

He steered his thoughts—and his gaze—away, settling his

attention on a faded black-and-white photo of him and his three siblings as kids. He and Geoff were holding their baby sisters in their arms. They were so young.

He considered for the millionth time ripping the picture from the wall. Somehow he couldn't bring himself to do it. He crushed the empty can. He needed another beer.

The doorbell pealed hard, as if someone had jabbed a finger on the button and held it there. Eric tried to ignore the sound echoing through the house, but it persisted again and again. He swore, rolled to his feet, and headed down the hallway to jerk the door open.

"I'm going to kill you."

Something smashed into his face. His world spun and then went dark.

A polar rage froze all rational judgment in Geoff's mind. Even seeing Eric sprawled on the floor, blood drizzling down his jaw, did nothing to restrain his fury.

He stood over Eric, reached down, and twisted the front of his shirt in his hands, hauling his brother back on his feet. His fist cocked back.

Eric just managed to block the move, but the dodge caused him to stagger back into the end table. A lamp crashed to the floor. Geoff shoved against Eric's chest and smashed him against the wall. His forearm found its mark and ground deep into Eric's windpipe.

Macabre satisfaction filled Geoff as Eric rasped in bits of air, struggling to get his fingers beneath Geoff's. *Arrogant s—*

Eric's foot lashed out and connected with Geoff's shin. Pain radiated up his leg, and Geoff shifted to avoid getting kicked again.

Eric gasped for air. "Are you insane? Get off me." His hands slammed upward beneath Geoff's, knocking his arm away.

Geoff lunged again. "Our baby sister! How could you do that to our baby sister?"

Eric's fists came up. He licked the blood away from the corner of his mouth as hardness collided with the astonishment on his face.

"I didn't do anything to our baby sister." His face darkened, and he dove toward Geoff. He rammed his fists like a jackhammer into Geoff's stomach.

Pain cramped in on Geoff's diaphragm and sucked the air and life out of his rage. His knees buckled.

Eric grabbed a handful of Geoff's hair and yanked his head upward, his hand jabbing out with his words. "You're the one that killed Shelly!" Eric's massive fist slammed into Geoff's face, and blackness cascaded over him.

July 31

"When I fall, I will arise; when I sit in darkness, the LORD will be a light to me" (Micah 7:8).

Twenty-Three

Mallory closed her eyes.

Jennifer's quiet voice intruded on her painful thoughts. "Can you tell me what you were thinking about just now?"

"Don't say anything, Jennifer. Please? I can't deal with this." A tear slid from beneath her lashes, and she swallowed hard. She had been determined to keep herself together, but there were times when just being in her therapist's presence was enough to send her emotions rocking.

"Mallory?" Jennifer's voice sounded like velvet steel.

"I don't know if I can describe how I feel. Empty." Mallory chanced a look at her counselor. Her eyes were sympathetic and understanding as she waited for Mallory to continue. "I told my parents about Eric."

Jennifer reached out and laid her hand on Mallory's arm; her touch commanded Mallory to look at her. "That took a lot of courage."

Mallory shook her head. "I was petrified. Afterward, I just fell apart. I ended up at Geoff's, and because I was such a wreck, he made me spend the night there. I don't know what I would have done if he hadn't been there, but he's been there for me all of my life. Even with Geoff's support I still felt so…abandoned."

"You may have been scared, but you didn't let the fear stop you this time. That takes tremendous courage. And it shows the growth that is taking place in your life."

Maybe what Jennifer said was true. Maybe Mallory was getting stronger, but she sure didn't feel that way. She couldn't stand up to her parents. Let's face it, she wasn't strong enough to handle her own emotions. "I've never been able to meet their expectations."

"Whose expectations?"

Mallory shrugged and picked at the nap on the fabric of the chair. "Everyone's."

"Tell me what happened, what made you decide to confront your parents?"

Do I have to? Mallory tried to describe the scene at her parents'. "They didn't believe me then, and they don't believe me now."

"I believe you. Mallory, I am so, so sorry that it happened to you. I am proud of you for speaking the truth. What others do is their responsibility, not yours. You can't change them—you can't even try—but you are changing you. The secret is out now. The bond of lies that Satan had over you is broken. Can you see that?"

She reached for a Kleenex and blew her nose. "I guess. I just feel so bad. If telling the truth is so good, why does it feel so bad?"

Jennifer was silent for a moment. "Mallory, the child in you needed to be believed. She needed to hear comforting words from your parents, and that didn't happen. You are grieving even as you are stepping out of the shell that had you locked up tight. Trust that God is leading you and your family to a new freedom. Look how far you have come in these last months."

Mallory shook her head. She hadn't come anywhere except full circle.

"When you came here, you were close to a breakdown."

Jennifer studied the yellow legal pad for a moment. "Your own words were 'I feel like I am living on a precipice, with only a black abyss in front of me and nothing to catch me if I fall.'"

Mallory found it difficult to look into Jennifer's brown eyes as she continued. "Since then you have told me what you never told anyone else. That you were raped. Then you had the courage to tell your husband. You've done every difficult assignment I've given you. You told your parents the truth. Hard as that was, it will eventually set you free."

Did Jennifer understand how hard it was for her to hear those words, as validating as they were? She wanted to draw encouragement from them, but she couldn't.

Jennifer paused. "I think you're ready to deal with Eric."

Are you nuts? She pushed her shoulders into the back of the chair, and her fingers curled into the armrest.

"How do you feel about it?"

"I-I can't."

"Why not?"

"I don't know how. I'm afraid. "

"I know, but the toughest part is already behind you. You told the truth. It gets easier every time you do so."

Mallory twisted her wedding ring.

"You've come so far, Mallory. Don't give up now. Why don't you try writing a letter to Eric? Put all your feelings down on paper. Everything you ever wanted to say to him. Then bring it to our next session. Can you do that?"

Mallory reached for her coffee that had grown cold. Her fingers trembled as she lifted the cup to her lips.

"Mallory?"

She set her cup down on the end table and forced herself to look at Jennifer. "I guess." Jennifer cocked an eyebrow at her, and Mallory amended, "Yes, I can do that. I think."

Jennifer let the last sentence slide and reached for Mallory's hand to end their session, as usual, in prayer. At the soft *amen,* Mallory stood and hugged Jennifer.

"You can do this."

"Thanks, Jennifer." All Mallory wanted to do was escape.

"Mallory." She stopped midstride. "Why do you think you're not good enough?"

"Wh-what?" Mallory's hands began to sweat. How did Jennifer know that? *I never told her about…* "I never said that!"

Said it, no. But she had thought it. Believed it, with all her heart. And the truth struck Mallory with such force that she couldn't breathe. No matter where she ran, no matter where she went to hide—she could never outrun herself.

August 4

Dear Jesus,

I have hated and blamed myself for so long. Even before I would let myself admit the abuse happened. The massive guilt, the unexplained fears and anxieties. The constant hovering over the girls… It makes so much sense now.

But where do I go from here?

Twenty-Four

The heat was oppressive. Jake pushed open the screen door and stepped off the porch of Joey's duplex. He trotted down the steps and around the side of the house. Joey had parked his beat-up Chevy truck, known as Old Tilly, beneath a towering tree, affording him some relief from the sticky heat.

Jake could hear the banging of metal against metal as Joey worked beneath the hood. Jake pulled his sunglasses from his nose and leaned a hip against the rusted fender. Joey's braid fell over one shoulder of his sleeveless T-shirt as he worked with a socket wrench. Tiny rivers of sweat were coursing down the younger man's face, but Joey hummed a nameless tune, while his foot kept rhythm.

"How's it going?" Jake ducked beneath the hood, and Joey looked up, gritted his teeth, and pulled hard on the wrench.

"Almost got it." The wrench gave way, and Joey pulled a spark plug out and held it to the light. "Looks bad. No wonder the ol' girl was wheezing and jumping when she was going uphill." Joey reached for the new packet of spark plugs and opened them. "What's up?"

Would Joey go with him? He hoped so. Joey was the best assistant he'd ever had, and Jake hated the thought of losing him. "I just got off the phone."

"Yeah?" Joey tightened down the spark plug then looked at Jake.

"Care to take a short trip with me to the West Coast in say, oh, three weeks?" *Say yes.*

"I got no other plans."

Jake smiled and took a breath. *Here goes.* "*World Graphics* wants to sign me on staff."

Joey looked up and high-fived Jake. "Way to go, man! Knew those photos of Malaysia would turn their heads." Jake looked at the grease that had been transferred to his own hand and reached to pull the rag out of Joey's hip pocket. He rubbed the grease off.

If only he could do that with the last year and a half of his life.

The smile faded from Joey's face as he turned and studied Jake. "Don't worry, Joey, I don't plan on leaving you behind."

Joey shook his head. "I ain't worried about me, boss. Doesn't matter whether I climb that ladder of success or not. I'm happy as I am. I'm worried about what this will mean to your relationship with Malo. Your travel with Point of View caused stress; what will happen when you start traveling with *WG*?"

"Joey, it's the opportunity I've waited for my whole life." Why couldn't anyone understand that?

Joey reattached the spark plug wires, then gathered his tools. "So have you told her?"

"No." Jake looked across the street. Late summer flowers were in full bloom in the neighbor's yard. The slight breeze wafted their fragrance in his direction. He breathed it in.

"Boss, you got to start communicating better with your lady if you ever hope to get back together."

I know. "It's hard when you keep hitting the same brick wall."

"I gotta say this, and I hope you don't hit me, but the only brick wall I see standing in your way is you."

Jake stiffened against the gentle criticism. "What's that supposed to mean?"

Joey reached up and slammed the hood down. "Maybe you need to give a little and go with your wife to see her counselor."

"No." He would not take the blame for the garbage going on in Mallory's life. Her issues were just that: her issues.

"What has you so scared of that lady?"

"I'm not afraid of her or any woman."

Joey stored his tools and slid behind the wheel. He turned the ignition, and the engine fired to life, purring like a contented kitten. Joey grinned. "Amazing what a little maintenance can do, eh?"

"Are you saying a trip with Mal to see this counselor will help?"

Joey shrugged. "Nope. Just sayin' it can't hurt."

"This reminds me of our college days. We haven't sat on the floor in ages. Why is that?" Mallory asked as she accepted the soda that her friend handed her. Heather sank down opposite her and adjusted a pillow behind her back, then drew her knees up to her chest.

"Maybe we grew up." Ice clinked against Heather's glass.

"Maybe we just got old."

"Remember our first few weeks of college? I wasn't sure I could handle you as a roommate." Heather laughed.

"Look who's talking! I feared I had a Bible thumping, Holy Roller, housemother on my hands, but I decided you might be all right when you helped me sneak back into the dorm after curfew."

"You'd been out with that jerk, Brad. You were depressed for weeks when he dumped you. You listened to your new stereo for hours."

"I guess I didn't have the best taste in men."

"You went for quantity, not quality."

Mallory threw a pillow at Heather's head. "Hey! I wasn't the only one that needed a little male comfort and companionship, Miss Goody Two Shoes."

"The difference was, I didn't hang out at the frat parties."

Mallory shuddered and covered her face with her hands. "Please! Don't remind me."

"You'd come in at three o'clock in the morning. In a pitiful voice, with your head hung over the toilet, you'd ask me where my so-called Christian love and compassion was, and if I had ever done anything bad." Heather shook her head. "It was a real wake-up call from God."

Mallory considered that. "How so?"

Heather grinned. "He wanted me to be a witness. Not judge and jury."

"I guess it was the difference in our backgrounds. Your family was so…perfectly Christian, while mine…" *Mine was so perfectly wicked.* Mallory's throat tightened.

Heather shifted back and lifted a hand. "Whoa. Stop right there. You know my family. Neither my parents nor my brother— or me, for that matter—ever qualified for sainthood. At least, not the man-made kind."

Heather lifted Mallory's chin and forced her to look her in the eyes. "Mallory, I don't pretend to understand why this happened to you, but I can see God using it to make you stronger. I want you to know how proud—and honored—I am to call you my friend."

Honor. Honor...

The word resonated in her head like the echo of a sonic boom. Mallory tried to shake her head, but Heather stopped her.

"Yes, I am. And you are strong now. You're not just hiding behind a mask of self-confidence or some phony feminist independence. Your strength is real."

Mallory leaned back, gazing around the room. The seascape she'd painted for Heather hung crooked on the wall. She rolled to her feet and reached to straighten it.

Heather watched her, and her slight smile made Mallory frown. "What?"

"I can always tell when something's eating you. You get restless. Are you going to tell me what's going on?"

Mallory looked back at the painting, but the blues and greens of the picture blurred. "Jennifer says I'm ready to confront Eric."

"Why?"

"She says disclosing the abuse, as I did to my parents, and facing my offender are both necessary for healing."

Heather got up off the floor and walked over to Mallory. "You know, at first I couldn't understand how you could forget something like what happened to you. But Yvonne explained that it's a survival technique. Now that you have remembered it, I believe God will help you forgive Eric."

He doesn't deserve forgiveness! Mallory shook her head. She didn't either, and wasn't that the point? God's love reached beyond all sin. Mallory knew she should forgive Eric.

But, dear God, there were days when she didn't *want* to!

August 11

The body remembers what the mind forgets.

Twenty-Five

Jake tossed the magazine on the coffee table in the reception area. He checked his watch.

Five more minutes and he was out of here.

He reached for another *Psychology Today,* flipped through the pages, then laid it aside as well. He crossed his leg over his thigh, but when he found himself shaking his foot, he put it back down on the floor.

Why am I nervous? He was just here for Mal. It wasn't as if this shrink was going to examine his head. Mallory had told him he could help her by being here today. So here he was.

What good it would do, he wasn't sure, but if there was a chance it would improve the one-step-forward-two-steps-back relationship they had, then he was all for it. He picked up a *Guideposts* magazine and found a story about an NBA player. He had just read the first page when the door opened and several women came in from the recessed hallway.

This must be Mallory's group. One woman was a tall blonde, beautiful enough to be a model. The others were well-dressed, attractive—normal. *What did you think, Carlisle, they would have "Victim of Sexual Abuse" flashing across their foreheads in neon?* Their chatter died when they saw him. A few nodded, the rest slid out the front door.

Mallory was the last one to come down the hallway. Dressed in his favorite shade of blue, she looked great. He rose to his feet, and she scooped her dark hair behind her ears.

"Hey. Thanks for coming." She wiped her hands on the sides of her shorts. "I appreciate this, Jake." She pointed over her shoulder. "Jennifer's ready if you are."

He cleared his throat and gave her an attempt at a smile. Maybe he should run while he still had the chance. "Uh, sure. Lead the way."

Jake shook Jennifer's hand. She had a firm grip, and Jake lifted his eyes to study her. She was not what he pictured. For one thing she was pretty, with dark brown eyes that sparkled with joy.

"Jake, it's good to meet you. Please, both of you, sit down and make yourselves comfortable. Would you like a cup of coffee or tea? I also have some Pepsi."

Definitely not what he expected. "Coffee, please." Jake sat down on the couch, and his tense back muscles began to relax.

Mallory sat next to him, about a foot away. Jake lifted his brow. For months she had wanted as little contact with him as possible.

Jennifer handed him a cup of coffee and sat opposite them with a yellow notepad resting on her knees. She spent a few moments in small talk, then she turned to Jake.

"As Mallory has explained, this session together will be helpful."

Jake squirmed in his seat. *Here it comes.* Jennifer was setting him in her sights.

"We want to deal with some of Mallory's triggers. That is, discover what things bring an immediate response connected with the abuse, even if it doesn't appear to be."

Jake lifted his ankle and crossed it over his thigh. "I'm not sure I understand."

"I have a colleague who has coined it *logical madness.*"

Mallory nodded. "I heard that at the seminar."

Jake thought Mallory seemed comfortable in this woman's presence, but then she should; she'd been coming here long enough.

Jennifer smiled. "It's like this: A person's actions or reactions, which appear to be crazy because they seem to have no connection to the reality of the moment, are in fact quite logical when you have all the facts, when you understand the background of the person responding. It might take a little detective work, but we can always discover reasons for our behavior." Jennifer leaned her elbow on the arm of the chair. "Let's start with you, Jake."

I knew it. Here comes the first volley.

"Are there any reactions or responses from Mallory that seem…unnatural or exaggerated? Or that just don't make any sense to you?"

Jake sat up straighter. He hadn't expected that. "Oh yeah. I touch her or come up behind her, and she jumps. We would go for a walk, and before we'd get back home, she'd be screaming at me. I'd have to take a shower as soon as I came home from work."

"Well, you stink after being at the office all day."

Jake glared at her. Her arms were folded over the pillow. He hated that posture. "Stink? I *stink?* What—"

"Mallory, let Jake finish."

Jake shifted to look at Jennifer. An unexpected ally. *Good.* Mallory was being brought down a peg or two.

"Go on, Jake."

"She won't let me turn the light off by our bed."

Mallory scrunched the pillow tighter to her chest. "So, I don't like tripping over myself if I have to get up at night."

"It's like I can't do anything right. I can't please her."

Her jaw line hardened. "That's not true!"

Jake leaned back and shook his head. She was being totally unreasonable. "See what I mean?"

Her voice rose over his. "You're being—"

Jake was relieved when Jennifer intervened. "One person at a time. Jake, go on. It sounds like you're frustrated. Can you expand on that?"

"I just don't know what she wants anymore." Jake threw up his hands.

"So you ran." A dull red stain flushed Mallory's cheeks, and those green eyes nearly flashed fire.

"I didn't run! I gave you the space that you needed to try to figure out what was going on in your life." His face heated.

Mallory's hands landed on her hips. "That was helpful. You abandoned me, Jake."

"Wait a minute, Mallory." Jennifer broke into the squabbling again. "Let Jake finish. I think what he has to say is important for you to hear." Jake hunkered back in his seat and folded his arms. He was beginning to like this lady.

"That's all I've got to say."

"Okay, Mallory. What did you want to tell Jake?"

Then again, maybe not.

Jake slid his gaze to his wife. Tears were gathering in her eyes. Wonderful. He was stuck in the room with no way out, and she was going to break down and cry. "He's never there for me. How can he expect me to respond to him when he's not investing anything in this relationship?"

This time he refused to give in to the guilt and pity that twisted in his gut every time she cried. "With your credit-card debt, I think I've invested plenty!"

A tear slid down her cheek. "This isn't about money, Jake. Why do you always go back to money? Everything is finances with you."

"Better be with me. Somebody has to—"

Jennifer's voice was quiet but firm. "Jake, let Mallory finish."

Mallory huffed. "If he's going to be like this, then forget it."

Jennifer shook her head. "Mallory, you had something to tell Jake. Tell him. He needs to hear you." She turned to Jake. "And you need to listen to what Mallory has to say."

"I forgot."

Yeah, right.

Jennifer's lips twitched. Apparently she didn't believe Mallory either. "I believe you were saying something about the pain you feel when Jake is gone. Tell him how you feel, not what he has done or hasn't done."

Mallory refused to look at either one of them. Jake clasped his knee with his hands. He didn't want to hear it. He was no better at fixing Mallory's problems than he had been at fixing his mother's.

Finally Mallory spoke. "I hurt when you walked away. I felt abandoned. I need…"

Jake stared at his wedding band and willed away the tears misting his eyes. He knew he'd hurt her. He just never realized how much. *I'm slime.*

"I feel," Jennifer corrected.

"I felt...alone. I ached to be near you."

His head jerked up and he stared at her. He was the one who ached to be near her, yet was constantly snubbed and given a cold shoulder. "You won't let me near you! I try! And every time I do, you push me away." Jake bolted to his feet. "This is a ridiculous waste of my time—"

"See what I mean? I told you he wouldn't stay." Mallory jumped to her feet and faced him. They stood glaring at one another like wrestlers in a ring.

"Actually, I think we're making great progress."

This was progress? Jake sure didn't see how. It was the same old argument, just in a new location.

"Sit back down. Let me explain."

Mallory plopped back on the sofa. *Like a teenager being reprimanded for something that wasn't her fault.* Jake glowered at her.

"Please, Jake." Jennifer nodded to the couch, and he eased down on the edge of the chair.

"You said she jumps when you come up behind her or touch her. She makes you shower when you come home. It makes perfect sense to me that Mallory would respond in that fashion." Jennifer shifted forward. "Mallory isn't rebuffing you. She's physically responding to memories she isn't even aware of. Mallory loves you. She just doesn't know how to deal with her own pain, and until she does, she won't be able to respond to you as you want her to."

"That doesn't make any sense."

"Think about it. It's that *logical madness* I was talking about. If I say 'Thanksgiving,' what's the first thing you think of?"

Jake hesitated, then with a sigh, answered her. "Football. Eating leftovers. A turkey roasting in the oven. Mom used to put it in just before we went to bed, and it would slow roast all night long. I'd wake up with my mouth watering."

"Like it's doing now?"

A slow smile eased over Jake's face, and he nodded. How did she know?

"You see? The body has a way of responding to memories. Scent is one of our most powerful senses. Just as the smell of turkey or pumpkin, or perhaps the sound of a football game on TV, might bring back childhood memories of Thanksgiving, ordinary, every-day things can produce a strong reaction in a survivor." Jennifer tapped her pen on the arm of her chair before continuing. "One of the most powerful triggers for most survivors is the male scent." She tipped her head in his direction. "Makes sense, doesn't it, when you think about what she has endured?"

Jake had to look away, but his own mind came to Mallory's defense. *You hate the smell of whiskey.* Jennifer was right. Scents *were* powerful.

"Mallory and I have talked a little about cues that she gave off as a child. That is, as a child, how she told the adult world around her that she was in pain. There are many ways a child tells this, usually through their behavior, which may seem strange or extreme until you see it in light of the abuse."

Jake shifted in his chair to look at his wife. "Why didn't you tell somebody, Mallory?"

Mallory plucked at the tassel of the pillow she held in her lap. She sounded like Angel did when she had done something bad. "I did."

Jake's mouth fell open. What? And nothing was done to stop it? He looked at Jennifer, but she gave no sign that the words had taken her by surprise. Maybe they had already discussed this.

Then Jennifer asked the question on Jake's lips: "Who?"

Mallory's head was bent, and a thick fall of hair covered her face. She wrapped both of her arms around the pillow and rocked back and forth.

Jennifer leaned forward to lay her hand on Mallory's arm. "Who did you tell, Mallory?"

Jake's heart began to pound in his ears. "And why didn't they do something about it?"

Jennifer sent him a warning look. "Mallory?"

"I told…" She began rocking faster, and it was a strain to hear her whispered voice. "I told Daddy."

Martin.

Jake still couldn't comprehend it. Why hadn't Martin torn Eric's head off? He slammed the basketball against the backboard and caught the rim on the way down. He missed an easy lay-up. He bent over to catch his breath and wiped the beads of perspiration off his forehead with the corner of his T-shirt.

Jake had stayed behind in the gym when all the other guys had left. He'd pushed his body hard for two hours but still didn't feel like going back to Joey's. He straightened up and went after the ball.

If only he could understand. The steady rhythm of the ball bouncing from hand to hand offered him no clues. Mallory had broken into sobs at the session, and he figured it was time to get out of there. Jennifer knew more about calming his wife down than he did. Mallory didn't want him there anyway.

He dribbled the ball close to the floor, then spun and took a shot at the basket. Missed again.

He retrieved the ball and walked to the top of the key. He and Mallory had come in separate cars, so he hadn't waited around for her to come out. Three of his foul shots bounced off the rim back to him. This was pathetic! He walked to the bleachers and picked up his towel, then cradled the basketball under one arm and sat down. Rubbing his face with the rough terry cloth didn't help.

He supposed some of what Jennifer talked about made sense. Just the fact he wanted to run every time a woman broke into tears could be called a trigger, he supposed. He spun the ball around in his hands, then bounced it once, hard. He spun it around and did it again.

And each time the ball pounded the floor, the same thought pounded his mind and heart: Why hadn't Martin Bennington done something—anything—about the abuse?

Martin Dale Bennington—her own father—the man she had trusted…loved…admired.

Mallory's stomach rolled, and for a moment she thought she'd be sick. She had told him what Eric had done, and he'd called her bad…wicked.

Her stomach twisted again.

Why, Daddy? Why didn't you believe me? The tears started again. They blinded her eyes and slid down her cheeks in a steady stream that soaked her shirt. A sob shook her body. Then another and another. Mallory pulled into a parking lot, dropped her forehead against the steering wheel, and allowed the torrent to spill out.

If she couldn't trust her father, who could she trust?

Mallory choked back the tears and reached for a tissue. She had to pick up the girls at her mom's. As much as she wanted someone to hold her, she had to be strong for her daughters. She put the car in gear and continued to her parents' home.

The hall light was on, but the house was quiet. Mallory checked her watch. It was early for the girls to be asleep. She padded toward the kitchen, heard the quiet buzz of voices on the TV, and veered toward the living room. Renee was curled up on a floor pillow, eyes shut, fingers tucked in her mouth. Mulan was battling the evil Hun leader, Shan-Yu. The movie was almost over.

Her father was asleep in his chair; a book lay open across his chest. Mallory's throat constricted. She couldn't deal with her father just now. She retreated, past the doorway, to the other end of the house, and climbed the stairs. A light was on in her parents' bedroom.

"Mom?"

"In here, dear."

Mallory peeked around the doorframe. Her mother was propped up against a pillow, needlepoint in hand. Angel sprawled beside her on the other side of the bed, her head nestled in her grandmother's lap.

The aching in Mallory's chest intensified. She envied her baby her ability to curl up and sleep in the security of her mother's embrace. She'd never been so fortunate.

"Everything go all right?" Mallory's mother eyed her above her reading glasses. "The girls lost the battle of waiting up for you."

"I'm sorry." Mallory once again fought her tears. "It was more…difficult than I thought. I needed some time to think. To pray."

Her mother set her work aside and removed her glasses. "What's wrong?" She laid her hand on the covers, and Mallory sank down on the edge of the bed.

"Oh, Mom…" The tears began again in earnest, and Mallory laid her head against the end of her mother's pillow. Strong hands touched her hair.

"I wish I knew what to say or do to make your pain go away, Mally. I don't pretend to understand, but I love you. Your dad and I are here if you need us."

Her mother's hand stayed on her head, and Mallory closed her eyes. The light ticking of her mother's clock was the only sound in the room. "Mom?"

"Yes, dear?"

"What was Gramps like? Early on, I mean. When he was younger." Her mother's light touch was gone, and Mallory ached to feel her caress again. She opened her eyes and stared at her father's shoes, lined up side by side in the closet. Why had her mother quit? Was Mallory onto something? "Gran said Gramps had a temper. Did you ever see him like that?"

"Once."

Mallory held her breath, willing her mother to continue. There was so much she didn't understand about this family. If her mother could tell her—

"It was before your dad and I were married, and I went out to the farm to have dinner with his parents. They had a couple of farmhands then. One of them was accused of starting a fire at the grange. Your grandfather caught him coming in late, and there was a terrible fight. He put the man in the hospital. The man lost his arm from a bad infection. Later we found out someone else started the fire. It did something to your grandfather. He was never the same after that."

Mallory pushed her face into the pillow. Did she have the courage to ask her? *I need to know!* "Is…did…was Daddy ever like that? Did he have a…a temper, I mean?"

"What do you mean?"

Mallory lifted her head. "I just meant—what Gran said at the farmhouse after Gramps's funeral, about Gramps being afraid Daddy was too much like him."

"That was a long time ago, Mallory. This…this obsession with the past has got to stop. It's making you miserable."

"I told him, Mom. I told Daddy what Eric did. Why didn't he believe me?"

"Lower your voice!" Her mother leaned forward and grasped Mallory's arm. "What kind of terrible things is that woman putting into your head?" *Mama, please don't do this!* "First you accuse your brother, now your father?"

Mallory's heart shredded. She pulled away and couldn't bear to even glance at her mother. Shame coursed through her. *I really am a bad, wicked little girl just like Daddy said.*

"Mallory! This has got to end. I will not allow this family to be torn apart by wild, unfounded accusations!"

Mallory slid off the bed. "I'm sorry, Mama. I'm sorry. I didn't mean to…" She had to get out, right now. Mallory gathered Angel in her arms and fled down the stairs.

August 18

God, You were there! You saw! You could have stopped him, but You didn't. Part of me hates You for that.

   I didn't mean that, Lord! I just don't know what to do with my anger.

Twenty~Six

"Eric—"

Mallory chewed on the end of her pen. *Where do I start?*

"*You abhorrent, merciless, slime ball...*"

She ripped up the paper. *Too nice.* This was supposed to be easy, this getting in touch with her anger. And she felt it, no question about that, but...

Mallory tried again.

"Eric—

"*This is the most difficult letter I have ever had to write.*"

Trite, but at least it was a whole sentence. It was her fifth attempt. The other four were crumpled up in the wastebasket. The anger work that they had done in group therapy had been nothing compared to facing her offender. And this was just a letter. How would she ever face him in person? *Just do it, just let it out.* Mallory bent over the sheet of paper.

"*I remember what you did to me. I remember how you hurt me. I hate you for it.*"

No, she didn't hate him.

Mallory made herself keep going. The fury was beginning to build, and she let it, writing faster and scribbling every thought that came into her head. She wouldn't quit. Not even the swear words would be taken out. She pressed harder on the pen, not caring when the words slanted downhill. Better to get it all out. Every memory, every thought, every question, every awful thing she ever called him—or wanted to call him.

Her fingers cramped, but she kept going. A wet drip blotched the ink, and still she kept writing. She didn't stop until, exhausted, she had spent every drop of rage in her. Then she folded her hands, lay her head down on the pages, and wept.

She hated the rage. She didn't want to admit it was there, but it was. And it was being dumped on the wrong people—on the girls, on Jake. It was eating away at her very life.

Please, God, just help me get beyond it.

The cathartic weeping left her drained but somehow more at peace. She wouldn't even rewrite her letter to make it legible.

Maybe the things she had to say were better left undecipherable.

Mallory put the car in park, but left the engine running. There was still time to turn around, to not do this. *No!* She had spent too many hours in therapy, too many months of struggling to understand…herself, her family, Eric.

Eric. Maybe he wouldn't be home. *Yeah, right. His Jeep's in the garage.* There weren't any good excuses; her mother had Lindsay, Renee, and Angel. Marty was with Catherine.

Eric was alone.

Mallory shivered. *I can do this. I can!* No, she couldn't. *God, why didn't you let me keep it buried?* Because it was the truth. And only the truth would set her free.

How she longed to be free! She turned off the ignition and got out of the car. She didn't know if her wet-noodle legs would make it up the sidewalk, or if her chicken finger would push the door-bell.

I don't want to hate you anymore, Eric. I just want... Her eyes smarted. *I will not let him see me cry.* She took a short step onto the patio brick walk. She had come so far. She couldn't quit now.

She remembered the glowing eyes of the woman who had been through therapy, who had come to talk to the group of women just starting the process. "The Lord helped me to persevere, to keep going. And it's worth it." Mallory had listened, trying to take it in. The woman's father had abused her for years, and yet they now had a growing relationship. "It's not where it should be, where I've always longed for it to be, but we'll get there."

How could anyone go through this process and look so optimistic? *Because there's hope.*

"Forgiveness is a process," she'd said. "You get there one step at a time. But first, you have to be willing. Let the Lord guide you. Everyone's journey is different."

That was why Mallory was here today. She didn't want to do this—she needed to. Eric wouldn't come to a counseling session any more than her parents would. Not that she'd asked him.

Chicken, that's me.

No. She would not let fear rule her life any longer. She would face Eric with the truth. She would confront him, not with anger, but with love. God's love.

He's my brother, Lord.

She wanted to have a relationship with him, whatever the obstacles, whatever it took. God would give her the strength she needed.

Mallory stepped up to the door and pushed the bell.

* * *

"Grow up, Eric. For once in your life, take responsibility for your actions."

Mallory raked a hand through her hair and paced across Eric's living room. *I can't do this. What was I thinking?* Her head pounded out a parallel rhythm with her heart.

"Mal, I feel for you, I do, but don't you think I'd remember these things you're accusing me of?" Eric stood silhouetted in the room's large picture window. As the evening sun sank from view behind his right shoulder, he folded his arms across his chest.

"Are you saying I've lost it?" Mallory braced herself against the credenza holding an array of family photographs. "That these memories are made up in my mind, or are not about you, but somebody else? I remember the gun, Eric. You said you'd blow my head off."

"Childhood games, Mal. A stupid prank. The gun wasn't even loaded. You weren't hurt."

"Not hurt? What do you call waking up dripping with sweat from night terrors? Being afraid of the dark because of the time you locked me in the cellar? I shove people away from me because I'm afraid they'll touch me. I have shaking spasms that are like convulsions."

"I just think you're dumping on the wrong person." The hard edge in Eric's voice softened. "Sis, I feel for you and the pain you must be going through. I've been there myself. And let's face it, whose childhood wasn't filled with a few ups and downs?"

Mallory closed her eyes. *This is so hard.* Was it possible that what she believed wasn't true? *God, help me see the truth.*

"I think this counselor of yours is leading you down the garden path. She's put this abuse thing in your head, and it's going to destroy our family."

"No! It's not my intent to destroy you or our family, but to make you see the truth." *Please, God, make him understand.* "Eric, this family has become expert at pretending. Tell yourself something long enough, and it becomes fact to you. The truth gets buried under the lies and pretense, and you begin to believe your fabrications are the truth."

"So what's your point? All this stuff you claim happened to you, that was a long time ago. What difference does it make now?"

"The truth is what's important, Eric. Because God is truth. Satan is the father of lies—and lies will only lead you further away from God."

"Here we go with the God thing again." Eric turned his back on her.

Mallory clamped down on her impulse to scream. She reminded herself of the group work they had done on confronting an offender. *Stick to the point. Don't let him sidetrack you. Deal with the facts.* If only they'd told her how hard those facts were to put into words.

"Eric!" It came out as a near shout, and Mallory tried for a more civil tone. "I'm trying to tell you that the consequences of what you did to me as a child are still affecting me today. It affects this whole family. There's a lot of pain in my life."

"You know what they say, 'one man's nightmare is another man's pleasure.'"

Mallory flinched. *God! Is he that cruel and heartless, or is he just that arrogant?* Through clenched teeth, she tried again. "Eric, I was seven, and you *raped* me. Only a sick person could find any pleasure in that."

Eric stood like granite. Immovable. No visible cracks. Mallory forced herself to go on. "I came here because, like you, I need to take responsibility for my actions. As a child, I was a victim, but I'm not a victim anymore. I won't deny what you did to me, not to anyone. I just wanted you to be prepared, because other people know."

"You're going around telling people this about me?" Eric whirled around to face her. "Who?" The last of the sun's dying rays were reflected in the corner of his eyes, and Eric blinked.

The familiar tug of pity and guilt pulled at Mallory, and she swayed for a moment beneath the pressure. *Wait a minute. He's the one who hurt me.*

"Eric, I've only told the truth, and only when appropriate. But I will no longer lie to the family about you or the past."

"You told Mom and Dad? You must be crazy! So that's why Geoff—" Eric shook his head. "Mal, I'm sorry you're going through this, but hanging the blame on me is not going to help anything. Like I told you, there are large chunks of my childhood I can't remember, but I would definitely remember something like this." Eric wrapped his arms across his body and turned back to the setting sun. "Switch therapists. This one is planting absurdities in your mind. Get some real help, Sis. You need it."

"We all need it, Eric. Denying the past won't get you anywhere, and you won't help your son get better until you deal with it. Think about it, Eric. Marty is following in your footsteps."

Eric stiffened, but wouldn't turn around, and Mallory continued. "Remember Harry Chapin's song? It fits you to a T. Your boy is just like you, Eric."

He cleared his throat and opened his mouth to speak, but nothing came out. He closed it, and a muscle jerked in his jaw.

Guard my tongue, Father. Help me with the anger; I can't do it alone. She softened her voice. "Eric, I did not come here to cause any more rifts in the family. I…I don't hate you." She dug for a Kleenex from her purse. "I just want…I just want to move on. I want to put this behind us, but I don't want to pretend it didn't happen. Keeping that secret has caused too many problems."

She wiped her eyes and nose. "Eric, I know you don't want to hear anything about God, but you need to know. I believe God can help me forgive you." She studied his stiff back and felt a wave of sadness…and compassion. "I'm not there yet. But by His grace I will be."

Mallory didn't know whether to laugh or cry.

She had done it! It had been tougher than anything she had faced so far, but she had done it. She had confronted Eric about the past.

She felt…good. Strong. In control. But sad at the same time. Tears swelled to puddles in her eyes.

Would the pain ever go away? The bitterness and anger? *God, I just want healing. And forgiveness. The road seems too long.* Weary with the stress of not only the conversation but also the anticipation of it, Mallory slumped behind the steering wheel of her car. She had tried to understand Eric. How many times had her mind screamed *Why?* Why would he hurt her? What had she ever done to him?

Pastor James had talked weeks ago about not being responsible for other people's actions, only for your own. It struck Mallory now that she was glad she was not Eric. If—no, *when*—he was honest with himself and with God, it was going to be far more painful for him than it had ever been for her. She did not have to live with the kind of guilt he would one day face. A holy, righteous God would be more terrifying than any vengeance she might plan.

If Mallory struggled with forgiveness for Eric, how could he forgive himself? How would he ever reconcile the massive destruction his actions had caused?

The answer was simple: He couldn't.

But God could.

August 22

I feel like Ezekiel in the valley of dry bones. No, I feel more like the dry bones. All around me is barrenness. Everything is dead or dying.
    Will this ever end?

Twenty Seven

"I said, 'But, Officer, I slowed down at that stop sign.' So the cop pulls out his stick and starts beating on me and says, 'Now do you want me to slow down or stop?'"

At Jake's roar of laughter, every head in the airport terminal seemed to turn in his direction. He wiped his eyes with the back of his hand. "I swear, Peterson, you are insane."

"Maybe, but I got a smile out of you, which is more than I can say about anybody else you hang with." Joey shifted his bag to his other shoulder and jogged to keep up with Jake's long-legged strides.

Jake transferred his overnight bag to his other hand and stopped to read the airport map. Joey nudged his arm and pointed to a direction sign above them. He swung left out of the terminal, and Jake followed but stopped when the PA system blared.

"Mr. Jake Carlisle, please come to Northwest ticket counter to meet your party. Mr. Jake Carlisle, your party is waiting for you at the Northwest ticket counter." *They're pulling out all the stops. Do they want me that bad?* Jake increased his stride through Seattle-Tacoma International Airport. "Come on, we don't want to keep them waiting."

* * *

A knife-sharp pain coursed through Mallory's abdomen, eradicating all conscious thought. She pushed away from her workbench, screamed out in agony, and doubled over as the pain intensified. She slid down the counter and curled into a ball on the floor.

Through the fog of pain she was aware of the sound of running feet and the door smacking against the wall.

"Mommy! Mommy! What's wrong?" Small hands grabbed Mallory around the waist, inflicting more pain. Mallory bit down hard on her lip, tasting blood as she battled to keep from crying out again. Renee shook her shoulders and sobbed in her ear. "Mommy! Mommy! Get up!"

She tried to speak to her terrified daughter, but the words couldn't get past the stabbing pain. Renee left, and Mallory thought she heard her talking to someone. When the little girl returned, Mallory felt a cold, soppy rag plop on her forehead. Water ran down her face. Another volley of searing pain racked her body, and Mallory surrendered to the encompassing blackness.

Jake leaned back in his chair and crossed one foot over the other, resting them on the railing of the balcony of his sixteenth-floor hotel room. The sultry breeze coming off Puget Sound held the scent of salt, seaweed, and fish. He filled his lungs. It would have been a perfect summer evening had his world not been gyrating out of control.

His thoughts spun at the lucrative offer the *World Graphics* people had laid on the table that evening. The salary alone would get him out of debt in five short months. He'd be able to provide a college education for his girls. Sure it would mean more travel, but the kind of money they'd offered would allow him to take his family with him on many of the shoots. He could photograph a location; Mallory could paint it. They would get to see the world. The girls would get the education of a lifetime.

There was just one thing wrong with the picture: He and Mallory were still separated, still struggling to rebuild common ground. *Oh, Mallory, I wish you were with me right now.* She would love this.

I'm so far away from you. I have been for a long time, haven't I?

He kicked against the railing, then rocked to his feet to lean his elbows where his heels had been. The wind played with his hair. *Maybe you were right. Maybe I have used all of these long-distance assignments to keep your pain and fears from ever touching my heart.*

He gritted his teeth until his jaw ached. It was so much easier to look at one small part of the world than to look at the whole picture. His eyes scanned the panorama of shimmering lights dancing on the bay waters. *I was so used to doing that with my work... I guess I fell back on that in my life and in my marriage.*

Images raced through his mind...images of all he'd missed, all Mallory had dealt with on her own. *I wasn't there when you had the miscarriage.* He couldn't—then or now—deal with the pain of it. *I wasn't there when Angel was born. I wasn't there when the girls were sick or needed discipline. Or when you had your emotional break and went into therapy.*

Nausea rose, bitter in his throat with the realization of what his absences had cost him and his family. He hadn't been there when Mallory got her job at the publishing company. He'd been gone for most of her birthdays and their anniversaries. How could he have been so blind? *I haven't been there most of our married life, have I?* He swore under his breath. Why had he let so much come between him and those he loved the most?

Well, that was going to change. Jake straightened. The lights glimmering off the bay were beautiful and filled his heart with hope. He spun on his heel. He was going home. *Home to Mallory.* Home to his life in his three-bedroom house. He would convince her that the choice he had made tonight was the right one. He would wine her. Dine her. Romance her. Just as he had done to win her the first time. It had worked before. It would work again.

Jake entered his spacious room and reached for the phone. He was going to set his plan in motion.

Geoff sprinted through the emergency room door and searched out the waiting area as he moved toward the information desk.

"Uncle Geoff!" He changed direction midstride at the sound of Renee's sobbing voice. He dropped to his knees, and Renee and Angel buried themselves in his embrace. He pulled them close, caressing their silky heads. They must have been terrified. As Geoff rose to his feet, four tiny arms tightened their grip on his neck until he could barely breathe. He shifted their weight and turned toward the older woman standing beside the plastic chairs. "Thank you for staying with the girls."

Mallory's next-door neighbor nodded her head. "It broke my heart when I got there and saw these two, so lost and alone, standing at the door of the ambulance. I have to go pick up my grandson. Now that you're here, I'll be on my way." She hugged them both. "Girls, you were very brave. I'm sure your mom will be okay."

"Thank you again." Geoff lifted Renee to a more comfortable position, then moved back toward the information area. He listened as they told him the doctors had just begun to work on Mallory. He sat down to give the receptionist the information she needed before returning to the hard plastic chairs of the waiting area.

Minutes later he saw Holly's petite frame, sporting surgical scrubs, moving in his direction. She reached out and engulfed him and the girls in a hug. "I just saw the ER admissions file. How is Mallory?"

"I don't know. I'm not considered next of kin, so they wouldn't tell me anything."

She smiled and ruffled his hair. "Good thing you know someone who can pull a couple of strings. Let me see what I can find out." She kissed the top of his head and turned to walk down the hall. "Be back in a bit."

Geoff saw his parents come through the emergency room entrance, followed by Eric. The way his mother's hand fluttered reminded him of a bird with a broken wing. She spotted Geoff and pointed, and he moved to meet them halfway down the hall. "I don't know anything yet." He spoke to his parents and ignored Eric. "The ER was crazy. They've been running tests, but I haven't seen Mallory."

He gave his mother a kiss, then ran a hand through his hair and watched his father pick up the sleeping Angel and cradle her against him. He blinked to dispel the ghostlike image of little Mallory on their father's lap.

"Holly is trying to find out something."

His mother's head jerked up. "Why Holly?"

"Because, Mother, she works here." Geoff walked back and forth in the confining space between the chairs. "She said she'd find out what was happening." He checked his watch. *She's been gone too long. I'm getting really scared.*

"Has anyone called Jake?" his dad asked.

"Call Jake? Why would anyone call Jake?" His mother's outburst rent the air. "He hasn't been a part of Mallory's life in months. If he cared, he would have been with her. Then maybe none of this would have happened."

I have to agree with you there, Mom. Geoff bit the tip of his tongue, then turned his attention back to his father. "I left a message with his answering service." Geoff shrugged. "Nothing yet."

Geoff turned to see Holly striding down the hall beside a woman dressed in surgical greens. The doctor didn't look old enough to be in charge of someone's medical care. Her oval face and petite frame made her look more like a china doll than a competent physician, but there was a firm, confident air as she spoke. "Mr. Carlisle?"

"He's not here. I'm Geoff Bennington, Mallory's brother."

"Her next of kin?"

"This is our mother and father."

"I'm Doctor Lorobaugh. A kidney stone brought Mallory in here."

Geoff sagged with relief. "It's not serious? She isn't going to die?"

"Once the stone passes, she should be fine. We have her on pain medication right now." The doctor motioned for the family to join her in a small cubical across the hall. Geoff looked at Mallory's two sleeping children. He couldn't leave them alone. Holly laid a hand on his arm. "Go with her. I'll stay here with the kids."

He nodded and touched her face. "Thank you."

Geoff crammed into the small room behind Eric, his parents, and the doctor. "Do you know when Mr. Carlisle will be here?"

His mother sniffed and straightened the collar of her jacket. "They're separated."

"All right. Mr. and Mrs. Bennington, the x-rays confirmed our original diagnosis, which was that Mallory has a kidney stone. However, the films showed something else."

Geoff's stomach tightened and rolled. His mother's face blanched, and his father's turned gray. He refused to look at Eric.

"What?" Geoff's dad finally managed Geoff's unspoken question.

"We aren't sure yet, but there is a dark spot on her left ovary."

"Oh, dear God."

It was as close to a heartfelt prayer as Geoff had ever heard from his brother. His mom began to cry.

"Mr. and Mrs. Bennington, it could be any number of things. A cyst. Scar tissue. An abnormal ovary."

Geoff clenched his fists. Or it could be the one thing the doctor hadn't mentioned…

Cancer. Mallory could have cancer.

"Her blood work hasn't come back from the lab yet, and it will be several hours before we can schedule the CAT scan. So for now we're not sure what it is. In the meantime we are pushing liquids through her in the hopes of getting the stone to move faster."

"How long before it moves?" The air had worked its way through Geoff's windpipe, and he could breathe again.

The doctor shrugged. "It's fairly far down the tube, so I expect it to pass in a few hours. We have her on IVs." She patted Geoff's mother on the arm on her way toward the door. "We'll do the CAT scan as soon as possible. Please, try not to worry."

Not worry? Why did doctors always say that right after they had given horrible news? "Can we see her?" Geoff steadied his trembling body against the doorframe.

Dr. Lorobaugh nodded. "She's medicated, so she may not be talking very straight. She'll be sent upstairs as soon as a bed is available. If you'll follow me."

Geoff motioned to Holly from across the hall. She laid her magazine down and hurried to his side. "We're going back to see Mally." His vision blurred, and his voice cracked.

"Geoff? What is it?"

"There was…a…" Geoff cleared his throat and looked up at the perforated ceiling tile. "They found something on the x-ray. A dark spot on her ovary."

"Oh, Geoff!" Holly wrapped her arms around his waist.

He buried his face against her neck. "What will I do if I lose my baby sister? What if she dies too?" Holly hugged him tighter.

"Geoff? Coming?" His father's words squelched the flow of emotions, and he pulled away from Holly and followed his parents.

When they reached Mallory, he leaned over and kissed her forehead. *She looks horrible. And this is only a kidney stone.* Her face was pale, almost sallow in color. Dark smudges beneath her eyes and small creases in her forehead attested to her pain. *What will she be like if she has to fight— No, she won't die! I refuse to let her.* An IV sent an array of medications into her system. A blood-pressure cuff was wrapped around her arm, and her finger glowed red from the small monitor connected to it.

Geoff's mother eased herself onto the chair by the bed, and his father stood behind her. Eric rested one shoulder against the doorway. Geoff took up residence on the edge of the bed and brushed Mallory's hair off her forehead. "She looks worse than when she showed up at my house a couple of weeks ago and told me about—"

A nurse peeked around the door. "We are ready to take her upstairs now."

He scowled up at the nurse, then leaned over to kiss his sister's cheek. "I love you, Mally. Please be all right. Please...please be okay." A tear slid down his face and dropped onto Mallory's pale cheek.

The early morning light peeked through the curtains of the hotel room as Jake made his way from the bathroom to the bed. He was fresh from his shower, and he felt great. He settled down on the bed and reached for the thick sheaf of papers to page through the contract, reading the fine print. He smiled. This could turn everything in his life back around.

His smile disappeared as he thought back on the previous night. Mallory hadn't been home when he'd tried to call, but he'd left a romantic message on the machine anyway. Should he try again this morning? He really needed to talk to her.

There was a knock on the door, and Jake moved to open it, hesitating when he saw Joey's sober face. Jake looked closer. It was beyond sober—Joey was scared. "What is it?"

"Check your pager."

"What?"

Joey went to Jake's open briefcase and pulled out his pager. He tossed it to Jake. "I had a message on mine. It said for you to call Geoff. Family emergency."

The pager slipped, and Jake fumbled to keep it from falling. Why hadn't he checked his messages last night? With shaking hands he turned it to the light. *Mallory in hospital. Call. Geoff.* Lead landed in the pit of his stomach. His heart stopped, then pounded against his rib cage. The room swam like heat waves in the distance. "Oh…God!"

Joey's hand pushed against Jake's shoulder, propelling him downward to sit on the bed. That same hand wrapped his around his cell phone. "Call Geoff. I'll get us on the next flight back."

Jake sat there. Joey's voice washed over him, but the words floated past his head. His brain had turned to mush. The weight inside him grew heavier and threatened to rip open his heart.

"Jake!" The roar of his name snapped him out of his stupor, and he stabbed the On button of his phone. Geoff's machine picked up: "I can't come to the phone. Leave your message. I'll contact you." Jake hung up and dialed Martin and Alecia's number, letting their phone ring and ring. He slammed his fist over the End button, then dialed Eric. His answering machine picked up as well.

Jake swore.

Joey returned from making his phone call. "We're on standby for a flight leaving in four hours."

Four hours! Four hours before he could even begin to know what was happening. That was an eternity!

By the time Jake and Joey arrived at the airport, Jake's frustration level had risen even higher. All flights had been delayed due to heavy fog that had rolled in off Puget Sound. Their standby status was even more precarious. Jake dialed Geoff's phone number again, and her parents, and Eric.

Still no answer.

What was going on? Jake stared out through the heavy mist. He didn't even know which hospital she was in.

"Hang on, Jake." Joey patted him on the back and leaned against the window overlooking the runways.

"I love her so much." He could see a ghost impression of himself in the glass. A pale, washed-out image of the man he thought he was. That's all he was without Mallory by his side. "What if something happens to her? What will I ever do without her? What about the girls? I-I'm so scared, Joey. I want her well. I swear I will do whatever it takes to make sure she gets better."

"Then pray, Jake, and ask God for the help you'll need. Because that's the only way any of this will ever work out."

Jake closed his eyes against the pain he saw in the faded image. He leaned his forehead against the glass. If he could, he would pick up the entire terminal and transport it to Cleveland.

"Ladies and gentlemen, this is your captain. We are going to make an unscheduled landing in Denver, Colorado. Our flight attendant dis-

covered a gas buildup in the belly of the plane, and we are landing to have the plane checked out. We are sure there is nothing seriously wrong, but we need to make certain before continuing. We ask for your patience and understanding. Thank you."

"No!" After finally getting off the ground, Jake couldn't believe he had to go back down. *This isn't happening. It can't be happening.* The very time when he needed to be with Mallory the world was falling apart.

Joey touched Jake's arm. "Hang tight, boss. We'll work something out to get you home as soon as possible."

The plane landed amid a swarm of emergency vehicles. He glared at the fireman that stood directing the passengers off the plane and brushed past him on his way out to find the nearest ticket counter.

"Look, boss, no reason for you to be standing here with smoke rolling out of your ears, waiting to blow up at the ticket agent. I'll deal with this. Get something to drink and try to rest. We'll make it back soon."

Jake glared into Joey's serene face and stalked away. He yanked his cell phone out and punched a number. The phone beeped twice, then flashed a low battery signal. He heaved it against the terminal wall. When the phone shattered, people near him moved farther away and gave him a wide berth.

"That ain't helping her." Joey's hand landed on his shoulder.

Jake shrugged it off and glared at his friend. "Don't give me trite words. If you want to help, pray to your God to get us there now."

Amazing how a smile could be both compassionate and smug. "I am, and He will."

Jake stalked to the windows and pressed his palms against the warm glass. He rested his forehead on the back of his hand and followed an outbound plane as it taxied off the runway and disappeared from sight. *Hang on, Mal.* He cursed the distance. All of it. The physical miles…the emotional void that had come so close to destroying his marriage. *I'm sorry for being so far from you all of these months. All these years…*

Tears slid down the crease of his cheek.

Joey joined him at the glass wall. His silence was a comfort. Jake shook his head. "I've got to do something!"

Joey nodded toward the bank of pay phones. "Call someone."

Of course! Jake slapped Joey on the back. "You're a genius, pal." He raced to punch in a number, grateful at least one of them seemed to have a brain.

Mallory drifted on a cloud. She tried hard to open her eyes, but they refused to obey the commands her brain sent. A soft sigh escaped her, and she felt the bed give beneath the weight of someone sitting on its edge.

Her eyelids fluttered open, and it took a moment to focus on the loving, blue-green gaze. "Geo?" The dimple in his cheek deepened. She tried to blink away the fog. "Where am I?"

"The hospital. Do you remember surgery? You gave us quite a scare." He tucked her hair behind her ear.

She looked around the unfamiliar room. The memories were coming back. "How'd I do?"

"Good. You were lucky you passed the kidney stone quickly

and they could get you into surgery right away. You came through just fine."

She lifted a heavy hand to touch his stubbled cheek, grateful he was there. But she couldn't hold back the question that mattered most.

"Where's Jake?"

Mallory watched Geoff's reaction to her question. His gaze slid away from her, and he shifted as though uncomfortable. "Geo, where's Jake? Does he know I'm in the hospital?"

"We've left messages with his service, but he hasn't answered his page." Geoff shrugged. "Maybe he's on his way."

Tears blurred Mallory's vision. *It's over.* She turned her head toward the opposite wall and swallowed hard against the lump in her throat. "He doesn't even care enough to come when I'm in the hospital. I guess that says everything, doesn't it?"

With that, she burst into tears.

August 24

*I'm doing the right thing. I know the path You have laid before me,
Lord. And You have shown me that no matter how difficult or painful
I may find it, You will go before me.*

You will never abandon me.

Twenty-Eight

"Hold tight, Mal. I'm almost there." Jake's whispered words felt flat, even to his own ears.

Relief had surged through him when he'd finally gotten through on the phone to Gran. Then she told him about the x-ray…told him that, even as they were speaking, Mallory was in surgery to have a mass removed from her ovary. Even after the CAT scan, they still weren't positive if it was a cyst or something more. *Cancer.* What an ugly word. An ugly disease. He'd begged Gran to get a message to Mallory, but she said a storm was wreaking havoc with her phone. Folks could call her, but she couldn't call out.

Jake had hung up, gripping the receiver so tight his fingers ached. "Why is all of this happening to me?" *Because God hates me, and this proves it.*

A bump of turbulence and the banking of the plane brought him back to the present. He stared unseeing at the seat in front of him. "What if it's too late? What if I never get the chance to tell her I'm sorry and I'm willing to change?"

Joey raised his hand to stop the flow of panic-filled words. "I told you that God is the God of second chances. Trust that and trust Him."

The *ding* of the bell through the intercom brought Jake to his feet. "C'mon, they're turning off the seat-belt sign." They hauled their gear from the overhead compartments, then made a dash through the congested foot traffic of Cleveland's Hopkins International Airport and raced outside to hail a cab.

When they arrived at the hospital, Jake tossed a wad of money to the cab driver, then sprinted through the lobby. *Let her be okay. Please...let her be okay.*

He bounded into her room with a bouquet of flowers in his hand, then stopped. She was sitting up! She looked...great. She was seated on the edge of the hospital bed in her street clothes, her overnight bag on the floor at her feet. Jake wanted to take her in his arms, hold her, kiss her, and will some of his strength and vitality into her body.

"Get out, Jake." Mallory's voice was flat.

He took a step further into the room. He must have heard her wrong. "Mallory?" His smile wobbled when he saw the coldness in her eyes. She meant it!

"I said get out."

"What? Why?"

"You have to ask why?" She stared out the window.

I don't understand. Why are you so mad? He held out the flowers in her line of vision. She shifted to look at them out of the corner of her eye, and hope coursed through him.

"My surgery's over. They removed a cyst, and I'm fine. As if you care. You needn't bother showing up now with flowers, phony concern, and some feeble excuse."

An arrow of pain lanced through his heart. "Babe, I got here as soon as I could. I've been on—"

"I don't really care." Her voice was monotone...almost dead. That scared him more than angry words ever had. Had she stopped loving him? He raked his fingers through his already messy hair. He needed a shower and a change of clothes, but even that had taken a backseat until he was able to see her for himself. Thanks to equipment and weather delays, his trip across the United States had been the longest he had ever endured. *I need to hold you, Mal. I need to touch you, to feel for myself that you're okay.*

"I was scared out of my mind when I got word that you were in the hospital. I left as soon as I knew something was wrong." He searched her drawn features for any sign of softening.

Her face was pale, and dark smudges circled her eyes. She'd lost even more weight, so that she appeared almost gaunt. But it was her eyes that made his heart constrict. They seemed dead, void of the sparkle of love that used to shine there when she looked at him.

"I don't care."

Fear landed hard on his hope. *Don't do this, Mal. Please don't do this!* He took another hesitant step.

Jake set the flowers beside her.

"Honey, I…" Where did he start? "This was the craziest trip I've ever experienced. There were all kinds of weather delays, and my cell phone quit working. I couldn't get hold of anybody. I was sick with worry. When I finally reached Gran, I found out her phone wouldn't let her call out. I swear, I got here as soon as I possibly could." *Believe me. You've got to believe me.* Jake compressed his hands together. His fingers twisted his wide, gold wedding band.

"There are always delays, aren't there? Whenever you need a convenient reason to be late."

"Mal"—Jake knelt before her and touched her knee—"I know what you must be thinking, but everything I said is—"

"You have *no* idea what I'm thinking or feeling or what I have been going through, Jake Carlisle." She pushed his hand away from her. "I had surgery! I needed you, and you weren't here."

"Mallory, if you don't believe me, talk to Joey—"

"It doesn't matter."

His jaw tightened; he lifted his hand. "Please, don't shut me out!"

"Me? Me shut you out? Jake, I…" Her voice wobbled and then hardened. "For once this isn't about your pain. It's about mine. It isn't about your feelings, it's about what I've been going through. You shut me out. You."

He folded his arms across his chest. How could she think that?

"You've been so wrapped up in yourself and your career and your little world that there wasn't any room for anything that didn't pertain to your work. You come and go in our lives as if we are some convenience store for your needs and comforts. Your world shrank to the point that it excluded your family, your wife, even your own children."

She finished with a tired sigh. "Go. Take your career and your life and stay out of mine. I'll be fine. Geoff is coming back to take me home. You needn't worry about me."

"Mal!" He surged to his feet. "I tried to get back. I've been arguing with ticket agents and fighting the elements to get back to you. Don't do this to us." Frustrated anger was eating its way through his desperation.

She swung to face him as anger dispelled the exhaustion from her face. "I didn't do this. It was what you wanted from the very beginning. You ran from me." She clutched the bedsheets as if to draw strength from them. "You've been running for months, and while you've been running, I've been discovering. I discovered that my strengths don't come from you, they come from God. I don't need you for my personal happiness and gratification."

I refuse to let you do this to us. "Listen to me—"

"No."

He stepped back as that one word slapped him in the face. "What?"

"I found out that I could survive on my own, without you in my life." Mallory rubbed her eyes. "So you got what you wanted, Jake. Space and time. They are all yours. Take all you need, because I don't care anymore."

With that, she hopped down from the bed. When she swayed and grabbed the bed for support, Jake sprang forward to catch her. Her hand jerked up to ward him off.

"Go, Jake."

He squared his shoulders and stiffened his spine. He was not going anywhere.

"Go away. I'm tired of the fighting, the anger, everything. I'm tired of you."

"Fine." Jake gathered his wounded pride around him like a shield and stalked out of the room. He brushed past Joey, who lounged outside the door. "Let's go, Peterson."

He didn't even wait for Joey to catch up. If Mallory wanted out, who was he to stop her? Who was he to ask God to stop her? Jake jammed a finger on the elevator button, then heard pounding footsteps.

Joey promised You were the God of second chances! He promised You wouldn't let this happen!

Joey sprinted in after him. Tears stung Jake's eyes, and he

fought them off. His hands itched to smash something...to punch a hole through the wall of the elevator. Instead he gripped the stainless steel rail that encircled the cubicle.

"Jake, Malo is hurting. So are you. Give God time to—"

"I don't need your God's help."

"Don't let your pain put up a wall."

"Too late."

Tense silence enveloped them as they left the hospital. As the taxi driver weaved the cab through the Friday night rush-hour traffic that snarled about them, Jake stared out the window and replayed the events from the last four days.

The car came to a stop, and Jake grabbed his bags and headed for the door leaving Joey to pay the driver. He entered the duplex and moved to the spare bedroom, pulling out the empty boxes that had transferred his belongings to Joey's in the first place.

"What are you doing?"

"Leaving."

A hopeful expression lit Joey's voice. "Going back home?"

Jake emptied the top drawer of the dresser into one of the boxes. "Back to Washington."

"Don't do something stupid."

Jake's head jerked upright and he glared at Joey. "How dare you tell me how to act?" It took all his self-control not to hit something, to feel some kind of physical pain to ease the mental turmoil. "I guess you agree with Mallory. All I've managed to do for months is make people's lives miserable, and make a certifiable fool of myself in the process. So leave me alone, and I'll be out of your life in no time."

Joey folded his skinny arms over his chest and rocked back against the doorpost. "I can't do that."

"Just why not?" Jake straightened as anger tore at his soul, and his hand knotted into a fist.

"Because I love you, Jake." The tenderness in Joey's voice stole the fight from Jake. He slumped back against the dresser as Joey continued. "You are the best friend I've ever had. You're the brother I never knew I could have. God placed you in my life at a time when my world was out of control, and I am not about to walk away from you when yours is in trouble. Man, I've seen the pain you've been in, and my spirit is bleeding for you. But your pride is like a fortress hiding that pain."

"Joey, she threw me out! You heard her."

Joey shifted his weight forward. "This isn't about Mallory, Jake. This is about you and your brokenness. I've watched you all these months going through the motions of living, but in reality you're reacting to your pain, just like Mal was reacting to hers. It's time to stop reacting and make a decision based on your spirit, not your emotions."

"I am not reacting! I'm deciding."

"Boss, I know the way your old man treated you and your mom. It wasn't right."

Jake flinched and stalked to the other side of the room. "What does that have to do with anything?"

"Everything, man. I don't know what your childhood was like, but I know that your father gave you one heck of a warped image of what fatherhood is all about. And in the process he messed up your spiritual view of the heavenly Father, to the point that you see God the same way you saw your dad. With aloof contempt."

Joey's eloquence captured Jake's attention, and he squeezed his eyes shut. *I don't want to hear this.*

"God isn't like your dad, Jake."

Little arms lifted high. "Hold me, Daddy!"

Crack! *Pain avalanched against his cheek. "Go away, you little—"*

"God will never hurt you. Abandon you. Threaten you. He loves the little boy who got hurt. He wants so much to pull you into His lap and tell you how special you are. Man, I've seen you with your girls. The kind of daddy you are to them is the kind of daddy God wants to be with you."

Little arms rose before him. "Hold me, Daddy."

He swung his daughter high up in a circle, then pulled her into a tender hug. He kissed her soft cheek and nuzzled her neck. She laughed and wrapped her arms around his neck. "I love you, Daddy."

"That's what God's like with us all, but we have to let Him in. Please don't shut Jesus out, Jake."

Jesus. Joey spoke that name with such tenderness—such intimacy—that Jake shut his eyes to the pain pricking his soul. "When did my life get so out of control?" Tears welled up in his eyes. "What will I do without Mallory? She and the girls, my work—that's all I've ever cared about in this world."

"Maybe that's why they're being removed. Jesus doesn't want them to be the center of your universe."

"Jesus?" He spat the name. "Joey, Jesus never cared for me. Not ever."

"Maybe it's you that didn't care for Him."

"What's that supposed to mean?" *I wanted You to love me, God, but I could never gain Your love, Your ear, Your help! I just wasn't good enough.* "I prayed to Him. I asked Him to make my dad quit drinking, to keep my mom safe, to keep my child alive. He didn't." Jake hunched his shoulders and stared out the window. Out of the corner of his eye he caught Joey's reflection in the dresser mirror. The younger man leaned forward, and tears filled his blue eyes.

"God won't make people do what they don't want to do. He gave them a free choice. Your dad wouldn't listen to God. But your mom is safe now, and your baby boy is alive in the heart of the Father."

A chilling emptiness collided with the wall around Jake's heart. It cracked, bringing an avalanche of pain as Joey continued.

"I don't pretend to have all the answers. All I know is that God loves you. He loves you so much that He has stayed away from you until you were ready to hear the truth about Him. 'Cause He's a gentleman; He will never barge in where you don't want Him to be. But He moved heaven and earth and gave His Son's life to prove His love to you."

"Stop, Joey." Pain. He was tired of the pain. It sledgehammered against his heart, broke through the years of barriers he had erected, and drenched his soul.

"God loves you so much that He's allowed you to fall. Because He knows there's nowhere else to look except up, into His face."

Jake crumpled, wrapping his hands over the back of his head. All the boyhood terrors tidal-waved over him, and he sank to the floor and buried his head in his arms. "Oh, God, what do I do?"

Joey knelt beside Jake and wrapped his arm around his shoulder. "Just what you're doing, man. Let Him into those hurting areas. Let Him do a good work in you, Jake. Let Jesus into those places you've never trusted to anyone else."

Jake didn't know if he could. But he did know this much: He was tired of fighting.

September 2

I hate myself for wanting him back. He's the one that deserted me, so why do I feel bad about telling him to get out? He deserved it.

   But the girls need their daddy.

   All right…I need their daddy.

Twenty-Nine

"If I didn't know better, I'd say you were jealous."

Geoff couldn't believe he and Holly were arguing over his care and concern for his sister. Didn't she understand what Mal had been through?

They were in Geoff's spacious living room, although the argument had started on the way home from Mallory's. It was true that since Mal's hospital stay he and Holly had spent more time with Mallory and had less time alone, but she had to see why Geoff was protective of his sister.

"Geoff, I'm just saying that perhaps your…" She shook her head. "Well, I'll say it. Your hovering over your sister isn't good for her."

"Hovering?" Geoff's voice rose. "Hovering? What's that supposed to mean? I know there are only girls in your family, so maybe you don't understand a big brother's role in his sister's life. Big brothers are supposed to protect and help their sisters whenever and wherever they need it. After everything Mally has been through these last few months, she needs to know that I'm there for her, that I support her."

"She's a big girl, Geoff, and doesn't need you fussing. Supportive, there for her, yes. But be realistic. We've been over to her place four out of the last five nights, and I know you've been visiting her during the day as well. Don't you think that might be a little too much?" Holly's sherry-colored eyes had deepened to a darker hue. Her styled cut had been tossed by the wind as they drove in his convertible, and now she stood before him, hands on hips, her resolute stance reminding him of a banty rooster.

"You're just being unreasonable. I know you were disappointed we didn't go to dinner last Friday, but I told you, it was a bad day for Mal. She'd been to see her therapist—what's her name? Jennifer. It's a tough time for her."

"What about Jake?"

"Jake?"

"You know, Mallory's husband?" Holly's biting words twisted in Geoff's stomach.

"There's no need to be sarcastic."

Holly expelled a huge breath of air and paced toward the large glass doors leading to Geoff's deck. When she spoke again, her voice had evened out. "Jake and Mallory are struggling with their relationship. I'm simply suggesting that having her big brother there to fall back on—as wonderful as that might be—may not be the best for them. Not all the time."

Geoff's anger flared to life. "I love Jake like a brother, but you've commented on his attitude with Mal too." He began to pace now as well. His living room had never seemed small before, but at this moment he felt like a caged animal.

"I know he hasn't always been there for Mallory." Holly's fingers ran through her short, thick strands, fluffing her hair for a few seconds before it tumbled back into place against her forehead. "I'm just trying to get you to back off enough to give their relationship a chance. Give us a chance, Geoff."

Geoff swung toward her. He had always admired Holly's independent spirit, and he was grateful for the way she had fit into his family when they had all gotten together, but this was going too far.

"I don't see it's any of your business, Holly."

"Not my business?"

Now her feathers are ruffled. Despite the seriousness of the conflict, he allowed himself a small smile.

"Come on, Geoff, I thought we were building something here! Now you say that your family—a major part of your life—is none of my business?" Her words rose with her agitation. "If that's the kind of relationship you want, Geoff, you don't need me."

She lifted her chin, her back rigid, and tufts of her red hair stuck out above her ears. Geoff chuckled, but remorse rose in him when he saw the hurt hiding beneath her unyielding features. Before he could apologize and explain that she just looked so darn cute when she was mad, she snatched up her purse and slammed out the door.

Geoff's amusement faded as fast as it had risen. *Women!* He headed for the refrigerator and a can of cold refreshment. Settling on the couch with his feet propped on the glass-topped coffee table, he flipped the remote. NASCAR racing he could understand.

What did she want from him anyway? Maybe it was time to cut loose from this relationship. He had been intrigued when he met Holly. *Not my type* had been his first impression, but he had been drawn by the fact that she was different from the other women he had draped on his arm.

Geoff was no fool. While his looks might not hurt, it was his money that drew women to him. But that didn't seem to matter with Holly. He admired how natural she was. Holly was a refreshing change of pace, someone intelligent he could talk to.

But the very things that attracted him to her had begun to irritate him. Holly seemed to enjoy his family gatherings; she was even a good enough sport to put up with his mother. But there was involved, and there was *involved*—and whatever Holly and he had been building together, he had never intended it to interfere in his or his family's life.

Geoff lifted his can for another sip as he contemplated the blur of figures moving across his forty-six inch screen. If he broke it off with Holly, he would bear the brunt of his parents' disapproval again. *Nothing new.*

When, in his thirty-six years, had he ever had their full approval?

"Mommy, you're crying."

A gentle brush of tiny fingers caused Mallory to shudder and sniff back the ever-present tears. The tiny hand moved and patted Mallory's stomach. "Does it hurt? Will you have to go to the hos'ital again?"

Mallory drew Angel up onto the sofa beside her, hugging her tight before kissing the downy softness of her hair. "No, sweetheart, Mommy won't be going to the hospital again."

Angel snuggled close to her mother, nestling her head under Mallory's chin. She seemed so tiny. She needed constant reassurance that her mother wouldn't leave her.

Mallory thanked God for the gift of her precious daughters,

but her heart squeezed at the thought of their pain. Their already rocky world had crumbled again when Mallory had been hospitalized. The separation of their parents had been hard on both of the girls, but Angel was the one who struggled most with the uncertainty. Renee was older, of course, but Mallory wasn't going to try to kid herself that Renee could understand why their daddy didn't live with them anymore. She seemed to cling to the fact that he would be home soon, while Angel just seemed to cling.

Mallory hummed to her daughter and wrapped the afghan around both of them. Angel's warm body relaxed against her. She should wake her up to go to bed. Renee had gone to sleep hours ago, but when Angel had come downstairs complaining of a tummyache, Mallory had put on a video for her to watch. The antics of the cartoon characters still flickered across the screen, but Mallory couldn't dredge up the energy to turn off the TV and take Angel upstairs.

She inhaled the fresh, baby scent of the tiny form next to her. A fierce wave of determination swept over her. She wouldn't let anything—or anyone—harm her daughters. She wouldn't be like her—

Mallory crushed the fleeting thought. She wouldn't go down that road. Not tonight. Her tears had dried, at least on the outside. Mallory shut her eyes. Losing Jake was bad enough. She didn't have the energy to deal with wounds from her past that were as sharp as when they were first inflicted.

When would it end? So much pain. The girls…Jake…

She shifted to a more comfortable position on the couch. Her arm had gone numb, but she didn't want to let go of the bit of human warmth available to her right now. She needed the comfort as much as her daughter did.

Loneliness pervaded every corner of her being. She hadn't seen Jake since he had walked out of her hospital room. *All right, since I kicked him out.*

Well, what else could she do?

Mallory rubbed her forehead. Maybe he'd told the truth, maybe he couldn't get to her any sooner, but it was too little, too late. Thank God that Geoff had been there. She didn't know what she would do without him...

Jennifer's words from their last session echoed in her mind. "Is it possible that Jake feels slighted by your lack of trust in him?" Mallory closed her eyes. No, she didn't want to think about that, but the memory of Jennifer's voice was relentless. "The root cause here is trust. If you feel you can't trust Jake, who do you feel you can trust?"

Geoff. Only Geoff.

It was her brother she turned to for support. He had always been her best friend. Always. He was the one she could count on. To be there. To love her.

It wasn't the same as Jake, of course. She'd said as much to Jennifer.

"Of course. Nor should it be." Jennifer had been quiet a moment before continuing. "Mallory, can you see how turning to Geoff instead of Jake could make your husband feel cut off or shut out? As though you're holding him at arm's length? Emotionally, even physically?"

The words seared Mallory's conscience, but she shook the feelings away. Jennifer didn't understand. Nobody did. Geoff was the one who had always been there for her. He was the one she could turn to. From the time they were kids, he had been the only one who truly loved her. He had always been her knight in shining armor.

Mallory hadn't thought there was anything strange about that until Jennifer had asked her how she would feel if Jake described his sister, Jill, as the woman of his dreams. When she put it that way, it sounded unnatural. Her abdomen clenched, pulling on her incision. Guilt flooded through her.

"How would you feel if Jake's sister had been the first person Jake went to see after being away from home for two months? What if she had called Jake back from a weekend away with you so he could be with her when she went into labor?" Jennifer's words fell like hammer blows. "Would you mind his sister being at your home all hours of the day or night? Would you care if he turned to her first for understanding? For each joy and sorrow in his life?"

Realization struck with Jennifer's final questions. "What do you think Jake felt when you turned to your brother instead of him after confronting your parents about Eric? When you lied to him about the money you owed, then ran to Geoff to bail you out? When you refuse to answer Jake's phone calls, but clearly want Geoff at your beck and call?"

The truth pierced her, and tears streamed down Mallory's cheeks. She made no move to wipe them away. Not even the rhythmic breathing of her precious baby could console her now.

Father...what have I done?

September 7

It's easy to fool yourself into thinking your decisions don't affect anyone else—no one gets hurt, right? Wrong! I don't want to cheat, lie, or deceive anymore.

My spending is out of control. Father, help put this right.

How honest do I need to be, and with whom?

Thirty

Jake followed Joey from the dimness of the church into the bright September sun. The girls tumbled out behind them. Who'd have believed it...Jake Carlisle in church. Mallory would probably fall over if she saw her husband now, carrying a Bible.

"I can't believe you did it, boss."

"What are you talking about?" Jake herded his daughters ahead of him and shielded the back of an innocent bystander.

"Work, man. I can't believe you—"

"Daddy, can we stop at Burger Boy?" Renee spun around in a circle.

"No. We're going home. Mommy will have lunch ready for you." *And I need all the points I can get.*

"Pleeease!"

"No." Jake made a playful swat at her with his Bible. "But we can go past the drive-through and get you both a Burger Boy Slurpy." Compromise. He was learning.

"Yea!" She skipped to the car, calling after her sister as she did so. Jake caught up with Renee and Angel at the car and helped them both get buckled in. He turned to lean his shoulder against the door. "That preacher sure gives a guy something to think about." It was all so new. Jake had a lot to catch up on.

Joey pulled the keys out of his pocket and took a step backward toward his truck. "That's why I go there. Comin' to the picnic later?"

Jake shrugged. "Depends on how things go with Mallory. I guess now is as good a time as ever to tell her what's going on. I'll see you later."

It was true. He'd put off telling her long enough. The decisions he had made in the last several weeks were major, and she needed to know, because regardless of what happened in their marriage, it affected her. His heart banged against his ribs at the prospect of talking to Mallory about the changes he'd made. What would she think? Would it be the final blow to their marriage? He clenched his Bible. What had the pastor said? "Cast all your care upon Him." *Trust is tough for me, God. But I'm going to try.*

The flower beds around the house were a profusion of color. They'd been extended. Jake squinted against the sun. The brass bell wasn't in its normal spot near the front stoop.

"Make sure you change your clothes before you go out to play, and let Mommy know you're here." Jake closed the car door behind his rambunctious daughters. He sniffed the air. Someone was grilling. It made his mouth water. A thin trail of smoke traveled upward from behind his house. *Mal.* Jake stepped off the sidewalk, heading around to the patio. She was standing with her back to him. How should he make his presence known without scaring her?

He cleared his throat. "Smells wonderful." She jumped and he cringed. *Great. Here comes another battle.*

Mallory turned, a towel in her hands. "You startled me."

"I'm sorry." He fought to keep his arms from folding across his chest. Joey had pointed out that it was a defensive posture he tended to use.

"It's not your fault. I know you didn't mean to."

Mallory? He raised a brow and moved toward the deck. "Just wanted you to know the girls are upstairs changing their clothes. They had a good time at church." He rested his foot on the bottom step and leaned an arm against his knee. "So did I."

She was wearing a pair of cut-off shorts and a white tank top in an effort to win the war against the heat. Her hair was pulled back into a ponytail, exposing the creamy expanse of her neck. Jake looked away. When he looked back, she was staring at him.

"Did you just say, church?"

His smile expanded to a grin. "Yeah. I've been going for the last two weeks. Joey's got a great church."

A warm glow extinguished the surprise in her eyes. "Good for you, Jake."

Mallory was happy. He hadn't felt that warm tension curling through him for months… Hope rose in his heart. Maybe there was still—

"Can I ask you a favor?"

Ask me anything. Ask me to come home.

"Go check on the girls. I don't want the burgers to burn."

"Sure." He vaulted up the steps and slid past her to the glass doors. She smelled of vanilla and barbecue. *Intoxicating.*

His steps clattered on the kitchen tile. Nothing had changed in here, but nothing seemed the same either. Jake stopped and frowned. No. Something was different. He turned and scrutinized the kitchen. What was it? His artistic eye focused on the sparseness of the room. Her collection of Longaberger baskets was gone. His frown deepened. Where were they? She must have moved them to another room.

He peeked in the dining room. Not there. The dark mahogany table and chairs, along with the china hutch, remained the dominant feature in the room. Jake moved out to the hall and started up the steps. He paused. Something was different here as well. What was it? He turned back down the steps to the end of the hall. The huge brass lighthouse was missing. So was the smaller collection of seascapes. In their place was a mural of a trellis framing a garden path. He smiled. He liked it. It lightened up the small dark space.

Jake jogged up the stairs to find his girls in the middle of a pillow fight. "Hey! That's enough. Get your clothes changed, and come back downstairs. Mommy has lunch just about ready." His children had the grace to look ashamed, and Jake turned away to hide his smile.

"The girls are fine," he said as he came back outside. "They're still changing their clothes." He perched on the end of the picnic table. "I see you've made some changes."

Mallory laid the spatula aside and pulled the lid down on the grill. "A few. Nothing major."

"Where'd you put the bell? In one of the flower beds? I didn't see it." Jake moved to the deck railing and leaned out to look around the back of the house.

"No. It's not in any of the flower beds." Mallory slid the screen door open.

He turned and hiked up his foot on the deck railing. "I like the mural in the hallway." He called out so she could hear him from the kitchen.

"Thanks." Her voice was muffled. "I like it too."

"What did you do with the lighthouse?" He tried to keep the

tone of his voice light, conversational, but he was itching to know why she had made the changes. Silence. Had she left the kitchen? No, he saw her figure through the glass. Maybe she hadn't heard him

Mallory returned with a bowl of potato chips and a glass of iced tea along with an envelope, which she handed to Jake.

"What's this?" He held it in his hands.

"Open it, please." She twisted her hands together.

Jake lifted his eyes to study her. She slid her hands along the back of her shorts. She was nervous. *What's going on?* He hoped it wasn't one of those situations where he was going to learn about trust the hard way.

He hopped down, set his glass on the table, then flipped the plain, white envelope over and over in his hands. *Please, Jesus, don't let it be divorce papers...*

"Mallory?" His voice quivered and he cleared his throat.

"Just open it."

He ripped the end open and upended it in his hands. Pieces of plastic landed in his palm, along with several receipts. His eyes slid up her body to examine her face.

"I don't understand."

"I sold the lighthouse."

"What?" He was confused. She loved it, why would she sell it?

"I've been seeing a credit counselor."

"Credit counselor?" What was she talking about?

Mallory nodded. "Jake, I was in serious trouble."

His heart began to hammer. "What kind of trouble?"

"Let me just get this off my chest. It's been eating a hole in me for a long time."

Jake crossed his arms, realized he had taken a defensive position, unfolded them and tucked his hands in his pockets. *I can handle this. Make that we can handle this. You and me, Lord. Please.*

"Besides the debt I amassed on our cards, I've had two other credit cards in my name and three other checking accounts that you knew nothing about."

"Three checking accounts?" Jake looked at the cut-up cards.

"My spending was…a little out of control."

"Why did you need three checking accounts?" Had he missed something here? Someone had fast-forwarded the conversation, and he had missed the punch line.

Mallory lifted the lid of the grill and a billow of smoke rolled out. "I was writing checks from one account and depositing them in another, trying to cover my expenses." She flattened the patties with the spatula, and grease ignited against the coals. Flames engulfed the meat.

Mal? Kiting checks? "But that's…that's a criminal offense. They could have put you in jail. Are you crazy?"

He wanted to grab the comment back as soon as it escaped, but she just smiled.

"I know. There is no excuse. I guess I was addicted to shopping the way your dad was addicted to alcohol. And, like with alcohol, my relief was only temporary."

Jake paced the length of the deck. "I can't believe this." When had all this happened? The answer stopped him in his tracks: *While I was gone. On the run.*

"I'm facing it now. I've closed out all the accounts, except one. And I don't use any credit cards."

"But, Mallory…" Realization was setting in. His heart sank.

What was he going to do? He had already made his decision. A decision he hadn't shared with her. *Okay, Lord. Now what?*

"Those receipts I gave you—the cut-up credit cards—those are my way of saying I'm taking responsibility for what I've done. It's going to take awhile, but we'll be all right. I'm on a budget."

He swallowed. Here went nothing…or everything. "A budget won't do us any good, Mallory." He met her slight frown. "I quit my job."

September 26

Lord, I know you wash away sin, but what about shame? It runs so
deep. It's like being sprayed by a skunk—the stink doesn't wash off.
    You can't scrub it off either.
    Will I ever be free from it?

Thirty-One

The leaves of the trees were beginning to turn color. Those that slapped against the pastor's study window were yellow at the edges.

School had started. Mallory felt ancient. Yesterday she had found a gray hair. Time had overtaken her and threatened to leave her behind.

She crossed her legs and eased back into the padded seat of her chair. She had been seeing Pastor James and Yvonne to answer some of her spiritual questions…questions that had plagued her since she disclosed her childhood abuse. Today they had been talking about dealing with her anger at Jake and her frustrations with their relationship. Several times they had discussed forgiveness.

She wasn't sure, though, how they had gotten to this present topic. "Did you say *soul ties?* What's that?"

"It's a term sometimes used to describe what can happen spiritually when two people are joined physically." Pastor James swiveled in his chair and put his elbows on his desk.

Mallory felt heat surge to her cheeks. What a thing to discuss with your pastor! But his voice was serious and matter-of-fact.

"The physical union was God's design. Marriage is much more than a physical union, of course, but when God declares that *the two shall become one flesh,* that's what happens." He shook his head and gave her a slight smile. "I won't try to make you believe I understand all of what that entails, but I believe it."

A sympathetic hand patted hers as she threatened to punch a hole in the vinyl armrest with her fingernails. Yvonne Gates was tiny enough to fold her legs up into her own vinyl chair. It amazed Mallory that she could sit still for any length of time. She buzzed circles around the women at the church, but Mallory had discovered that she listened with equal intensity. "It's an emotional and spiritual bond, not just a physical one."

Mallory frowned. "I'm not sure I understand."

Pastor James leaned back in his chair and pressed the tips of his fingers together. "I often think of the words *what God hath joined together, let no man put asunder.* I don't think man can put it asunder if God has sealed the relationship. I think man has the mistaken idea that sex was his invention, not God's." The pastor's deep chuckle filled the small office. "Human sexual intimacy goes beyond just the sex act itself. Animals mate, but God created man in his own image, and so we are on a different plane than a mere animal."

"It's man— Excuse me, honey." Yvonne gave her husband a quick wink and looked at Mallory. "It's man and *woman* that pervert God's design. The spiritual and emotional bonding that takes place during the physical act is a gift from God. A man leaves his mother, and a woman leaves her home. That's the breaking of the bond of the parental and family ties. When a man cleaves to his wife, that's the bonding we're talking about. That's what God desires for you and Jake."

"The word in the original language means *adhering* or *being joined together.*"

"Sort of stuck like glue?" Yvonne laughed at her husband, who smiled despite the seriousness of their discussion.

Mallory's mind was whirling. "Okay. I think I understand what you're trying to say, but imagining Jake and me getting to that point is difficult."

"What do you think is blocking that?"

Mallory pondered Yvonne's question for several moments before she replied. "It seems we're striking out on all counts—spiritual, emotional, and physical." Mallory scooted further back into her chair. "I think Jake is trying to deal with my past, but…" She struggled to express what she was having trouble defining in her own mind.

"I think you'll find that your past will be something you'll always have to deal with, because it affects every area of your life. It may even be a large part of the problem with your relationship with Jake."

Pastor James nodded in agreement. "There can be blocks in our relationships, not only with people but often with God. The Bible talks a lot about this matter of joining ourselves. It's serious business. We're warned in Proverbs about joining ourselves to a harlot. When we put our faith in Christ, the Holy Spirit then resides in us, and our bodies are no longer our own."

"Oh." Mallory's body stilled. She could feel her blood inching along her veins. Time had slowed to milliseconds. It was several moments before she could respond with a question. "Does that…I mean, are you"—she took a deep breath—"can you be joined or bonded or whatever to more than one person?" Mallory couldn't still the tremor that went through her.

Pastor James tapped his finger on his desk blotter. "It's possible that any physical union"—he held up his hand—"setting aside for a moment all the ramifications when sin is involved, can be a soul tie. God intended that in a physical union, a man and a woman would be joined together as one flesh."

Mallory turned as Yvonne added in a soft voice, "I think you can have a soul tie with anyone you are physically joined to. God created us that way. Maybe that's what lies at the key to your emotional distance from Jake."

"It's not a mystical thing, Mallory. A mystery, yes, because we don't understand all of God's ways. But the term *soul tie* is used to describe God's means of uniting us together."

"But…well, are you attached for life or what?" Eric's image haunted her.

"That's what we're talking about. You can't cleave only unto your husband if you are already bonded to someone else."

"But what do I do?" Mallory shuddered, and Yvonne took her hand.

"You can pray." There was gentle pressure on Mallory's fingers. "We believe that God can break those soul ties so that you can be free of the past, and your relationship with your husband can be without barriers."

"We often find it's a way to break the shame barriers as well."

Her tears came without warning. Yvonne took Mallory's hand, and Pastor James stepped from behind his desk to kneel beside her. His hand was a firm, comforting presence on her shoulder. Her sobs filled the room. Mallory didn't even know why she was crying, but the release was immediate and immense.

* * *

"Have you ever heard of praying for soul ties to be broken?"

Mallory wasn't sure of the response to expect from Jennifer. It was all she had been thinking about since the conversation in the pastor's study.

Her therapist's eyes widened a fraction, then a smile chased across her rounded features. "Yes, I have, but where did you hear about it?"

"My pastor. The last time I met with him and his wife."

"Go on," Jennifer urged when Mallory dropped her head in her hands.

"I don't want to be attached like that!"

"Mallory, look at me." Jennifer waited until Mallory lifted her head. "Look me in the eye." It took every bit of Mallory's courage to do so.

"The shame isn't yours."

She was flooded with tears once again. "You don't understand."

"Explain it to me."

Mallory attempted to laugh, reaching for the tissue box on the table beside her. "All I ever do is cry."

"You have a lot to grieve over. Someone you trusted betrayed you and hurt you. It was his sin—"

"You…don't…understand." The words were wrenched from her.

Jennifer closed her notebook and laid it to the side of her chair. "Tell me, Mallory."

"Gotcha! You're it, princess. Come on. Betcha can't get me. Naa-nanna-naa."

Her big brother chased around her, turning her in circles, and Mallory laughed. She'd show him! Her little legs pumped as hard as they could, and she slammed into his thighs. He laughed and fell hard, taking her down with him.

Mallory giggled. She got him! His chest jiggled beneath her, making her laugh harder. He began to tickle her sides and she rolled off of him. He always made her laugh. Eric was wonderful. He was big and strong and helped her with everything.

His hands went to her belly and lifted her shirt. "Don't do the raspberry, Eric!" She rolled away from him, and he grabbed her, pulling her back to him. "Okay, okay! I give up!" His lips vibrated on her bare tummy, and she giggled again. He moved his lips around in a circle, razzing her again and again. It tickled. She pushed against him, and he rolled over, pulling her with him. Her legs straddled his tummy and she bounced up and down. "Yea! I win. I win. I got you now."

His hands moved against her leg and it felt warm. Good. "I love you, Eric."

"I love you, too, princess. You know that, don't you? I would never hurt you."

"Eric…" She moved away from his hand, but he put it back. Her eyes widened. "Wha…what're you doing?"

"Shh, it's okay, princess."

"Shh. It's okay."

The gentle words pulled Mallory from her memory, and she realized Jennifer was beside her, stroking her hair away from her face, holding her. Mallory leaned into her shoulder, hiding her face.

"Can you tell me what happened?"

The words were lodged in the deepest crevices of her innermost being. "I remembered—"

"You remembered something just now?"

Mallory nodded and began to cry again. Ripping the words out by the roots was less painful than trying to keep them hidden any longer. Her face flamed, but once started, she couldn't stop the confession. "It's not Eric's sin I'm worried about. It's mine. It's mine."

The agony of the truth consumed her. "I wanted it. I liked it. Dear God, I might have even asked him for it."

She was engulfed in a fierce hug. "It's okay, Mallory. It's going to be okay."

As her shuddering sobs subsided, Mallory felt a strange mixture of shame and relief. "I'm sick. But maybe now I can get help."

"You need help, Mallory, but you aren't sick." When Jennifer saw Mallory had composed herself, she moved back to her seat.

"I think you should buy stock in tissues. If your other clients are as weepy as me, you could make a killing."

Jennifer laughed, but her gaze never wavered from Mallory's. More than anything, Mallory wanted to run and hide. In the months since she had started therapy, she had discovered that was one thing Jennifer would never allow her to do. Her counselor prodded, nudged, cajoled, did whatever was needed to draw the truth from Mallory, but she never let her hide.

"You do the work yourself, you know."

Mallory stared at her. "How do you do that?"

"Do what?"

"Read my mind!"

"Would you believe me if I said your face is an open book?"

Jennifer grew serious. "Mallory, don't put me on a pedestal. I'm not God. I don't work miracles. I haven't done the work. You have."

Mallory nodded her head but wasn't sure she agreed.

"Let's talk about this." Jennifer's pen scratched on her yellow notepad. "This flashback you just had…what was it?"

In halting words, Mallory described the scene.

"How old were you when that abuse happened?"

Mallory sat up straight. "Abuse? But I just told you that I liked it—"

Jennifer held up her hand. "We'll get to that. How old were you"—Jennifer paused until Mallory looked at her—"when this abuse happened?"

"Seven."

"And Eric, how old was he?"

"Thirteen. Just a kid. He didn't hurt me, not then. Later I made him angry, and he…" Mallory drew in a shuddering sob. "It's my fault."

"Mallory."

"What?"

"How old is Marty?"

"He's twelve, but wh— Oh." Mallory blinked hard and forced herself to say it. "But it wasn't like later, when he hurt me." She dropped her head into her hands. "I told you I-I liked it." *It was my fault!*

"We're looking at two sides of the same coin here. Just a different cause-and-effect, if you will." Jennifer waited for Mallory to look up. "Violent abuse will often produce anger, while coercion produces shame."

Mallory shut her eyes. Shame. She knew all about that.

"Mallory, do you believe God created our bodies?"

"Yes." At last, a question with an easy answer.

"Do you believe he designed sex to be pleasurable?"

Mallory squirmed. Not so easy. "Well…"

Jennifer smiled. "Believe it or not, our bodies were designed to experience pleasure during the sexual act. Physical union is God's idea. Done His way, it is an incredible, wonderful gift. Desire and pleasure, our bodies responding the way God intended them to—that, Mallory, is no cause for shame."

"But—"

"You don't have any control over your body's physical responses, any more than if somebody stuck pepper under your nose and you sneezed."

"But…but I *wanted* it." The words—the shame—stuck in her throat.

"Isn't that the point? He wanted you to respond, to manipulate you into having sex with him. At thirteen I would say he knew better. Marty's in the detention center. He's the offender. We don't blame the little girl; it wasn't her fault. Why is it any different for you and Eric?"

Mallory didn't answer. She could see what Jennifer was getting at, but knowing it in her head and feeling it in her heart were two different things. The guilt she had carried for so long was not so easy to erase.

"Man often twists what God intended for good, but it doesn't have to stay twisted." Jennifer tapped her pen against the notebook on her lap. "God can take what man tries to pervert—what man intends for evil—and make it good. Remember that verse I gave you? The one that talked about shame being turned into honor?

That's not something we do, but what God does for us. If we let Him."

Mallory shook her head. Wasn't that too much to ask of a holy God, to somehow forgive what she had done and make her whole…clean again?

October 5

"For I was envious of the boastful, when I saw the prosperity of the wicked.... When I thought how to understand this, it was too painful for me—until I went into the sanctuary of God; then I understood their end" (Psalm 73:3,16-17).

Thirty-Two

A solitary gull dipped its wing toward the surface of the lake and gave a shrill cry before it tilted its wing once again and swooped upward. The breeze had freshened, and Mallory pulled up the collar of her jacket. The sun slid lower in the sky.

She closed her eyes. She had smelled the water long before she had arrived at the lake. She loved it here. In the past, she and Jake had rented a cabin just down the shore from where she stood. The memories of those times together both warmed and saddened her.

She had driven up alone today. She needed time to think. Time to pray. It had been difficult to tell the girls they couldn't come, but she had to do this for herself.

For them too, she decided, and made her way along the rockstrewn shoreline. Where had the summer gone? There were few people left at the island on Lake Erie. Only year-rounders and some like herself who desired the solitude.

The isolation was a haven, a respite from the chaos of her life. She had choices—decisions—to make, and she needed to get away to do that. Usually she was an avid beachcomber, but today she shuffled through the dried bulrushes and kicked at the driftwood lying in her path. Finally she found a sheltered cove and tugged a large fallen limb next to the eroded cliff. She sat on the log, leaning back against the sandy outcropping.

Her thoughts were jumbled, confused. *It seems like I've been confused most of my life!* One more thing to attribute to her childhood, Jennifer said.

Jennifer had given her much to think about. So had the session with Pastor James and Yvonne. Mallory was at a crossroads, and she knew it.

Pastor James had reminded her that she needed to make decisions based on what God said, not what she felt. The crux of the matter now was Jake.

And Geoff.

Eric seemed to have made his own choices.

Restless, Mallory stood and began to walk along the water's edge. This stretch of the island was dotted with summer cottages, empty now that the season was over. It was too cool to walk in the water, but Mallory loved being at the edge of its great expanse. She halted and looked out at the horizon.

The waves had increased their motion, and whitecaps dotted a choppy line along the shore. Dusk came earlier now, and the wind picked up even more as sunset approached. It was Mallory's favorite time of day. Something about the strength of the wind, its bracing purity, gave her courage to hope.

God, what do I do now? She was sure God would answer, but was she ready to hear His words? Deciding to do right was easy; doing it was another matter. The waves lapped at her feet, and she watched the relentless water. She spotted an unusual stone and reached for it, rolling it over in her hands, rubbing its surface with her thumb.

She'd never given much consideration to the rocks on this beach. The multitude of pebbles was just a backdrop to the scenery.

There were so many that in some places very little sand could be seen. She turned the stone in her hand and examined it. One edge was rough, with sharp angles and planes, but the other side looked as if someone had sanded it, blunting the jagged points.

I'm like that. Tossed and tumbled by life, with the friction of adversity rubbing against her like the gritty grains of sand that had worn down these edges. Mallory picked up another stone, this one smooth all the way around, polished by the silky water and the tumbling friction of the sand. She rubbed its softness against her cheek.

Could God do that with her life? Take all the rough edges and smooth them? Could the very things that hurt her be what God used to shape her? She weighed the stones, one in each hand. The rock with the uneven edges needed to go back in the water, to be buffeted by waves and sand until it, too, was sleek and without blemish. The polished stone would just continue to be perfected.

How long would it take for the sharp edges to be worn down, for the stone to be finished? The apostle Paul had promised the Philippian believers that "He who has begun a good work in you will complete it until the day of Jesus Christ." Could that be true for her, too?

Mallory bounced the unfinished stone in her hand, then reached back as far as she could and flung it out over the crashing waves, watching it arc in the air and drop into the water. The other stone she put in her pocket, rubbing its glassy surface between her thumb and finger. She turned back along the shore toward her car.

She had made her decision.

October 11

"Not by might nor by power, but by My Spirit, says the LORD of Hosts"
(Zechariah 4:6).

    Strength—power—control. These I have gained as I submitted
myself to God's strength—power—and control. I still don't know how
He redeemed my shame, my weakness, my powerlessness…but He has.
He is beautiful beyond description, and I only want to know Him
more intimately.

Thirty-Three

Mallory picked up a box of toys to move from the garage steps to the folding table. The brightness of the sun's rays made the shadows in the garage even darker, and she paused to roll her shoulder, wiping away the sweat that trickled down her temple. They had almost everything sorted for the auction. She'd been ruthless; she had to be.

She dropped the box on the table and sorted through the stuffed animals. New. All of them. She remembered how she'd vow to use the hidden surplus for gift giving, but always found something new she had to have. So many things she didn't need. *All to numb the hurt and appease the hunger.* What a waste. She went back for another box.

"Baby, you aren't supposed to be lifting anything heavy yet."

Baby. Am I your baby, Daddy? Pain collided with a surge of peace. She knew whose child she was. *"When my father and my mother forsake me, then the Lord will take care of me."*

Her father came and lifted the box from her arms. "Where do you want it?"

She motioned to the one spot on the table that was still empty. "Thanks, Daddy."

"You're working too hard. Let me carry the boxes. Or wait for Geoff, he should be here soon. You're supposed to just be directing the work crew, remember?" He brushed the back of his fingers against her chin.

Oh, Daddy.

"Mallory? Are you all right?"

Would he answer if she asked? Did she even have the courage to ask? Mallory folded the top of the box together and tucked in the corners. "D-dad? Why didn't you believe me?"

"Believe you about what?"

Mallory looked at him, and hesitated. Beads of moisture had popped out on his forehead. He used his handkerchief to mop his face and smiled at her.

"Eric." The word came out soft, choked, full of sadness. *Why, Daddy?*

The smile melted away. "I…Mallory…I'm so sorry." His eyes closed. "I couldn't." He looked at her, and stark pain etched a fine line between his brows. "I guess I didn't want it to be true. And if it was…"

He turned toward the open garage door and the brisk fall air. He stood with his back to her, his hands clenched into fists. "And if it was true, then I was afraid I might kill him."

"Daddy…" Mallory stepped toward him just as he turned to face her.

"I was wrong, and I am so sorry! If I had—"

The door to the kitchen banged, and Mallory jumped. Her mother carried a box of crystal from the house. "Why you chose to have this auction so close after your surgery is beyond your father and me. Why didn't you tell us you were having financial trouble?"

Her father took the box of glassware as her mother shifted it into his arms. He looked at Mallory and gave a slight shake of his head.

She recognized the pleading in his eyes. He needn't worry. *I won't tell her, Daddy.* She followed her mother back into the house.

"What's up? Are you moving?"

Geoff toed a box as he threaded his way through the minefield of clutter overflowing every flat surface of the driveway and garage. "Dad called and said you needed help with some heavy lifting."

"Just getting ready for an auction." She turned to another box. This one was filled with small porcelain pieces. Geoff had been called out of town three short weeks after her surgery. During that time she had dealt with her spending addiction and…

The other she didn't want to think about. But Geoff was here, so she knew it was coming.

She watched him run his finger over the bronze eagle. Of all the things going into the auction, that one hurt the most. But it would bring in the most money. The other bronze pieces would too, no doubt. They were Callie Foster's work.

"What auction?" Geoff settled into a brand-new deck chair and folded his arms. "Just cleaning out the house and getting rid of old stuff you no longer want?" He swiveled his head at all the boxes piled around him.

"Not old stuff, but stuff I no longer need." Mallory took a deep breath. She had to tell him sometime. "I need the money."

"Well, why didn't you say so?" Geoff reached into his dark blue jacket. "How much?" He clicked his silver pen.

Mallory sighed and shoved her hands into the back pocket of

her jeans. "I don't want your money." *Don't you get it? I need to stand on my own.*

"If you're in a financial bind, I can't stand by and do nothing to help you out. Now how much do you need?"

"No." He paused in writing, and she continued, "I appreciate the offer, but the problem is mine, not yours. And so is the solution."

His head snapped up, and those blue-green eyes seared her soul with the hurt and confusion she saw there. She shoved against the guilt. *Geo, I have to do this.*

"Mally, I have more than I need. I don't see what the problem is."

"I know." She knelt down at his feet on the cold cement and took his large hand in hers. "Oh, Geoff, can't you see? I've taken so much from you in the past that it's become a problem for me. You've always been there for me, and I love you for that. But I can't keep running to you every time I have a problem." *Please, Lord, give me the words.* "I have to start fixing my own problems. You can't keep doing it for me."

"Since when is helping someone you love a problem?"

She drew a steadying breath. She had to tell him the truth. "When you never let that person grow up and make choices, or mistakes, or take responsibility for their actions."

He pulled his hand away. "Is that your shrink talking?"

Mallory smiled. "Truth is truth, no matter where it comes from."

Geoff bolted from his chair. "I still don't see what this has to do with my helping you!" He weaved his way through the boxes and leaned his shoulder against the back door of the garage.

It stood open, letting a breeze through the heated garage. The maple trees in her backyard had deposited colorful mounds of red, gold, and orange. The girls had made a lopsided pile of the leaves to jump in. They were with Jake today, and right at that moment Mallory wished she were with them.

Anywhere but here.

"It's taken most of my therapy to face this truth, Geo." His back stiffened, and her stomach constricted. *What if this destroys our relationship? Who will I turn to? Geoff's the only one...*

No. She had the Lord. And she had to face this. As did Geoff.

"I loved you so much growing up. You were my best friend, and in so many ways you still are. But Geoff, our relationship isn't any healthier than the one I have with Eric."

Geoff spun around, and the fury in his face slapped at her. "There's no way you can compare me to Eric! I would never hurt you. I love you. You know that!"

"It's not a matter of love, it's a matter of facing the truth, of taking responsibility for our own actions and letting go of the family secrets that have held us in bondage all these years."

"I wasn't the one abused."

"But it's affected everyone in our family. It's twisted us, and we all need to look at it."

Geoff slammed his fist against the drywall, rattling the bicycles hanging on hooks from the ceiling. "This is all Eric's fault!"

"This has nothing to do with Eric. It has to do with you and me." With all of her being, Mallory longed to comfort him, but she knew she had to be honest about their relationship. Somehow the abuse had warped it. Geoff wanted to do everything for her, and she was too willing to let him. "Geoff, you can't protect me from life."

"I should have protected you from Eric!"

"That wasn't your job."

"Yes, it was. I didn't protect Shelly, and I didn't protect you."

What's he talking about?

Geoff paced the garage. In his agitation, he had ruffled his hair, and the tail of his shirt was sticking out. A dark smudge stood out against the knee of his tan pants, where he'd brushed against the grease in the doorway.

"Eric blames me for Shelly's death, and he's right. I killed her." His cry came out half sob, half yell.

"Geoff?" Was he crying? Mallory put her hand on his bent back.

"I should have stayed. Dad told me to take care of her. I left, and she died."

Geoff's words at Christmas came back to her with startling clarity: *"I think we all blame ourselves for her death."*

Oh, Geo, no wonder you never talked about her.

"Is that why you've always taken care of me?" Mallory whispered as she wrapped her arms around his broad back.

"I told Eric to watch her. I wanted to come home. He said he wouldn't, that she was my responsibility, that Dad had given me the job of watching her. He went up the hill…and I just left. I left her!"

"Geoff, Shelly's death wasn't your fault. It wasn't anybody's. It was an accident. You aren't responsible for carrying the entire burden of our family. It's not yours to carry. That belongs to God. And I've got to let God help me handle my life, not you."

Geoff straightened. "Are you saying you don't want me to be a part of your life?" The rims of his eyes were red, and his strong jaw jutted out at her.

"No! That's not what I'm saying. I just need a little distance and some time to rebuild my life."

"Without me in it?"

He looked like a lost little boy, and she hugged herself to keep from backing down. *Oh, Geo, don't you see? I have to do this.* She made her answer as gentle as she could, knowing it could never be gentle enough. "Just for a little while." He blinked, and she knew he hadn't expected her to say that. The blow hit him hard, and she wanted to grab back the words, but it was too late.

Geoff studied her face, then turned and walked away.

He's really leaving. She was frozen in place until he slammed his car door shut, then she ran after him. She couldn't let him go like this.

"Geoff?"

He looked up, his expression stone-faced, giving nothing away.

"I love you."

He hesitated, gave her a silent nod, then drove away.

October 19

Father!

I have heard You speak. Although the words weren't audible, I know they came from You.

"O Beloved,

"You have released your healing into My hands. Accept the gentle caress of the Holy Spirit upon your soul. Accept My gift of sweet forgiveness as you reach out in forgiveness to others.

"You have accomplished much. You have walked through difficult places and persevered. Though hard days may be ahead, the hardest are behind you. You have been diligent in accepting truth and confessing lies. You have been obedient when it would have been easier to rebel.

"You, beloved, have learned to trust Me! You have received My grace, you have offered My mercy to those who hurt you. Do you hear My joy? Listen with your heart. It beats with Mine."

Thirty-Four

Jake looked up at the sound of the sharp rap on the apartment door and made a mad scramble to catch the box of slides as it skidded across the table and teetered on the edge. He shoved them back against the light box, laid his magnifying loupe next to a stack of papers, and called out, "Coming!" as another knock sounded through the room. He studied the slide on the examining box one last time and stripped off his cotton gloves, sprinting to answer the door.

"Mallory! I didn't…I wasn't expecting you."

She tucked her hair behind her ears. Her features were soft and open. He couldn't believe she was here. "Can I can I come in? Or are you busy?"

"I was culling some of my pictures. Getting them ready to present to a client."

"Oh, well, then I won't bother you. I know how time-consuming that can be." Her glance fell away from him, and she turned to leave, but not before he saw the disappointment sweep across her face.

Jake touched her shoulder. "You're not bothering me." Her eyes roamed over him, and he kept his smile fixed. "Come on in."

"Are you sure?" To answer, he stepped back to allow her to enter.

She stopped just inside and looked around. "Joey has a nice place."

Despite Joey's lack of inhibitions and sloppy wardrobe, he did keep an immaculate apartment. Jake's work, spread out over the large oak table, was the only disarray.

"Joey's not here right now. He said he had to run some errands."

"I know. One of his stops was to see me. He made it very clear that he would be gone the rest of the morning." She turned back toward Jake and brushed her bangs off her forehead.

She had regained some of her lost weight, and her figure was a perfect fit in her stonewashed jeans. The pale green cashmere sweater brought out the color in her eyes. Her hair was longer now and curly. But what Jake reacted to wasn't anything physical or tangible. It was something deeper, though he couldn't distinguish what it was.

He inhaled and caught the scent of his favorite perfume.

She settled on the overstuffed couch as he perched on the edge of the matching chair. Once more, her eyes drifted over the room. "Where do you sleep?"

A smile played along the corner of his mouth. "You're sitting on it. The couch pulls out into a bed." He gestured behind her. "The kitchen's back there. And Joey's room is over there." He pointed off to the right. "He has a spare room, but it's filled with his—well, our gear, for now. Would you like something to drink?" He was halfway up before she responded.

"No, nothing for me. I drank my fill at Heather's before I came here." A long pause filled the air. As one, their voices broke in on each other.

"Jake."

"Mal."

He shifted and rested his arms on his knees. "You go first."

"It's a beautiful day. Would you like to go for a walk with me?"

Anywhere. There was a warm light in the depths of her eyes, and a tremor coursed through him. What would she tell him? "I'd like that." He stood and grabbed his jacket off the coat tree by the door. He waited until she had moved out in the hall, then closed the door and stepped out beside her.

Thick, white clouds played tag in the cobalt blue sky. Sunshine spilled its warmth through the tangled, bare branches of the trees. Autumn had painted the hillsides in rich, vivid color. Mallory's and Jake's footsteps kicked up leaves and sent them swirling down the path. The wind lifted and teased their hair as it danced over them. The faint sound of children's voices shouting and laughing drifted on the breeze.

Jake fell into step beside Mallory, allowing her to set the pace and the direction of their outing. They traveled several blocks, down tree-lined streets, past homes and storefronts, in silence.

"Let's sit over here." Jake pressed his hand into the small of Mallory's back and steered her toward a small duck pond. She sat down and gathered a handful of gravel, then tossed the pea stones one by one into the dark green water.

Jake sent a smooth, flat stone skipping across the mirrorlike surface. Ripples coursed outward and sent water lapping onto the shore.

"You were always good at that. What's your record anyway?"

Jake squinted against the glare of sunlight refracting off the water. "Six skips. I beat out Evan Braxton. We had a bet on who would take you to the Christmas dance."

"You what?"

He grinned. "I loved you more. I tried harder. I sacrificed my lucky flint to the murky depths of Salter's Pond for you, and it didn't fail me."

Her sparkling laughter eased his tense muscles.

"Well then, God was listening. I prayed that you would ask me before Evan did." Mallory's laughter died. "I've never been sorry I said yes to you, Jake. I've never regretted our marriage." Mallory shoved her hands in her pockets and took a deep breath. "I need to ask your forgiveness."

Had he heard her right? Jake shifted his feet. "There's nothing to forgive."

"Jake"—Mallory held his gaze—"there's plenty that needs forgiveness in our relationship. I'm asking you to forgive me for all the ways I failed you, the ways I failed our marriage commitment. I thought you had abandoned me, but I see now how many times I pushed you away. I realize how unhealthy I've been for years and how that has damaged us."

Tears thickened in Jake's throat. As much as he had longed to hear her say those words, it was hard to see her so vulnerable. When he started to speak, she stopped him.

"Hear me out." Mallory had turned to watch the ducks gliding across the pond. "This is hard, but it needs to be said, so don't say anything until I get it out, okay?" He smiled and nodded his encouragement for her to continue.

After a quick look in his direction, Mallory went on. "Geoff and I were always close, I guess because after Shelly died, our family became so splintered. He has always been there for me. He felt he had to protect me, and I needed that protection."

Her head bowed, and Jake had to lean forward to catch her next words. He longed to hold her, to tell her it would be all right, but he kept his hands in his pockets. "Jake, I realize now that I defrauded you. I cheated you out of what was yours."

He looked away as a single tear slipped down her cheek, but he made himself look back, made himself connect physically with her pain, her vulnerability.

"Jake, I'm sorry I gave my trust to Geoff instead of you. I even trusted him above God. I know it sounds crazy, but to me it was just normal." Mallory touched his arm. "I didn't realize how unhealthy a relationship it was."

He shook his head. "He's your brother…"

"I shared with him what I should have shared with you. I turned to him when I should have been leaning on you. I told him I was pregnant with Renee before I told you. I asked him for advice on whether to leave the art gallery and go to the publishing house. I called him about fights with Mom and Dad and borrowed that money from him. I was shredding the fabric of our marriage every time I turned to Geoff instead of you."

It made a certain kind of sense, he supposed. Jake remembered being on the road once, and Renee had cut her hand, requiring twelve stitches. He hadn't found out about it until he'd gotten home. "You were gone, what could I do?" Mal had said, pointing out that Geoff was closer, claiming she couldn't remember the number Jake had given her for his hotel.

She was being more honest than he could ever remember. Could he do any less? "I've always liked Geoff, but I admit there have been times I've wished him to the farthest reaches of the earth. I just never understood why I felt jealous. It seemed so stupid."

"It's not stupid at all. The emotional support I got from Geoff took the place of what I should have let you give me. Somehow, the healthy emotional bond Geoff and I should have shared got all twisted up with the abuse, the pain, the shame; it severed any ties I tried to make with you."

Mallory followed Jake as he began to move around the pond. "It hit me when Jennifer asked how I would feel if you were always leaning on your sister."

Like his mother leaned on him. Jake's strides lengthened. He thought of all the ways he had tried to escape his mother's clinging. Just as he'd tried to escape his responsibilities with Mallory. No wonder she had never been able to lean on him. It wasn't all Mallory and her problems. All the assignments, all the long hours—they were a way to keep anyone from leaning on him, to calm his fear of being smothered.

Jake's pace came to an abrupt halt and he turned to face Mallory. His hands slid up her arms to her shoulders. "Mal, now it's my turn."

Jake avoided Mallory's gaze, and she held her breath, waiting to hear what he had to say. Could he understand the confusion of her past, or would he tell her it was too late?

"I need to ask your forgiveness for running out on you and the girls."

She heard Jake's voice break and saw his eyes brim with unshed tears. She blinked back her own as he wrapped his arms tightly around her and continued, "I was so afraid I'd lost you!"

Mallory leaned her head against his chest, loving the warmth of him and the steady rhythm of his heart as it beat against her ear. He stroked her hair, then lifted her chin to meet his tender gaze. "I'm sorry for all the ways I added to your pain. I abandoned you when you needed me most. I was scared."

"Of what?"

"Of not being able to meet your needs." Jake pulled her closer. "As a kid I never knew how to help my mother. I guess I was afraid I would fail you, too."

Mallory began to cry. "Oh Jake, you—"

"Shh." He put a finger to her lips and whispered in her ear. "I need to say this. I did fail you, Mallory. I failed you in so many ways. You needed me to be strong. I should have been the one to take you and the girls to church. I know now that God wanted me to share this incredible spiritual journey with you, wanted us to learn about Him together."

She felt the muscles in his shoulder tremble.

"I should have been there for you to lean on. I should have been there to protect and comfort you, and I wasn't. It was my pride. My ego was hurt. I quit my job, so I could go to *World Graphics,* but then I realized that it would be the same thing all over again. I'd be gone from you and the girls. I don't want that. That's why I decided to start my own business. I'm stepping out in faith, Mal. I don't know where God will lead me. Maybe you can't believe this, but I don't want to run anymore. Except home to you."

Mallory eased back so she could see his face. *It was true; he wanted to come home!* Her fingers trembled as she caressed the rough stubble on his chin and smiled at him through her tears.

"Jake, I know we're not done. We haven't finished our journey yet…"

Apprehension filled his eyes, and she smiled. "But you know what? That's okay. We can go forward from here together."

Just before her lips met his, she whispered, "It's time to come home, Jake."

Two years later

"Now the LORD blessed the latter days of Job more than his beginning"
(Job 42:12).

The meeting room was large, with floor-to-ceiling windows lining the wall that overlooked the small, man-made lake. Mallory could see drops of water still running in rivulets down the panes of glass. The recent rain had left branches dripping, soaking the bed of fallen, brown leaves. Weak rays of sunlight penetrated the density of the tree-shrouded lodge. The sky was growing lighter, and she could see patches of blue breaking through the clouds.

It might turn out to be a beautiful day after all.

She twisted her fingers in her lap, and Jake reached over and took her hand. She tried to concentrate on what Pastor James was saying, but it was difficult when she knew she and Jake would be sharing soon.

Lake of the Shepherd was a rustic retreat center with simple amenities. Mallory loved it. She had never been here before, but Pastor James had spoken here often.

How did I let him talk me into this?

Mallory's attention was drawn back to the small group of people gathered in front of the blazing fireplace. Folding metal chairs were scattered about, but more than a few opted for the plush carpeted floor. The whole scene gave her the feeling that they were gathering for an informal time of fellowship, rather than listening to a teaching session. Not that she and Jake would be teaching anything. They were just here to share a few words.

When Pastor James had approached them about speaking at this retreat, Mallory had hesitated. She hadn't been sure whether she wanted to spill her guts about the intimate details of her life. He had assured her that she could share as much or as little as she wished. What he wanted was for her to share how the Lord had helped her, healed her, and eventually changed her.

"Do it. Let's do it." Jake's words had more than taken her by surprise; they floored her. He had approached this the way a little boy would run toward a mud puddle. Mallory smiled at the memory. God was doing amazing things in her husband…and amazing her in the process.

"I've known Jake and Mallory for close to five years, but it wasn't until the last three years that I got to know them well." At Pastor James's words, sweat popped out on the palms of Mallory's hands. She tried to wipe them dry. Jake reached over and patted her knee.

He had been sprawled back in the metal chair until Pastor James introduced him. Now he rose and stepped up to the lectern. He wasn't the least bit nervous! Mallory wiped her hands again.

"I'm Jake. She's Mallory."

A light ripple of laughter went through the crowd as he jerked his thumb in her direction.

"Three years ago if Pastor James had asked me to speak at a retreat, I wouldn't have known what one was." His boyish grin twisted Mallory's heart. How she loved him! "In fact, I would have been the one retreating!" At the second wave of chuckles, Mallory felt her shoulders start to ease.

What Jake said was true. But his penchant for running had been replaced by a surprising determination to stand firm.

"My work was all-consuming. And I never realized it was my coping mechanism when I was faced with things I couldn't handle. It was where I ran to. Oh, I provided for my family materially, but emotionally I neglected my wife and my two children." Mallory's eyes misted. "I thought I was a good husband. I loved my wife. My girls. Life was good." Jake paused and let his gaze touch those who were listening. "But I was empty. I couldn't face that emptiness, so I ran to every photo assignment that came my way, using the travel to exotic places as a buffer between me and pain. Between me and the struggling relationship with my wife. Between me and God."

His smile was a thing of pure beauty. "But God wouldn't let me hide. He pursued me." Jake turned his grin to Mallory. "And when I hit the wall and could no longer run, God was there, and He was the only place left for me to turn."

Jake's easy confidence gave Mallory courage, and she felt God's peace settle over her. *I can do this.* Jake smiled and held out his hand for her to join him.

"Stay here," she whispered when she joined him.

He wrapped his arm around her waist. "I'm not going any-where, babe."

Mallory looked out across the sea of faces that were staring at her. How many of them were like she had been, locked in a cycle of pain, anger, bitterness, and self-defeating behavior?

"I wasn't running." Mallory winked at Jake. "I was hiding." She was rewarded with Jake's rumble of laughter. She looked back at the audience and took a deep breath. "I was sexually abused as a child and was in denial for years." Her gaze landed on Heather, who leaned back on her elbows, stretched out in the front row. She smiled, gave Mallory a thumbs-up, and mouthed the words *Go for it.*

"Because of the abuse, I was insecure in relationships and I avoided emotional intimacy, with my husband, and even with God. I had so much shame that I second-guessed myself at every turn. I was afraid for my children and didn't know why. I was angry, but didn't know how to express it. It was directed at the wrong people." She squeezed Jake's hand. "Most of it got dumped on my husband. No wonder he ran! I would have too, but I couldn't run from myself. So I hid.

"But you can't hide from God, any more than you can run from Him. Only by turning around and facing my past was I able, with His help, to move forward." Mallory shifted her feet and stepped closer into Jake's embrace. How thankful she was for his presence. "When I went into counseling, I was given a Scripture verse. It's found in Isaiah. 'Instead of your shame you shall have double honor, and instead of confusion they shall rejoice in their portion…everlasting joy shall be theirs.' I couldn't see how God could make joy come out of such pain, but I clung to that thought, even though I didn't understand it."

Help me make them understand. A spring of joy welled up within her. "God gave me back the years the locusts had eaten. The shame was broken! I can't explain it, except that God shattered the prison of guilt and anger I lived in. I'm free!"

Mallory straightened her shoulders. "I'm standing in front of you today without the burden of anger. My journey of emotional recovery began with that spiritual healing. And now…now I know that God loves me, that nothing can ever take that love away from me. Not my sin, not anyone else's. His forgiveness is eternal, and Christ's payment covers it all. For too long I believed I had to somehow earn His love, but I couldn't. No one can."

Mallory looked once more around the room. "I don't know what your hurts are today. I only know that we all have them. And I know that God can heal and will heal you, if you let Him."

She turned to Pastor James. "That's all. I'm done."

Spontaneous applause broke the silence as Pastor James came forward to hug both her and Jake.

He thanked them and then opened the floor up for questions. A woman seated at the back of the room raised her hand. "Pastor James, if the abuse is incest, how do you deal with your family? Does the relationship have to be broken, or is it possible to maintain it?"

Pastor James looked at Mallory and she answered the woman. "My abuse was incest. I was abused by my brother." Jake rubbed her shoulder. "I believe God wants to heal that relationship. At this point in my life, my relationship with my family is strained." Mallory shook her head. "I don't believe it will ever be the same, but it can be better. With God, all things are possible. But it all depends on the individuals. Everyone has a choice. My brother had a choice. I had a choice. Jake had a choice. I chose to face the truth, to work on my relationship with my husband. I desire to be close to my family and am praying that it will happen one day."

A woman right in front of them spoke up. "Mallory, where was that verse you mentioned in Isaiah?"

"The verses are found in Isaiah 61." Pastor James reached for his Bible, turning to the book of Isaiah. "This whole chapter is a profound one for victims—for all of us who need healing." He glanced down at the pages open before him. "It says, 'The LORD has anointed Me to preach good tidings…, to heal the broken-hearted, to proclaim liberty to the captives, and the opening of the prison to those who are bound.' It goes on to say, 'to console those who mourn…, to give them beauty for ashes, the oil of joy for mourning, the garment of praise for the spirit of heaviness.'" He shut his Bible.

The words soared through Mallory. Isaiah may have been speaking to the children of Israel, but the principles held true. So many suffered, as Jake and she had, because of sin, their own or others'. But through it all, God's grace prevailed over the lives of those who suffered. Hadn't she seen that? And the time would come when God, in His mercy, would say his people had suffered enough.

God had promised Israel double what had been taken from them…and when Israel chose to rejoice in God, He became their "portion." His blessing was heaped upon them.

Mallory hugged herself, and her spirit sang with praise. She could see her past now, with all its pain, and her future, with all God intended for her life.

She looked at the woman, blinking back tears as she spoke. "Don't you see? Although my childhood was a life of confusion that lasted into adulthood, that confusion is now being trans-formed into an everlasting joy. I want to allow God to finish the good work He has begun in me. And He will."

Jake wiped away the tear rolling down her cheek. "If Mallory's family will choose to allow God to work in their lives, their shame will be gone, and they, too, can possess double honor."

With all her heart, Mallory wanted her family to discover what

Jake and she were learning about the Father's love. The gift of healing would be lifelong and only achieved in God's perfect timing, but blessings waited for those who persevered and sought God's truth. She had experienced those miracles firsthand.

Mallory smiled at Jake and slid her arms around his waist, hugging him close. All she had to do was look at him, to see the love in his eyes, to be reminded of what God could accomplish when a heart fully surrendered to Him.

Double honor. That's what God had promised, and she knew… God's promises never fail.

About the Authors

Susan Stevens holds a B.A. in psychology and is working on her master of divinity at Ashland Theological Seminary. She pastors a United Methodist Church in Holmesville, Ohio, and lives with her cat, Oscar, and her computer fish, Italics. If she had any free time, you would find her horseback riding, swimming, painting, or photographing landscapes and seascapes.

Missy Horsfall is a published magazine and greeting-card writer. She and her husband have three children and live in Baltic, Ohio. She grew up an army brat, traveling extensively, but her heart remains on the shores of the Great Lakes. She loves the wind, the waves, and the palette of the sky at sunset.

Friends for years, Susan and Missy started out by encouraging each other's writing dreams with regular 3 A.M. writing marathons and eventually began to toss around the idea of authoring a book together. The story for *Double Honor* came from their shared counseling experiences, Susan with her church and Missy in her role as a pastor's wife.